Coincidences

by

Maria Savva

Printed and bound by Lulu.com 2012

First Edition published in hardback by: The Book Guild Limited (2001) ISBN: 1 85776 566 4

This edition: Second Edition
Published by:
Rose & Freedom Books
P.O. Box 55285
London N22 9EU
England, U.K.

A catalogue record of this book is available from the British Library

ISBN: 978-0-9564101-6-0

Author's note & acknowledgements:

I would like to thank everyone who has read the original version of Coincidences, especially my friends, Sheri Wilkinson, Calum McDonald, Carol Perry, Jerry Travis, Julie Elizabeth Aldridge, Benjamin Jones, Katherine Marple, and Shenaka Singarayer. It is thanks to all the positive feedback and reviews from all of you, and seeing other readers' comments and ratings on various websites, that I decided to make this second edition available as a paperback and e-book so that it could be more widely read.

Thank you to everyone who has ever proof read any of my books for me, helped me to edit them, or written constructive reviews. I am indebted to you all. You have all contributed in some way to making me a better writer. When I first started writing Coincidences I had no idea about what it takes to write a novel. Over the years, I have learnt so much about editing and grammar from fellow authors, and friends, and just through the process of writing and editing on an almost daily basis. One thing I have learnt over the years is that all art remains a work-in-progress in the mind of the artist who creates it. For me, at least, no novel or short story is ever really finished; we just have to stop editing at some stage to avoid going completely mad. Most of us are already slightly mad which is why we write ;).

I first started writing Coincidences towards the end of 1997, and it was published in hardback in 2001. It is now out of print, but continues to be quite popular in UK libraries. I wanted to make the book more widely available and decided to publish a paperback and e-book version. When I looked for an electronic copy of the book on my computer, I could not find one. I contacted The Book Guild who had originally published the book, but they didn't have a copy. I then decided to start typing the book up from scratch. Whilst doing that, I noticed that there were things I would have done differently, and I also had the idea of adding more scenes and background to the story without changing it. This second edition of Coincidences stays true to the original, but has extras, and I have used the editing skills I have developed over the years to tighten up the prose and hopefully make it a smoother read. I still love the story, after all these years, and hope that you will too.

It was interesting for me as a writer to see how my writing style has developed over the years. Perhaps readers of the original edition will also find it interesting to see how my writing has changed over the years.

I would like to thank the following people without whom I would not have finished this edition:

Darcia Helle. Thank you so much for proof reading the final draft. Thanks for reading the book so thoroughly and for giving me such constructive feedback. Your comments and suggestions helped me to make the book more realistic, and prevented Alice eating too much food before her big date LOL. Thanks also for spotting so many annoying typos. You are the best.

J. Michael Radcliffe. Thank you so much for proof reading the book and finding lots of typos. Thanks also for spotting the chapter heading mix-up with the Monday that was supposed to be Wednesday LOL, and Alice's cup that kept changing into a glass as if by magic :) I'm sure that must have escaped from one of your fantasy novels!

Can I also thank all my fans, friends, and readers, who tell me they enjoy my books, and write such wonderful reviews (you know who you are. There are too many to mention and I don't want to leave anyone out!). You are the reason I carry on writing. I love you all.

For Evita, Brenna and Tadhg
Follow your dreams

Chapter One

Monday 11th August 1997

Alice Turnbull lay in bed shaking, too scared to move, perspiration cold on the back of her neck. A lock of her hair fell onto her face, covering her eyes. Alice jumped. Her heart began to palpitate. As she caught her breath, and moved the hair away from her face, she noticed something red from the corner of her eye. Instinctively, she turned towards it, and breathed a sigh of relief when she saw the luminous red numbers on her radio alarm clock. It was 12.15 a.m. She seemed to be strangely drawn to stare at the clock. As she did so, she felt that the clock was almost staring back at her in the pitch black, as if it had taken on an existence of its own. Panic gripped her.

Continuing to lie in bed, as her eyes adjusted to the dark, she became more aware of her surroundings. Everything was shrouded in shadows, and she had a hazy feeling as though she were trapped in a nightmare and could not wake up. Alice felt frightened as she recalled the noise that had shaken her from her sleep. It had sounded like an explosion of some kind. Had someone broken into the flat? She lay frozen, unable to move, straining her ears to detect any sound. But she could hear nothing. Feeling restless and uneasy, she knew that she would not be able to get back to sleep until she checked her flat to make sure she was alone—but she still felt too scared to move.

After a few moments, she somehow managed to summon up the courage to reach out of her bed and switch on the bedside table lamp. Her arms continued to shake. The soft lighting of the lamp, with its familiar orange glow, brought with it a warmth that comforted her. Sitting up, she continued to listen for any noise. She noticed the time again: it was 12.38 a.m. Slowly, she forced herself to get out of bed.

Putting on her slippers, she hesitantly walked towards her bedroom door. It had been almost half an hour since she had woken, but she still felt strangely scared and anxious. Taking hold of the knob on her bedroom door, she nervously pulled it open. For a few moments, she stood at the door, on constant alert for any sound, but all she could hear was the beating of her heart in her ears and the ticking of the kitchen clock. The clock had been a moving-in present from her mother when Alice had left the family home six months ago. Each tick of the clock in the darkness now reminded Alice of the countless times her mother had begged her to come back home. *'You shouldn't be living alone, a girl of your age. I worry about you'.* The clock seemed to tick more loudly as Alice's fears grew. Tick, tock, tick, tock... Taking a few steps towards the kitchen, she switched on the light, hoping that it would somehow detract from the sound.

Finding courage in the light, she proceeded to switch on all the lights she could find. Once she had checked every corner of the flat, and assured herself there was no one else in there, she could breathe easier. She returned to her bedroom, and although she had now switched off all the other lights in the flat, she could not quite bring herself to switch off her bedside table lamp. Her unusual awakening had disturbed her inner peace, and she still felt an unnerving fear deep inside her mind.

She could not forget the loud, banging sound that had echoed in her head when she had awoken. She recalled fragments of her dream: she had dreamt of a fire, she had heard screaming, there had been lots of water... a sea. Eventually, Alice drifted back to sleep.

When her alarm clock sounded at 7.30 a.m. that morning, she woke up feeling refreshed. She had managed to sleep well, despite the incident in the early hours. She remembered the fear she had felt, but it had lost its hold on her; it was like an old memory, as distant as a dream. If her bedside table lamp had not still been on, she would have thought that she had dreamt last night's disturbance. Alice shrugged, turned over in bed and reached over to the lamp to switch it off.

At twenty-one years old, Alice Turnbull was a Law student, due to start her final year of studies in October. During the summer break, she worked part-time at a local bookstore; *Bairns' Books.* On the morning of the 11th of August, she was sitting in the kitchen of her flat, eating her breakfast. It was 8 a.m. when she looked at the kitchen clock. The round, bright yellow clock, which was framed with a hand-carved wooden hen, hung benevolently from the blue, painted wall. The ticking of the clock, which had been so loud in the darkness, was hardly audible now above the daytime sounds of people rushing off to work. Turning away from the clock, she almost laughed at herself for being afraid of the ticking during the night. Casually, she reached over and switched on her portable radio. Yawning, she continued to eat her corn flakes. The news on the radio told of a plane crash into the Atlantic Ocean. Alice was only half-listening to the radio as she thought about what she would be doing that day, and was at the same time thinking that there always seemed to be chat or news on the radio; she would have preferred a bit of music to start her day. But the following announcement caught her attention:

'The plane crash, which happened at a quarter-past twelve this morning, claimed the lives of at least thirty people. Air-Sea Rescue operations are still continuing in an attempt to locate survivors...'

She didn't hear the rest of the story. All she could think about was that when she had looked at her alarm clock last night, it had been 12.15 a.m. The same time as the plane crash. Images from her dream coursed through her mind. The fear she had felt now seemed more real. 'Quarter-past twelve,' Alice said to herself, as she sat alone at the kitchen table. Her words reverberated in her head, like an echo, and as she closed her eyes she could see the red numbers on her alarm clock staring back at her.

Whilst on the bus, on her way to work, Alice could not stop thinking about the night before. Something was nagging her at the back of her mind, but she could not quite understand what it was or why she felt so confused.

'Hi, Alice,' Charlotte, her colleague, greeted her cheerfully as she arrived at the book shop.

'Oh, hi,' replied Alice, still in a bit of a daze.

'Well, do you notice anything different about me?' Charlotte was pointing to her new hairstyle and posing. She'd had most of her once long, tousled, blonde hair cut off, and Alice had hardly noticed.

'Oh, yeah, it looks nice,' responded Alice, coming back down to earth.

'You're very observant today,' giggled Charlotte.

One or two customers had come into the shop now, so the girls settled themselves behind the counter. It was never very busy in the store on weekdays, so much of their time was spent chatting. Charlotte liked to talk about herself.

Charlotte Wade was twenty-two years old. She worked part-time at the bookstore, and was also a part-time film extra. She was forever telling Alice about her latest "roles". Charlotte's aim was to become a famous actress. She had changed her name a few months ago. 'Well, no one has ever become famous with a name like "Susan", have they?' she'd said to Alice. Alice was tempted to mention Susan Sarandon, but thought she would let it slip as the deed had already been signed and "Charlotte" had a new name.

Charlotte had an interesting social life, and it seemed that she always had a different boyfriend. She would spend ages telling Alice all about them. Alice didn't have anyone special in her life. There was a boy at university called Andrew, whom she liked, but she had kept it to herself. Somehow, she didn't feel she was ready for a relationship and preferred to dream about such things.

'So how was your weekend, Alice?'

She knew that Charlotte was probably only looking for a reason to talk about her own weekend by asking that question; she always liked to be the centre of attention. Alice replied: 'Oh, it was fine, how was yours?'

'Oh, mine was great!' Charlotte began to talk at length about the new film she was going to appear in, which according to her was "sure to become a blockbuster".

Alice breathed a sigh of relief that she would not have to talk about her own weekend; all she could remember about it was the nightmare, which seemed to be following her like a black cloud above her head.

'I'm playing a waitress. I've actually got some lines! I'm so excited,' gushed Charlotte. 'I have to take an order in a really posh restaurant from the two main actors. Can you believe it? Obviously, they saw that I have star potential! I might be discovered and become famous. Imagine, Alice, you'll be able to say you knew me before I made it!'

'That's nice,' said Alice, smiling, not having heard much of what Charlotte had said, her mind being elsewhere.

'You're not even listening to me, are you?'

'Oh, sorry.' Alice felt guilty for offending her. 'I was listening. Er... but I just noticed your dress, it's really nice, I was a bit distracted.'

'Thanks!' Charlotte beamed. 'It is nice, isn't it? It's designer.' She went on to describe how she had chosen her bright red nail varnish to match her dress and lipstick.

Alice's concentration drifted once again.

It wasn't long before Charlotte realised she didn't have her full attention. 'What's wrong, Alice?' She clicked her fingers above Alice's head as if to indicate that she needed to wake up.

Alice sighed and stood up. 'Nothing's wrong.'

'You can tell me. It's man trouble, isn't it, honey?'

Trust Charlotte to think that. 'No, don't be silly. It's nothing. I... I didn't sleep well last night, that's all.' She forced a smile. She had been thinking of her nightmare again. It was as if the news of the plane crash this morning had triggered off something in her mind. She noticed that she was able to remember more and more of her nightmare as the day progressed. It bothered Alice that she now knew she had dreamt of a plane crashing to land. The voice from the newsflash resounded in her head.

At lunchtime, she was glad to get out of the bookstore for some fresh air.

She'd arranged to meet a university friend, Jenny, in *McDonald's*. When she arrived at the restaurant, she was waiting for her outside.

'Hi,' said Jenny, taking off her sunglasses. 'How are you? You're looking well.' She was in a cheerful mood, as usual, which helped to lift Alice's gloom slightly.

'Thanks, yeah, I'm fine,' she replied, her eyes unable to meet her friend's.

The two girls entered the busy restaurant and ordered their meals. They pushed through the crowds of lunchtime customers and managed to find two empty seats close to the entrance.

Jenny Callum was Alice's closest friend at university. They usually studied together. Jenny had just returned from a trip to France. She'd gone to Paris with her boyfriend, Frank, who was also a student at the same university. The girls spent their lunch hour chatting about Jenny's holiday and looking at snaps, and they talked about university and mutual friends.

'Oh! I almost forgot! Guess what?' exclaimed Jenny. 'I found out from Frank that Andrew told one of his friends that he fancies you.'

'You're kidding,' said Alice, blushing and trying not to choke on her hamburger. Alice had fancied Andrew for a few months. He was tall, with dark, shoulder length hair, and striking blue eyes. She had told Jenny in confidence that she liked him, not knowing that her boyfriend knew some of Andrew's friends.

'It's good news, isn't it? I swear, I didn't say anything to Frank about you fancying Andrew.'

'Good,' said Alice, not really knowing what to say. She felt embarrassed. 'Don't say anything to him.'

Jenny laughed.

By the end of her lunch hour, Alice had managed to put the plane crash and her nightmare to the back of her mind. Her disrupted night was once again like a distant memory.

Stephanie Turnbull was on her way home from work. At fifty years of age, she was the owner and manager of a hairdressing salon in East London. She had a journey of about forty minutes on the London Underground to her flat in North London. Before getting on the Tube, she bought a copy of the evening paper.

After standing for fifteen minutes, lodged uncomfortably between a huddle of rush hour passengers, Stephanie managed to get a seat on the train. The heat in the carriage was unbearable and the air was thin; thankfully she had a bit of air space now that she had finally sat down. Her feet were killing her from standing in the salon all day.

The worst part of the day for her was always the journey to and from work. There was never any space to move in the overcrowded trains. It was especially uncomfortable during the summer months when the temperature inside the carriages would far exceed the temperature on the streets. She stared at the briefcase belonging to a harassed-looking man in a business suit. He was standing just in front of her, trying to avoid hitting her on the head with his briefcase each time the train jolted. On days like this she regretted selling her car and opting for Tube travel to work.

No sooner had she sat down, she had to get up again to change onto the Northern Line train to continue her journey. Luckily, the next train was not as full and she managed to sit down upon boarding the carriage. She began to read her newspaper. The headline on the front page read: *"Air Disaster: Forty Feared Dead."* With interest, she read about the desperate attempts to locate survivors of the crash. The ill-fated jet had plunged into the Atlantic Ocean in the early hours of the morning. Stephanie noticed a picture of a young girl being carried out of the sea to safety, her hair dripping with water. It was a dramatic scene with smoke in the background. Sitting on the Tube train, staring at the picture, Stephanie began to think of her own daughter, Alice, and a tear came to her eye. The girl in the picture looked about the same age as Alice. She prayed the girl would be all right.

Her thoughts turned to Alice now, as she closed the newspaper and placed it on her lap. Stephanie was forever worrying about her daughter ever since she moved out of the family home six months ago. Stephanie had been against the move, but Alice had said she wanted her independence. The more she tried to dissuade her, the more determined she had been to move out.

It had proved very difficult for Stephanie to adjust to living without her daughter. She almost felt abandoned. Living on her own was something she had never done. She had gone from living with her parents, to moving in with Roger, Alice's father, when they married. Roger had left home when Alice was only eighteen months old. Alice was her only child. Even though she had not moved very far away and visited often, Stephanie still felt a great sense of loss. She had built her world around her daughter. One of the causes of friction in her marriage had been the fact that she was unable to have children; when Alice came along it had been nothing short of a miracle as far as Stephanie was concerned. She'd been so grateful and felt so happy and privileged to have a daughter, she wanted to keep her by her side for ever. She just didn't feel ready to let go of her only child yet—not after she had gone to such lengths for her to be born.

Stephanie arrived home at 7.45 p.m. Slumping onto her favourite armchair, she put her feet up onto the coffee table and kicked off her shoes. Reaching over to the side table, she grabbed the telephone and dialled her daughter's number.

'Hello,' said the familiar voice on the other end of the phone line.

'Hello, darling, it's Mummy,' said Stephanie. 'How are you? I haven't seen you for a few days.'

'Oh, I'm fine, you don't have to worry about me.'

'But I do worry. I'm your mother, that's my job.' Stephanie caught sight of the newspaper lying on the coffee table where she'd left it when she'd walked into the room. 'Did you hear about that terrible plane crash?'

There was silence on the phone line.

'Alice? Are you still there?'

'Yes.'

'Well anyway, there was a picture in the paper of a girl who looked about the same age as you, being rescued from the crash. She looked so young and helpless, she reminded me of you. That's when I started to think about you and realised we haven't spoken for a few days.'

Alice had almost forgotten about the nightmare and the fear she'd felt, but the phone call had brought it all back, and she found she was unable to reply.

'Alice?'

'Yes... Listen, Mum, I'll come and see you tomorrow at the salon. I'm not working tomorrow.'

'Okay, sweetie.'

When Alice hung up the phone, she regretted not telling her mother about her nightmare, but at the same time, she knew her mother would only worry even more about her if she told her. It was probably best to keep quiet.

Alice did not sleep well that night. Each time she drifted off to sleep, she would see herself screaming or unable to breathe under water. Alternately, she would see a plane crashing to land with great flames and smoke consuming the atmosphere. Eventually, she decided to try to stay awake. Turning on her bedside lamp, she stared at the ceiling and tried to think of other things. She thought about her meeting with Jenny and for a while she felt better remembering what she'd said about Andrew. Her mood lifted as she began to imagine what it would be like meeting Andrew again after the summer break from university. Feeling less frightened, she turned off the table lamp and tried to get some sleep.

Chapter Two

Tuesday 12th August 1997

Alice woke up at 9 a.m. Upon waking, she remembered her nightmares. It seemed impossible for her to forget about the plane crash, no matter how hard she tried. It was like an obsession, haunting her mind, ever since she heard the newsflash on the radio.

She went into the kitchen to make her breakfast, and switched on the radio, as usual. She listened intently for some more news about the plane crash; perhaps if she had some more details she would be able to work out why it had affected her so. But there was no mention of it in the news. It was "yesterday's news" to everyone else, but felt so ingrained in her mind. Sighing with frustration, she opened the fridge door and saw that she had run out of milk. She had meant to buy some yesterday. It bothered her that this incident was now getting in the way of her concentration, making her forget to do things. It was as if, no matter what else she was doing, some part of her brain was constantly thinking about her nightmare and the plane crash—like a track on a CD on repeat playback.

She sat down at the kitchen table after making some toast for breakfast. As she looked through the local newspaper, she remembered her mother telling her that yesterday's paper contained a news story about the plane crash. Alice felt a compulsion to find that newspaper and read all about it. Picking up the last slice of toast from her plate and grabbing her bag, as if in a mad rush for an appointment, she hurried out of the front door.

Once on the Tube train, she noticed that a few people were reading newspapers. She tried to see if any of the papers contained stories about the crash, but it was difficult to tell. A middle-aged woman, wearing a floral-patterned summer dress, got on at the next stop and sat next to her. The woman opened a copy of the *Daily Mail*. Alice saw that there was something about the crash on the front page. She leaned forward, trying to read the story, but this movement seemed to annoy the woman, who took a sharp sideways glance towards Alice. The woman then sighed and moved further along the Tube train, quite a few seats away from her, so it was impossible for her to read anything. Feeling embarrassed, Alice spent the rest of the journey staring at the floor.

Arriving at her mother's flat, Alice opened the door using the key her mother had insisted she retain when she left home. Upon entering the flat, she walked into the living room and spotted the newspaper lying on the coffee table. When she picked it up, her eyes immediately fixed on the picture of a young girl being rescued from the crash. She remembered her mother mentioning it. Alice stared at the picture. It was grainy and slightly out of focus, but she couldn't help noticing that the girl bore a resemblance to her. She began to read the news story with heightened interest.

"Flight 764, took off from Boston USA at 11.45 p.m. GMT, and was a direct flight to London Heathrow. The pilot reported some trouble with the engine just ten minutes before the recorded time of the crash. This is still under investigation. The plane was to make an emergency landing, but lost control and crashed into the Atlantic Ocean in the early hours of Monday morning."

There was no mention of the exact time of the crash. Alice felt she would be able to relax a bit now. As there was nothing in writing to say it had occurred at 12.15 a.m., she told herself that it was quite possible she had misheard the newsflash on the radio. She placed the newspaper back onto the table and made her way out of the flat.

Alice arrived at *Stephanie's,* her mother's hairdressing salon, just as her mother was getting ready to leave for lunch.

'Oh, Alice, darling, you look so tired. You haven't been looking after yourself, have you?' The words bombarded her as soon as she stepped through the salon door.

Alice felt embarrassed, as two of the customers who were seated in the waiting area were now looking at her. She felt her cheeks redden and tried to avoid looking at the women.

Stephanie ran towards her daughter and hugged her. Then stepping back to look at her, she said, 'I just knew you'd be no good at looking after yourself. Maybe you should come back home.'

'Mum,' said Alice in an almost-whisper, 'stop fussing, I'm fine.'

'Come on, I'll buy you lunch. You look like you've been starving yourself. Are you eating properly?' She was almost pushing Alice out of the salon as she spoke.

They went to a local café, and after purchasing their sandwiches, they sat at a table near the window.

'I've missed you, love,' said Stephanie. 'You really should keep in touch more.'

'Sorry, Mum.' Alice smiled.

'You really do look tired, darling. Are you staying up late partying and going to night-clubs? I know what you students are like. But you need to make sure you get enough sleep.'

Alice wanted to tell her mother about her nightmares, and she almost did, but she stopped herself. Her mother already worried about her living alone, and would find any excuse to insist that she should return to live with her.

Just as the two women were finishing off their meals, they heard a voice calling out.

'Steph! Steph Forester? Is that you?' The accent was not a London one. It had a northern tinge.

Stephanie had not used the surname "Forester" for over fifteen years. It had been Alice's father's surname. Stephanie had reverted to using her maiden name after the divorce.

A plump, middle-aged woman, with short, dark-brown hair now stood beside the table.

Stephanie appeared quite shocked, Alice noted.

'Rita, hello... er... what a nice surprise. How... How did you recognise me after all this time?'

Alice had seldom seen her mother like this; she seemed nervous as she spoke to the woman.

'Steph, it's been too long, hasn't it? We should never have lost touch!'

Rita Smart had once been Stephanie's closest friend, but they had not seen each other for about twenty years. They had met at school and had kept in touch until Alice was about a year old. Rita had moved to Birmingham for work, and they lost contact after a few months.

When Alice looked up at Rita, she noticed that the woman

was staring at her as if in awe. Alice blushed and Rita seemed to then realise that she was staring. She smiled quickly and looked away to address Stephanie: 'So, this must be Alice.'

'Yes,' Stephanie replied and then coughed, appearing nervous again and fidgeting in her chair.

'She looks so much like Roger,' commented Rita. 'It's like looking into his eyes when I look at her.'

But Rita did not look at her; she kept her face firmly fixed in Stephanie's direction, as if to make up for the earlier bout of staring.

'How is Roger these days?'

'We're divorced.'

'You're kidding?' Rita seemed genuinely shocked. She almost gasped the words. 'After... After everything you two went through, you know, after—' She seemed to be jerking her head sideways towards Alice.

'Yes,' said Stephanie, quickly. 'It didn't work out between us.' Her cheeks and neck reddened.

'I'm sorry to hear that,' said Rita, smiling sympathetically. She then turned towards Alice and smiled at her. Alice still thought that the way she was looking at her was unnatural. It was as if she knew something about her... about her father... something that was making Stephanie uncomfortable. Alice frowned.

Looking back at Stephanie, Rita said, 'We must keep in touch now. I'm living back in London—have been for the past two years. I tried to find you at your old address when I first came back. Where have you moved to?'

'North London; I'll write the address down for you. Where are you living?'

'Not too far from here, actually.' Rita fished out a pen from her handbag and picked up one of the napkins from the table. She scribbled down an address. 'I'll put my phone number on here, too.'

The two women exchanged addresses and phone numbers, then Stephanie explained she had to get back to work.

'Oh, where are you working?'

'I own a hairdressing salon on the high street. It's called *Stephanie's*. You must come in and see me sometime.'

'That's *your* salon?' Rita stood open-mouthed. 'Can you believe I've walked past it so many times and thought of you when I read the name, but I've never been in there. My cousin's a hairdresser, so she always does my hair at home. Last year, when my cousin was in hospital for a few weeks, I almost made an appointment for a hair cut at your salon! If only I had done.'

'That would have been nice. But never mind; the main thing is that we've found each other again,' said Stephanie, smiling.

Alice wondered if her mother was just being polite. Was she really happy that she'd found this woman again, or did Rita know some deep dark secret about her that her mother would prefer stayed hidden?

When they'd left the café, and were alone again, Alice asked her mother who Rita was.

'Just an old friend, dear,' replied Stephanie.

'She seemed to know about me, but I don't remember you ever mentioning her before,' said Alice.

'Oh, I'm sure I must have. Anyway, it was a long time ago. Rita and I lost touch about twenty years ago; you were just a baby.'

They arrived at the salon door.

'Alice, I'm going to be very busy this afternoon. You're welcome to hang around if you like, but you'll probably get bored.' Stephanie seemed distracted and Alice felt as if she did not really want her to hang around. Perhaps she was concerned that she would ask more questions about the mysterious Rita?

Feeling perplexed, Alice shrugged and said, 'I have to go shopping this afternoon. I need some milk and stuff. I'll come and visit you again soon.'

'Okay, dear,' said her mother, disappearing into the salon.

It surprised Alice, how her mother's mood had changed so dramatically since seeing her old friend at the café. Alice recalled how Rita had seemed almost too surprised that her parents had divorced. Having never met her father, she was naturally curious about Rita, as she was someone who had known him a whole world away when Stephanie, Roger and Alice had been a real family. Rita's appearance in her life seemed to signal an opportunity for her to learn more about her own past and her parents' relationship. But there was something that slightly unnerved Alice about Rita; it was the way she had looked at her when they first met. She had been staring—almost as if she were looking at a curiosity rather than a person.

Alice went shopping and arrived home late in the afternoon. She sat down to watch the *Ricki Lake Show* on TV. The subject under discussion was teenage pregnancies and the ensuing problems. Whilst she was watching a story about a girl who had chosen to have her first child at the age of twelve, the telephone rang.

'Hello,' she said, still trying to listen to the TV.

'Allie!' It was Jenny.

'Oh, hi. How are you?' asked Alice, still half tuned-in to the TV show.

'I'm fine. I can't talk for long—I'm getting ready to go out—but I just *had* to call you!' said Jenny in her usual loud jovial tone. 'Frank's been invited to a friend's birthday party next week and I'm going with him. Andrew is going to be there! I asked Frank if it would be okay for you to come, and he said yes! You've got to come.'

Alice soon lost interest in the TV programme. 'Oh, when is the party?' she asked, trying to sound indifferent.

'Next Tuesday. You will come, won't you?'

'Um... okay, yes.'

'You don't sound very enthusiastic,' said Jenny, disappointed. 'I thought you fancied Andrew.'

'I do think he's good looking and everything, but I don't know him,' said Alice.

'Well, here's your chance to get to know him!'

'Okay.' Alice smiled to herself. 'I'll look forward to it.'

'We'll come and pick you up about seven-ish. I'll call you again to confirm the time. Make sure you dress up!'

'Okay, Bye, Jen.'

Alice felt excited at the prospect of seeing Andrew again. She often thought about what it would be like if they got together. She began to plan in her mind what she would say to him if she had the chance, what she would wear... When she came back down to earth, she realised that the programme she had been watching had finished.

She reached towards the coffee table to pick up the newspaper she had bought on the way home. Her mind was still full of fantasies of Andrew, and she felt in high spirits. As she reached out, she felt a pain in her lower right arm that seemed to spread to her elbow. The pain was so intense that she grabbed her arm with her left hand and screamed. After a few moments, the pain disappeared as quickly as it had manifested itself. She pulled her sleeve up to check if her arm was bruised, but she could see nothing. With no memory of having hit her arm anywhere, she felt confused as to why she had felt the pain. *Maybe I strained something when I was reaching out?* she wondered. But that seemed unlikely as the table was so close to her.

Trying to forget about it, she read her newspaper. There was a story about the plane crash on page five. She decided not to read it, not wanting to be reminded of her nightmares. After cooking her supper, she watched her favourite soap opera, *EastEnders*, and went to bed early to catch up on the sleep she had missed over the past couple of nights.

Chapter Three

Wednesday 13th August 1997

Alice arrived for work at *Bairns' Books* at 9 a.m. Charlotte was already behind the counter.

'Sophie and Rob were asking where you were,' said Charlotte as Alice settled herself behind the counter. Rob and Sophie Bairns were the husband and wife team who ran the bookstore.

'Oh... the bus was late,' explained Alice, trying to think of a plausible excuse. Then, she saw Rob Bairns looking at her from the corner of the bookstore; he didn't look happy and began walking towards her.

'Alice,' he said, as he got closer to her, 'you're late. You know you're meant to be here by 8.45. Don't let it happen again.'

'I won't. I'm sorry, the bus was late. I'm sorry,' Alice repeated as he walked away.

'Alice!' exclaimed Charlotte, when Rob had disappeared into a corridor of sci-fi books.

The sharp tone in Charlotte's voice almost made Alice jump. Turning towards her colleague she saw that she was holding a copy of the *Daily Mirror*. Alice squirmed.

'Look!' said Charlotte, continuing in a shrill, voice. She pointed to the picture on the front page of the newspaper. 'Look at that girl. She's the spitting image of you!'

The headline read: "*Plane Crash Survivors Speak Of Air Tragedy.*"

'Er... she does look a bit like me,' replied Alice, fumbling with her words. She hoped Charlotte would change the subject.

'A bit!' Her colleague laughed excitedly. 'She must be your double. Everyone has a double somewhere, apparently.' Charlotte continued to stare alternately at the newspaper and then at Alice as if she were comparing the two girls.

'She doesn't look that much like me, and anyway, the picture is unclear; it's all grainy,' said Alice defensively. She was glad when a customer approached the counter to purchase a book, forcing Charlotte to put the newspaper to one side.

Alice had left her flat at the usual time for work that morning. She'd been walking past the local newsagent's on the way to the bus stop when she'd noticed the headline on the front page of the *Daily Mirror*, on the rack of newspapers outside the shop. Still curious about the details of the plane crash, she moved closer and then noticed the picture on the front page. Her first reaction was shock; looking at the girl in the photograph was like looking in a mirror. The resemblance was overwhelming. As if in a flashback, Alice's mind returned to the night of the crash and she began to feel dizzy as she stared at the newspaper.

Taking a deep breath, she took the newspaper out of the protective plastic cover on the rack and read the words printed below the picture. The girl's name was "Jane Forester". Upon reading that, Alice gasped loudly. A man wearing jogging pants and a bright red T-shirt was walking past her at just that moment and he noticed her anxiety. Turning to look at her, he saw the newspaper in her hand. 'Yes, that was a shocking accident, wasn't it?' he said, looking sympathetic. 'I'm flying to America next week. Makes you think, doesn't it?'

Alice nodded at him. She was glad when he disappeared into the shop. Looking back at the paper, she again saw the name "Forester" as if it were the only word printed on the page. Her father's surname was Forester. The thought flashed through her mind, *Could this be my sister?* Almost immediately she felt foolish for thinking it. But something was nagging her. Her father had never kept in touch; her parents had separated when she was only two years old. He'd never tried to contact her. Alice had often wondered whether he'd remarried and had children, so it was unsurprising her train of thought would lead her to think this girl might be her sister: she looked so much like her.

Alice had never tried contacting her father for fear of upsetting her mother. But as she continued to stare at the picture in disbelief, she couldn't help feeling the need to find out more. She looked up and saw the man in the red T-shirt exiting the shop. Feeling self-conscious and not wanting him to see her still holding the paper, she rushed to place it back in the holder.

As she turned around, she saw her bus disappearing into the distance; she hadn't even heard it arrive...

Whilst Charlotte was busy serving the customer, Alice folded the newspaper and placed it out of sight under the counter, wanting to avoid any further discussion about the photograph. Charlotte turned to face Alice when her customer had left, and her eyes searched the counter, looking for the newspaper.

'I've been invited to a party,' said Alice, hoping that this would distract her.

'Oh? Tell all!' Charlotte sat on a stool facing her, waiting for her to continue.

Alice blushed as she remembered that Andrew would be at the party. She coughed to try to hide her embarrassment. 'It's a friend's birthday party.'

'What are you going to wear? Now let's see... do you have a gold dress? It would set off your eyes so well, and you look so good in dresses. You should wear them more. You're always in jeans. And you'll need to wear make-up. I bet there'll be lots of boys at the party, right? You want to look your best. It's time we got you a boyfriend.'

'Well, Andrew will be there,' said Alice turning away towards the counter, hoping she hadn't turned too red.

'Is he that boy you fancy? All the more reason for you to dress up and try to catch his eye. Don't worry, I'll give you some great tips. He won't be able to resist you.'

Charlotte chatted away happily, dishing out advice to Alice in between serving customers. She soon forgot about the picture in the newspaper, and so did Alice; her mind far away dreaming of Andrew.

Alice passed by the newsagent's on her way home. Once more, she felt overwhelmed by the feeling that she had to find out more about the plane crash and about the girl on the front page. She decided to buy a copy of the newspaper.

When she got home, she scoured the newspaper, reading

every word of the story about the plane crash survivors. She wasn't sure what she was hoping to see written in the paper, but was left feeling disappointed. The only mention of Jane Forester, apart from her photograph on the front page with the other survivors, was a quote from her, when asked about her experience. *'It was very frightening. We thought we would all die.'* The paper described her as "traumatised" and "tearful". Alice read the paragraph at least three times, and then stared at the photograph again. She took the newspaper with her into the kitchen to prepare her dinner.

As she stood stirring her pasta, her mind was going over the possibility of Jane Forester being related to her father. She knew her father's parents lived in America—she had heard her mother talk about it when she was younger. She was sure she could remember her mother saying that they lived in Boston. But the information was very fuzzy in her mind, almost as if she had made it up to suit her purpose. Could she ask her mother about it? She felt unsure. If it was true, perhaps Jane Forester had been to Boston to visit her grandparents and was returning when the plane crashed. Or, could Jane be an American cousin? Maybe her father had brothers or sisters in America. The newspaper had not said whether she was American or British. Alice felt excited, but also slightly confused and disconcerted because she didn't like the way she seemed to have developed a fascination with the plane crash and this girl. A splash of boiling water hit her hand and she was awoken from her daydream to see that the water in her pasta had started to boil over while her mind was miles away. She shook her head as she turned down the heat.

Just as she sat down at the table to eat her dinner, the telephone rang.

'Hello, darling, it's me.'

'Oh, hi, Mum. How are you?'

'I'm fine. I was just calling to make sure you're okay.'

'Yeah, I'm fine.'

'Good. Listen, I'm sorry I couldn't spend much time with you yesterday. I feel bad.'

'Oh, that's okay.'

'Are you working tomorrow, Alice?'

'No.'

'Great, why don't you come over and spend the day with me? I'm not going in to the salon; I'm taking a couple of days off.'

'Okay, great, because I was meaning to come and see you

anyway. I'll come over at about ten, is that okay?'

'Yes, that's fine. I'll see you then. Bye.'

'Bye, Mum.' Alice placed the handset back onto the telephone and as she did so, she felt the sharp pain in her right arm again, starting from the wrist and ending at the elbow. She screamed out loud and grabbed her arm. This time the pain lasted for about ten seconds and she could hardly bear it. Her arm felt stiff. She rocked backwards and forwards until the pain stopped. When it did stop, her mind was filled with concern. There had been no reason for the pain and it had come on so suddenly without warning. The day before, when it had happened, she thought it was because she had stretched her arm too far reaching for the table, but she had not had to stretch her arm at all when she replaced the handset just now—the telephone was right in front of her.

She sat at the kitchen table, hesitating to pick up her fork to continue eating her meal, half-expecting the pain to return; she was on edge as if waiting for it. But it seemed to have disappeared as quickly as it had come. She slowly flexed her arm and it felt fine, so she decided to try to put it to the back of her mind.

As she ate her pasta, she flicked through the rest of the newspaper, trying to avoid the story about Jane Forester, but thoughts of her father taunted her mind. She wanted to find out more about him. Would her mother be willing to talk about him? In the past eighteen years, she had hardly spoken a word to Alice about him. The odd bits of information Alice did have had been gleaned from listening in to her mother's conversations with her friends. As the years went by, her mother had lost touch with people who had known her when she was married. Whenever Alice had asked her mother about him in the past, she had found ways to skirt around the subject. She'd told Alice that the reason her father left was because they had drifted apart. In the past few years, Alice had been busy with her studies and her friends, so she had not been concerned about her absent father; she had settled into a pattern in her life and felt quite happy as she was. She'd always told herself that his rejection had never really affected her because she was just too young when he left home for it to have had an impact on her life. It was hard for her to relate to those people she would see on daytime chat shows who wanted to find their long-lost parents; his absence had not left a hole in her life. But now, suddenly, some part of her had been awakened, the curiosity too loud to be ignored.

As she lay in bed that night, she resolved to try to find a way to ask her mother about Roger Forester, the man who had once been a part of their lives. After tossing and turning in anticipation of what information she might uncover, she eventually drifted off to sleep. She dreamt she was in a large building, which looked like a hospital, and she saw a long needle. A doctor was trying to find a vein to give her an injection. She saw herself screaming. She woke up to find that she was actually screaming and grabbing her right arm. The pain had returned, but as soon as she realised what was going on, it subsided. She felt afraid to go back to sleep in case the pain came back again.

Chapter Four

Thursday 14th August 1997

Alice telephoned the doctors' surgery in the morning to book an appointment to see her GP, Dr. Small. There was an appointment available for 3 p.m. that day. After booking it, she set out to meet her mother.

As Alice ascended the stairs at the Tube station, she saw a newspaper salesman standing outside. She then remembered that she'd forgotten to bring yesterday's newspaper with her. It would have been easier to explain to her mother why she wanted to find her father if she could have shown her the picture of Jane Forester. Having the newspaper with her would have helped her to bring up the subject.

For a moment, she thought about going home to get the newspaper. As she stood, unmoving at the top of the Tube station exit, unsure what to do, busy commuters rushed past her. One man said 'Sorry', when his briefcase hit her leg; this roused her from her rumination. She noticed how everyone seemed to be in a hurry to get somewhere. This focused her mind on the time. It was 10 a.m. Her mother would be wondering where she was, and she didn't really feel like taking the Tube back home again. Shrugging her shoulders, she realised that she wouldn't be able to talk to her mother about her father today. In a way, it brought a sense of relief; part of her didn't quite feel ready to ask her mother about him.

Alice found her mother in the kitchen, eating breakfast. Stephanie was wearing a long peach-coloured silk dressing gown. 'Darling!' she exclaimed as Alice walked into the room. She stood up, still holding a slice of toast, and gave her daughter a hug and kiss. 'How are you?'

'I'm fine, Mum. How are you?'

'Oh, I'm okay.' Stephanie sat back at the kitchen table and

gestured for Alice to sit next to her. 'I've decided to treat myself to a couple of days off work. We're not busy at the moment. Have some toast, Alice.' She pointed to the pile of toast on the table—much too much for her to eat alone. It was obvious she had prepared extra for Alice, always worried that she didn't eat enough.

Alice took one slice, even though she wasn't hungry, so as not to offend her.

'So, Alice, what shall we do today? We can go shopping; I could buy you some new clothes. Or, we could go to the cinema; there's a new romantic comedy I want to see... what's it called? Oh, I'll remember in a minute. Or, we could go to the park.' Stephanie leaned to look out of the window as if to check the weather. 'It would be a pity to miss out on catching a bit of sun. It looks like it's going to be a warm day again today.'

'I don't mind. Anywhere you want to go. But I have to be back early. I've got a doctor's appointment at three.' Almost as soon as she'd said it, Alice wished she could take the words back. She saw her mother's face drop. Ever since Alice had been a young girl, Stephanie had worried too much about her, fearing the worst every time she had a bit of a temperature. Alice was kicking herself for mentioning the doctor's appointment; her mother would now be imagining all sorts of things—it was bound to ruin her day.

'Why? What for? What's wrong?' Her mother's eyes penetrated deep into her own.

'It's nothing, Mum, just a routine trip. Um... a blood pressure check.' Would that ease her mother's concern?

'There's nothing routine about a blood pressure check. Oh my God! I'll come with you. Do you feel okay?'

It seemed that her little white lie had only made things worse. 'You don't have to come with me. I just got a pain in my arm a couple of days ago and it came back yesterday—'

'A pain in the arm? Which arm?' Stephanie's eyes were open so wide, Alice could see the whites all around them. 'A pain in the arm could be your heart. Is that why they want to take your blood pressure?'

'They don't want to take my blood pressure.'

'But you said—'

'I know; I only said that so you wouldn't worry.'

'Let me see your arm, where was the pain?' She took Alice's left arm and rolled up her sleeve.

'It's the other arm,' said Alice tugging her arm away and

rolling her sleeve down.

Her mother instantly took her other arm, only for Alice to pull it away. 'Please don't fuss, Mum. I think I just pulled a muscle or something. I'll be okay.'

'Does it hurt?' asked her mother, her face full of concern.

'No. The pain comes and goes. I shouldn't have said anything; you always worry too much about everything.'

'Of course I do; I'm your mother. You'll understand when you have children of your own.' Stephanie finished drinking her coffee. 'Are you sure you don't want me to come with you to the doctor?' she asked, after five silent minutes had passed. Her mind had obviously still been ticking away, imagining what could be wrong with Alice.

'No. I'm not a child.'

'Right, I'll go and get changed, then we'll go out. I won't be a minute.' Stephanie disappeared into her bedroom.

Alice started to clear away the breakfast plates. There were a few old photographs displayed in one of the glass cabinets above the dishwasher. The photographs caught Alice's eye as she was placing the plates and cups into the dishwasher. She had seen the photographs a hundred times but they somehow seemed more significant at the moment. Her mind went back to something Sophie Bairns had said at work the week before:

'You see that painting up there,' said Sophie, pointing behind her to the canvas depicting an old cottage by a stream. It was a fairly run of the mill type of painting, hung above the counter where they served the customers. Alice hardly ever noticed it.

Alice looked at the painting and smiled at Sophie. 'It's nice,' she said, as if seeing it for the first time.

Sophie nodded. 'Yes, it is. The funny thing is, no one ever notices it; but today everyone has been saying to me, "that's a nice painting". Isn't it odd?' Sophie laughed it off as another customer walked up to the counter.

Odd. That's how it felt to Alice now, looking at the photographs that had been in the background for years, but which now screamed out for attention. Two of the photographs were of Alice from her school days, the other was a picture of Alice with her mother, taken a few years ago. It suddenly occurred to her that, as far as she could recall, she had never seen any photographs of her father. *That* was definitely "odd"; after all, her parents had been together for years.

She now had an overwhelming desire to see a photograph of her father. In the past, she had not given much thought to him, perhaps because of the negative way he had been portrayed by her mother; a man who had walked out on his family, deserting his only child and never trying to contact her. Alice had grown up only knowing Stephanie and not overly concerned about not having her father around. Of course there were the times when she would visit her friends' houses and watch them interacting with their fathers; at those times she had wondered what it would be like to have a father at home. When she had argued with Stephanie over one thing or another, she had sometimes wished she could leave her and go and stay with her father. At other times she had almost had a fantasy image of what he was like, and dreamed that one day she would meet him; but her thoughts of him had flittered in and out of her mind never really leaving any lasting impression. She had never seriously wanted to see a photograph of him, until now.

Just as she was turning on the dishwasher, her mother appeared in the kitchen. 'Okay, I'm ready. Oh, Alice, thank you, but you didn't have to tidy up, dear, I would have done it later.'

'That's okay; I wanted to do it.' Then she decided to jump straight in, rather than think about it and risk losing her nerve: 'Mum? Do you have any photos of my dad?'

The colour appeared to wash out of Stephanie's face. She sat down, as if to prevent herself from fainting. 'You've never asked to see photographs of your dad before,' she said.

Alice felt uncomfortable. 'Um... I know. But, I just realised, when I saw those old pictures; well,' Alice pointed at the photographs displayed in the cabinet above the dishwasher, 'I realised that I haven't seen any pictures of him... I don't know what he looks like.' She paused.

Stephanie's gaze fixed on the photographs in the cabinet. The colour had returned to her face now, but she was gradually turning redder and redder. Alice was not sure if she was embarrassed or angry.

Alice coughed to try to get her mother's attention. Then she continued. 'The other day, in the café, your friend, Rita, she said I look like my dad.'

Stephanie sighed deeply and stood up. 'I don't have any photos of him.' There was an apologetic tone to her voice, but then she looked directly at her daughter and said: 'I didn't really want to look at any photos of him when he left us. Can you blame me?' Her cheeks were still very red.

Alice looked away. 'I suppose not,' she muttered, disappointed. Unsure whether she should continue, she decided to take the risk: 'Do I look like him?'

'Well, yes, I suppose so. Yes, okay, you do,' said her mother, begrudgingly.

Looking at her mother's face, she saw that her colour had returned to normal. Perhaps she would be okay to talk some more about him. Alice was curious. Now that she had started to talk about him she felt a need to find out as much as she could; it was like unwrapping a gift in a "pass-the-parcel" game—each answer unwrapped a further truth and brought her closer to the mysterious man who was her father. 'Why did you split up? I mean, your friend seemed really surprised that you were divorced. Why was she so surprised?'

'Oh, I don't know. Alice, do we really have to talk about this now? It's not important.' Stephanie sighed again. 'Let's go out.'

'But, Mum, wait!' She felt a longing in her heart to find out more, but her chance was slipping away, out of her grasp.

Stephanie turned to face her.

'It's important to me. I need to know about my dad.'

There was a look of anxiety in her mother's eyes. 'It must be hard for you,' she said, looking past Alice at nothing in particular. Then she shook her head as if to rid it of painful memories. 'Look, just forget about him,' she said quickly, smiling to hide any other feelings. 'He's not part of our lives. He's the one who decided to stay away. I never tried to stop him seeing you, he just never made the effort. He left us. He's not worth worrying about. You're an adult now, darling. You don't need him. We're happy, aren't we?'

'Yes, but...'

'You don't need him,' repeated Stephanie, as if trying to convince her.

'Lots of children try to find their parents... It's something I want to try—'

'I don't think you should,' said Stephanie, bluntly.

'Why not? Is there something you haven't told me about him? Was he violent?'

Stephanie laughed. 'No, nothing like that.'

'Well... I'm not being disrespectful or anything, but just because you two didn't get on, that's no reason for me not to know him... He's my dad. He might want to know me, too.'

'If he wanted to know you, he'd have contacted you before now. He knows where we live. Please, darling, I just don't want you to disappoint yourself. He wanted a divorce so he could remarry; he didn't want us anymore. See how selfish he was? He's stayed away for so long.'

Alice began to think that her mother might be right. The sad truth was that her father had never once even thought of sending her a Christmas present or birthday card. He didn't care. She felt upset and disheartened. 'Sorry, Mum, I shouldn't have asked you about him. Let's go out and forget about this.'

Stephanie put a hand on Alice's shoulder. 'I'm not trying to stop you, dear. You know that if I thought it was a good idea for you to contact your father, I'd help you, really. I just don't think it is.' She smiled and turned towards the door. Alice could not tell what thoughts were going around her head, but she seemed positively relieved that Alice had changed her mind.

They spent the day in Regent's Park and then had a meal in a restaurant beside the Thames. Despite the fine weather, there was tension in the air between mother and daughter. Alice could tell that her mother was feeling insecure about the fact that she was showing an interest in finding her father. The afternoon had only reinforced Alice's suspicion that there was something she had not told her about him. This served to stir her curiosity further. At the same time, she knew that any mention of her father seemed to upset her mother, and that was something she did not want to do. She felt trapped in an in-between place; wanting to know more about him, but not wanting to destroy the relationship she had with her mother. As she made her way to the doctor's surgery for her appointment that afternoon, she felt tearful.

Alice returned home at 4.30 p.m., after her visit to the doctor. Dr. Small said he was unsure about what could be causing the pain in her arm. He said he would refer her to the local hospital for some tests; she would receive a date for the appointment in due course.

Sitting on the sofa in the living room, her feet on the coffee table in front of her, Alice noticed yesterday's newspaper lying on the table. Her thoughts went back over the events of the day. Feelings of guilt rose to the surface when she remembered how her mother had seemed to be on the verge of tears for most of the day. If she was going to look for her father, she knew she would have to do it on her own.

Her heart felt heavy as she recalled how her mother had inferred that she would probably end up disappointed if she did look for him; he might not want to know her. But Alice knew that was a risk she would have to take. She didn't want to live her life wondering "what if?". All the coincidences surrounding the plane crash had kick-started her curiosity. Was Jane Forester somehow related to her? Was she a half-sister she had never met? Her father could have a whole other family. Somehow, Alice had started to feel incomplete as soon as she had decided to try to find him; it felt as if part of her background had been blotted out and it was up to her to fill in the gaps. Her father was a part of her; if he hadn't existed she would never have been born. Part of her imagination that had rested dormant for years had now begun to stir; she knew she would have to continue in her journey to the end, no matter what the consequences.

That evening, Stephanie sat alone in her kitchen, eating a bowl of spaghetti bolognese. Spread out in front of her on the table were the last few photographs she had of Roger Forester. They were old, black and white, and slightly faded. She stared at the photographs, scrutinising Roger's smiling face as he held Alice in his arms. Would others be able to see what she saw behind the smile on his face? Was that why she did not want to show the photographs to anyone else... even Alice? Stephanie could see that he was faking the smile; but was that just something her mind had conjured up because of everything that had passed between them? Was her imagination reflecting back to her what she thought she knew when she looked at the photograph? Would someone else just be able to see a smiling man, happy to be holding his tiny daughter in his arms?

She felt insecure when she thought about Alice's new found interest in her father. She was twenty-one years old, and up until now she had never really asked any questions about him. Stephanie had always known that the day might come when Alice may want to know more, but as the years had rolled by she had become more hopeful that perhaps it would never happen. It had come as more of a shock to her than it should have when Alice asked about Roger; after all, she did have the right to know the truth about her father—but at what cost?

Her meal continued to grow cold in the bowl in front of her as she contemplated the photographs and thoughts about Roger swirled around her mind; thoughts that had been packed away in a box, hidden in the depths of her memories, sealed tightly. As Alice grew up, Stephanie became too complacent, she realised, imagining that she would never have to think about the secrets locked away, buried deep where no one could find them; but now she sensed that the box was like a ticking time bomb, gathering dust, but nevertheless ticking away, and one day the time would come for all to be revealed.

Standing up, she lifted her bowl with the half-eaten pasta and placed it absent-mindedly in the sink. Her mind wandered to a time long ago when Alice had asked about her father. She had only been five years old at the time.

'Mummy, all the other children at school have a daddy. Why don't I have one?'

Stephanie felt a lump in her throat as she continued to get Alice dressed for school. Looking into her daughter's innocent eyes, she didn't know what to say. She began tying the child's shoelaces, looking fixedly at the laces as if directing the reply to them. 'Well, darling, a daddy is just the same as a mummy really. It is just a name for someone who looks after you.' Stephanie smiled, and hoped that Alice would not ask any further questions. 'Come on, let's go and have breakfast.' She lifted Alice off the bed.

'But, Mummy, why does everyone else have a mummy and a daddy? Karen said I should have a daddy too. She said maybe he died. Natalie's daddy died. What does that mean, Mummy? Did my daddy died?' Alice's forehead creased into a frown, her brown eyes waiting for a reply.

'No, your daddy... You don't have a daddy. You only have a mummy. Not everyone has a mummy and daddy. When you're older you'll understand.'

Alice then saw her cat run up the stairs to greet her and she began to play happily with the creature, forgetting her questions, and leaving Stephanie to worry whether she had said the right thing and what she should say the next time.

When Stephanie thought Alice was old enough to understand, she explained that Roger had left them, telling her that their relationship had broken down, they had grown apart and could no longer live together. In a way, Stephanie preferred it that Roger had cut himself off from them completely; it made things less complicated.

Stephanie emerged from Alice's bedroom. It had taken longer than usual to settle her to sleep, as Alice was teething and didn't want to be left alone. Eventually, after Stephanie read her a story, the child had fallen asleep. As she stepped out of the bedroom, her head throbbing, she wondered how long it would be before Alice started crying again; she prayed that she would somehow sleep through the night tonight. For three nights now, Alice had woken her up throughout the night and she had hardly been able to get any rest.

Stephanie walked into her own bedroom, ready to collapse onto the bed. Roger was packing a suitcase. 'Roger? What are you doing?' In her groggy state of mind, she wondered if she was dreaming. For the past couple of days it had been hard to tell if she was asleep or awake half the time.

'I'm leaving you,' he said, throwing the final items of clothing into the suitcase and slamming it shut.

She stood at the doorway, now holding on to the door handle to steady herself. 'What do you mean?' she heard herself say, but it was more of a mumble, and she could not be sure if she had said it or thought it. He didn't appear to have heard her.

'Excuse me,' he said gruffly, as he approached the door. He then indicated with a gesture that he wanted her to move away from the door so that he could leave.

'Wait, what's happened?' she asked, unable to believe that he was just leaving, without warning. Things had not been going well between them; there had been a lot of rows over trivial things, but she hadn't expected this... Tears filled her eyes, threatening to spill.

He stood up straight and looked her in the eyes, his gaze was cold, unemotional. 'Don't pretend you didn't know this was coming. This marriage isn't working. We both know that. We hardly speak to each other—'

'We have a small child—'

'We both know you wanted a child more than I did.' He

pushed past her, forcing her to let go of the door handle. She turned around quickly to face him, and saw stars before her eyes. She took a deep breath to settle herself. The lack of sleep was making her woozy. Now, what she was hearing from Roger didn't make sense. She thought he wanted Alice, too. She thought they'd both wanted children. 'You... You never wanted her? Is that what you're saying?'

'I never said that.' He began walking down the stairs.

'Why didn't you tell me before?' Stephanie hurried after him, turning towards Alice's bedroom door, speaking in a low voice to avoid waking her, praying she would stay asleep.

'Your heart was set on having a child, remember? It was like it would be the end of the world if you never had one.' Roger was talking to her from the bottom of the stairs.

She stood holding onto the bannisters, looking at him. He had made up his mind, he was leaving; he didn't even want to discuss it. She didn't want to let him go.

He reached towards the front door.

'Roger, please.' She wiped her tears on the sleeve of her dressing gown. 'Don't leave, not like this; let's talk.'

'You haven't wanted to talk to me for the past couple of months, why start now?' he huffed.

'I've been moody sometimes, yes, but so have you. It's Alice, she doesn't sleep well. I'm up half the night.'

'You've got time to sleep during the day; you're not working.'

'It's a full time job running the house and looking after a small child; looking after you.'

He fished inside his coat's pocket for his car keys: 'Well, you won't have to worry about looking after me anymore. I'm going.' He opened the front door.

She ran down the stairs and tried to hold onto his arm, but he pulled it away.

'Stephanie, stop fooling yourself. We're living separate lives already. Think about it, when was the last time we had sex?'

'Is that what this is about—'

'No, that's not it! We're different people. It'll never work. We hardly talk to each other anymore. We're better off apart.' He stepped outside the door.

'But, Alice... What will happen to Alice? She's your daughter...'

'Take care of Alice. Good-bye, Stephanie,' he said, pulling the door closed behind him.

She stood alone, the slamming of the door resonating in her ears. Alice began to cry.

As Stephanie sat in the kitchen and recalled the memories, she wondered whether she had pushed things too far. Roger had never been as keen to start a family as she had. She began to think that maybe he had not wanted Alice from the start. Perhaps they should have been trying to work out the problems in their relationship, before thinking about having a child.

Stephanie's mind went back to the conversation she'd had with Alice earlier that day. What if Alice found Roger, and what if she got to know him? Surely, he wasn't a threat to her now... or was he? She couldn't be sure what he would tell Alice about the reasons he left home. *Would he tell her about—* Just at that moment the telephone rang, interrupting Stephanie's train of thought. She walked into the living room, sat on the sofa and picked up the phone.

'Hello,' she said absent-mindedly.

'Steph, hi, it's Rita,' said the friendly voice on the other end.

Rita's voice brought Stephanie back down to earth. 'R... Rita,' she stuttered, 'how nice to hear from you.'

'It was so nice to see you again on Tuesday; it brought back so many memories. I can't believe Alice is already so grown up. It seems like only yesterday she was just a baby. Doesn't time go too quickly?'

'Y... Yes, it does.'

'We really must meet up soon,' Rita babbled on, unaware that her voice was making her friend feel uncomfortable.

Such timing, Stephanie couldn't help feeling edgy; she had just been thinking about events from years ago, and now she was hearing the voice of someone who knew everything... all about her secret. The truth now seemed to be bubbling under the surface ready to reveal itself, like a chick cracking through the shell of an egg, slowly chipping away until soon all that was left would be shattered remains.

'We used to be so close; it's such a shame we lost touch.' Rita's words awaited a response.

Perhaps this was a good thing; maybe Rita walking back into her life now was a blessing—after all, she was the only one who ever knew.

'Rita,' she began tremulously, 'I'm sorry if I wasn't very friendly when I saw you on Tuesday. I just hadn't expected to see you, and it brought everything back—all the memories. Sometimes, I think I'd prefer to forget.' She laughed to hide her nervousness.

'Steph, don't worry. It was as much of a shock for me seeing you. It did upset me to hear that you and Roger split up. I don't know if you want to talk about it. I knew you had problems when I was around, but I really thought that would change when Alice came along. I mean, you both wanted a child so badly, didn't you?'

'Hmm, it's funny. I was thinking about that just before you phoned. I'm not sure. Maybe Roger didn't really want Alice. She asked me about him today. Of course, I expected her to ask about him sooner or later, but it still came as a shock. She's never really seemed that bothered about him not being around. I'm sure if she finds him and finds out everything, she'll hate me. What do you think? I've been going crazy all day worrying about it.'

'Why would Alice hate you? I don't understand. Of course, I don't really know much about what went on after I left town. How old was Alice when Roger left?'

'She was about eighteen months, I think.'

'That's a long time ago.'

'It is.'

'And Roger has never kept in touch with you or Alice?'

'No, never. He just disappeared. I heard from him a couple of years later; he was getting remarried, and wanted a divorce. It was a bit out of the blue. I'd moved from the home we'd been renting together, to this flat. Apparently, he'd got my new address from a mutual friend. You know, he didn't even once ask to see Alice while the divorce was going through the Court. Once the divorce was finalised, I never heard from him again.'

'So, why would Alice want to see him? He basically abandoned her.'

'She's curious.'

'Yes, well, I suppose he *is* her father. Maybe it's because she wants to meet some of her family. Being with you, she hasn't really had any of that; well not *real* family. Maybe that's what it is. But it is, as you say, probably just curiosity.'

'No... you don't understand. Alice doesn't know about... well, about any of that.'

'What do you mean?'

'She thinks I'm her real mum.'

'You never told her about Miranda?'

'No. Do you think that was wrong?' Stephanie felt a strange mix of emotions when she heard Miranda's name. It brought back old, distant feelings of insecurity, defensiveness.

'Well, it's not really for me to say.' Rita's voice brought her back to the present. 'But, I had presumed that you would have told her everything by now; I mean, how old is she? Twenty?'

'Twenty-one,' corrected Stephanie.

'She's an adult. She's entitled to know,' said Rita. 'When were you planning to tell her?'

'I don't know if I was. I hadn't really thought about it. After Roger left, Alice was all I had. He obviously didn't want her. I was the one who cared for her. It was an agreement. Alice was *my* child—mine and Roger's. Anything else is too complicated.'

'Look at it from *her* perspective. If it was *you*, wouldn't you want to know?'

'She doesn't need to know. Anyway, I could never find the right time to say anything. She'd been rejected by her father at such a young age, I just couldn't bring myself to tell her. I came close a few times, but what was I supposed to say? "By the way, I'm not your real mother"? I couldn't do it to her. As time went by and I never heard anything from Roger—or Miranda for that matter—it became less important. As far as I am concerned, she's my daughter and I'm her mum. Miranda never wanted her. It was a surrogacy agreement, that's all. It wasn't my fault I couldn't have children.'

'Steph, Alice knows you're the one who brought her up. She'll understand. I think she should be told,' said Rita. 'These things should be out in the open, or they could cause problems.'

'But, Rita, I'm the one who raised Alice. I don't want her to end up seeing me as a stranger. I couldn't cope with that.'

'Look, let's meet up tomorrow and talk about it. We can't discuss something like this over the phone. You sound upset.'

'I'm okay.' Stephanie took a tissue from the box on the coffee table in front of her and held it against her nose. 'Meeting tomorrow would be a good idea. I'm glad we met again. I don't think I could do something like this on my own.'

'Shall I come to your house?'

'Yes,' said Stephanie.

After the telephone conversation, Stephanie mused that although she hadn't spoken to Rita for nearly twenty years, she had been able to talk to her as if they'd never lost touch. It calmed her nerves to know that she would not have to make any decisions on her own, although she felt slightly concerned that

Rita seemed to be pushing her to tell Alice everything. In her heart of hearts she did not feel that she was ready. She remembered the feeling she'd had years ago, when she had been sitting in a helicopter, harnessed to an instructor, ready for a skydive. Roger had booked the experience for her as a gift for her birthday. That had been a time when she was younger and willing to try new things. Even then, when it was time to jump from the plane she didn't feel ready; she wanted to change her mind and call it off, but suddenly she was out there floating high above the ground, miles from anywhere. It felt the same now, as if she was on a precipice of sorts. But if she took the chance and revealed all, would this be a safe landing or a crash landing?

She walked back into the kitchen and picked up the photographs that were still lying on the table. She put them back into the old shoe-box, where they had been hidden for years, and decided to keep them out of sight.

Chapter Five

Friday 15th August 1997

When she woke up, Stephanie felt tired. Her night had been one of tossing and turning; not only physically, but also mentally. She had been thinking about her conversations with Alice and Rita. She could hear Rita's voice in her head: *'She's entitled to know... She should be told'.* But Stephanie still felt reluctant to tell Alice about the surrogacy agreement. One thing was certain, Alice had made the decision to try to find her father, so the problem wouldn't just go away. Stephanie was racking her brain to try to find a way to explain things to Alice without revealing too much.

It felt as if she was excavating a tomb that she had hoped would stay buried for ever.

She recalled how when she was still married to Roger, when they were agreeing the surrogacy with Miranda, they had both said that when Alice was old enough they would tell her everything. Her mind went back to a late summer evening when she was seated next to Roger on the sofa, a glass of red wine in her hand...

'So, are you sure about this, Steph?' asked Roger, taking a sip of his beer.

'Absolutely. Miranda seems like a nice girl, and she's willing to do this for us. She doesn't want children; she said it herself. I don't think there'll be a problem.' Stephanie tried to push any niggling doubts to the back of her mind. She had been questioning how any woman would give up her child for money. What if Miranda is just desperate for money now, as she is a student? What if her situation changes in a few years and she has a change of heart? *Would she be able to take back the child? A child that Stephanie would have taken in as her own and fallen in love with? She knew she could not afford to think about any of that. The most important thing was that this young girl was offering her the chance to be a mum; something that she*

had dreamed of. Her focus was on that goal.

'Yes, but she's young. What if she changes her mind?' Roger voiced one of Stephanie's greatest concerns.

'That's a chance we have to take.' She sat back and took a mouthful of wine, trying to think positively, not wanting this chance to slip through her fingers.

'But I mean, what if she comes back a few years from now and asks to see the child? I'm not sure how watertight these agreements are.'

Stephanie sat forward and looked at Roger. 'I've thought about all that too, but I'm willing to risk something going wrong. I have nothing to lose. If we turn down Miranda's offer, what chance do we have of ever being parents?'

'We could adopt, or foster a child. There are always children being abandoned,' said Roger.

'But when I suggested those options to you before, you always said that if we couldn't have a child of our own—'

'Then we shouldn't have one,' he completed her sentence.

'But, Roger, don't you see? If Miranda has your child, it would be a part of you. This way we have a chance for a child of our own, or as near as possible.'

Roger looked uncomfortable.

'You know how much I want children.' Stephanie stared into her now empty glass of wine.

'I'm just not sure we're going about it the right way. We don't know Miranda.'

'Well, we'll be meeting her soon, and then I'm sure we'll be able to get an idea about whether she can be trusted or not. You do still want to meet her?'

Roger stood up and looked down at her. 'What do we tell the child when it grows up? Are we going to pretend that you are its real mother?'

'I hadn't thought about that.'

'It's something we have to think about. If we do go ahead with this plan, I think we should tell the truth to the child; tell him or her about the surrogacy agreement.'

Stephanie felt as if her dream was being watered down with a dose of reality. She wanted a child of her own and had seen the surrogacy agreement as a way of getting that—after all, Miranda didn't want the child; it would only be born because Stephanie had asked for it. 'Would it be absolutely necessary to tell the child? Wouldn't it be better to say that we are the real parents?'

'No,' said Roger, sitting on the edge of the sofa. 'That wouldn't be right. The child should be told.'

'We can deal with that when the time is right. The child would have to be old enough to understand.'

'I think you're living in some fairy-tale land, Stephanie. You do realise that this child won't be yours, and you can't buy a child and pretend it's yours?'

His words further diluted her dream. 'Why are you being like this?'

'Like what? Realistic?'

'No. You're treating me as if I'm stupid.'

'I know what you're like, Steph. I won't agree to this surrogacy arrangement unless you agree that we'll do things properly. I want this child to know everything when he or she is old enough. Everyone has a right to know who their real parents are.'

'Okay.' Stephanie stood up. 'I never said we wouldn't tell the child about the surrogacy'. But deep inside she was questioning why it was necessary. Miranda didn't want the child; why should she have any rights?

Reflecting on her thoughts, Stephanie realised that if she'd still been with Roger, Alice would probably have known about Miranda by now. She began to question herself. Had she been selfish, keeping the truth from Alice for so long?

Lying in bed, she thought back to the one and only occasion she had come close to telling Alice everything. Alice had been thirteen years old. It was late October or early November; the leaves were falling from the trees outside. Alice and Stephanie sat together close to the gas fire. They had made some popcorn and settled down to watch a rented video. Alice had chosen the video on the way home from school. It was a popular film amongst her school friends; the story of an orphan girl, adopted and brought up by a couple who treated her badly. The girl had eventually managed to run away. Thinking back, Stephanie could not remember the details of the film, but the thing that stayed in her memory was the conversation she'd had with Alice that night.

'What did you think of the film, Mum?' Alice asked, cheerfully, as she pressed the rewind button on the video recorder. 'It was good, wasn't it?'

'Yes, darling, it was very good,' Stephanie said, wiping away tears.

'Typical of you to cry at the end.' Alice laughed.

'Well, it was so sad.'

'Yes, but it was a happy ending. I'm glad she got away from those people,' commented Alice.

Stephanie nodded.

'I felt sorry for Amy. The people who adopted her were so cruel.' Alice took the video tape out of the machine and placed it back in its box.

Stephanie found Alice's comment moving, and the thought occurred to her that maybe it was the right time to tell her the truth about her birth. Standing up, Stephanie walked over to the light switch and turned on the lights. Alice had wanted the lights off during the film to create a "Cinema" effect.

'Alice, dear,' she began, 'do you know any children who have been adopted? For example, someone in your class at school?'

'No.' Alice shook her head. She was now seated on the sofa with her legs resting on the coffee table in front of her.

'Take your feet off the table,' scolded Stephanie.

Alice sighed and curled her legs up on the sofa instead. She reached for the television remote control.

Stephanie sat on the sofa beside her. 'Not all children who are adopted are treated badly, you know.' She waited anxiously for a response.

'I know that,' said Alice, switching channels on the television. 'But it's not the same as having real parents, is it? I mean, I know I don't know my dad, but at least I have you.' She smiled through her brown eyes. She seemed contented with her life, and Stephanie felt it would be cruel to now tell her that she wasn't her mother, especially after what she had just said.

She leaned back on the sofa, feeling torn between wanting Alice to know the truth and yet wanting to protect her from it.

She made one last effort: 'Alice,' she fiddled nervously with the fringes of the purple velvet cushion on the sofa, as she spoke. 'Wouldn't it just be the same if you had been adopted by me? I'd still be your mother if you didn't know your real mother.'

Alice looked at her in the eyes, and Stephanie held her breath, feeling suddenly as if she'd said too much.

'No, Mum, it wouldn't be the same.' She turned back to face the television. 'I think it's good that people adopt children that haven't got parents, but I don't think it could ever really be the same as having real parents, do you?' She seemed to be awaiting a reply. The innocence in her eyes made Stephanie feel like weeping. There was no way she could even consider telling her about the surrogacy now.

Stephanie turned towards the television, unable to meet her gaze. 'I'm not sure,' she said. 'Oh, Alice, isn't this that programme you watch every week?' She made an effort to stop her voice breaking as she stood up and walked towards the door.

'Yes, it is. Don't you want to watch it, Mum?'

She was already at the living room door, her back towards Alice. 'Er, no, dear. I'm going to bed. I feel a bit sleepy; it must have been the dim lighting when we were watching the film.'

Stephanie had cried herself to sleep that night and made the decision that she would wait until Alice was older, or if necessary she would never tell her the truth.

Her thoughts returned to the present day as she wiped a tear from her eye. Alice's interest in her father was something she had convinced herself she would never have to deal with, but here it was staring her in the face, taunting her, stirring up feelings of guilt and regret. Her selfishness may have denied Alice the right to know her real identity, and the thought that she had made the wrong decision haunted her, giving her no peace.

She turned to look at her alarm clock and saw that it was 12 p.m. She had been awake for most of the night and felt tired still. Suddenly she panicked, remembering that she had promised to meet Rita at the Tube station at 1.30 p.m. She forced herself out of bed and hurriedly prepared for her meeting with her old friend.

Rita introduced Stephanie and Roger to Miranda Carey in early 1975. Stephanie had been at her wits' end at that time; she had spent endless hours talking with Rita, her best friend, about her problem. She could not have children, and it was something she was having a hard time facing up to. She had suggested adoption to Roger, but had been met with a cold hard stare. He'd crossed his arms in front of him: 'Stephanie, do you realise how desperate you sound?'

'I *am* desperate!' she'd screamed, and then saw that look of disdain in his eyes that brought her down to earth. Part of her could see what he was seeing; she hadn't been able to hold a rational conversation since being told she was infertile. She was screaming inside, angry, and in denial; refusing to give up or to accept that she would remain childless. Her mind was constantly whirring, trying to think up the best way she and Roger could have a child. Fostering or adoption—they seemed like good options—but Roger wasn't convinced. 'If we can't have a child of our own, I don't think we should have a child at all,' was the only thing he would say when questioned. He was like a brick wall when it came to discussing the matter.

Stephanie knew the reason Roger was being so obstinate, but at the time she didn't want to face up to it. Their marriage was on rocky ground. They hardly spoke to each other and seemed to have very little in common. At first, Stephanie had thought having a baby would focus their attention and bring them closer; after all, they had been in love once. But after trying for a baby unsuccessfully for months, her nerves were frayed, and Roger was ever more distant. Looking in his eyes sometimes, she thought she could see him consciously planning a way to get out of the marriage. To stay sane, she ignored the signs.

In the midst of all this turmoil, and as her mind was restlessly going over it all again for the hundredth time, she overheard a conversation on the bus one day on her way to work. She was seated behind two young women; one of them was blonde, with a bob-cut hairstyle, and the other had permed light brown hair. Stephanie always noticed hairstyles before anything else, being a hairdresser. She had been trying to distract her thoughts by looking at the girls' hairstyles when she heard something that caught her attention.

'Well, you know how much Josie has always wanted children of her own,' said the blonde girl.

'Yes,' said her friend. 'I must admit I was quite surprised when I first heard what you were planning; but I suppose if she's happy, and you—'

'She is. I think it's all worked out well. I haven't seen her so happy in years. She has a child. It's her dream come true.'

On hearing that, Stephanie couldn't help feeling the stab of pain associated with the knowledge that she could never have a child. The doctor had been clear about that: 'I'm sorry, Mrs. Forester, I'm afraid you will never be able to have children.'

It had been such a final blow. Like someone had taken a baseball bat to her dreams. Knowing that she would never know the joy of holding her own child was a burden she carried with her every day. Every time she saw a small child playing, or a baby in a pram, she would be back there in the doctor's surgery, tears flowing from her eyes, shock taking hold and refusing to let her go.

'But how do you feel?' asked the girl with the brown hair, bringing Stephanie out of her trance.

'Oh, I'm fine,' said the blonde girl. 'It's a wonderful feeling. I've given my sister something she's always wanted—a child of her own.'

'But... it's not really hers.'

The blonde girl took a tissue from her bag and blew her nose.

'Sorry, I didn't mean to upset you, Stacy,' said the brown haired girl.

'No, no, you haven't. I just get a bit emotional...'

'Well, yes, I suppose you would. It must be the hormones. I'm not judging you or anything, but I really don't think I'd be able to give my baby away to someone else.'

'It wasn't hard to do. Josie isn't a stranger; she's my sister, and we're very close. Throughout the pregnancy I told myself the baby was Josie and Paul's. It is Paul's baby, and I'm sure Josie and Paul will make the best parents. I don't regret it for a minute.'

When Stephanie got off the bus, she felt a new sense of hope surge within her. It was raining and she had to open her umbrella, but it seemed to her as if the sun was shining. Roger hadn't agreed to adoption because he didn't want a baby that wasn't theirs. He could still have a baby. Someone could have a baby for her and Roger. She smiled to herself.

Stephanie mentioned the surrogacy option to Rita and she actually asked Rita whether she'd consider having a baby for them. Rita declined, saying she didn't think it was a good idea. However, a couple of months later, Rita phoned her:

'Steph, remember you were telling me you wanted to consider surrogacy as an option?'

'Yes. Have you changed your mind? Oh, Rita—'

'No, no. I'm not offering. But I talked to a friend of mine and she said she knows someone who might be interested.'

'Oh. Do you know her?'

'No. She's a student, apparently. She has plans to travel abroad but is short of money. She mentioned to my friend that she'd be willing to have a baby for you if you pay her.'

'Well, how much does she want? We have some savings, but bringing up a child is expensive and we'll need money.'

'She hasn't said how much, but she'd like to meet with you and maybe you could discuss it with her. Her name is Miranda Carey.'

Stephanie told Roger about it when he came home form work that night:

'Are you going completely crazy?' was his initial reaction.

'You know how much I want a child,' she said. 'I thought you did, too.'

They were sitting in the living room on the brown leather sofa. Roger was smoking. He put out his cigarette and turned to face her. He saw how his comment had upset her, as her eyes were welling with tears. He reached out and touched her face softly.

'Darling, you have to admit this is a crazy idea. What woman in her right mind would give up her baby to a complete stranger?'

He was talking softly, but Stephanie felt that there was a patronising tone to his voice. She reached for a tissue from the box just in front of her. As she pulled out a tissue, the box fell onto the floor. Roger picked it up and looked at her sympathetically. Stephanie felt that he was inwardly laughing at her. He was treating her as he always did every time she had an idea; as if she was a little girl, unable to make decisions about anything.

'Now, let's forget about all this, shall we?' He seemed pleased with himself.

Stephanie took a deep breath. 'There is someone who is willing to have a child for us; so it's not a crazy idea. I'm not just going to forget about it.' She sat back on the sofa, folding her arms, and waited for his response.

'You're not thinking straight, darling.' Roger stood up, he seemed agitated, restless. 'You are asking me to have a baby with someone I've never even met.'

'It's not as if you have to sleep with her. You just donate your sperm.'

He turned to face her, and looked directly in her eyes, making her feel uncomfortable with his hard stare. 'I won't do it,' he said, angrily, folding his arms and sitting back down on the sofa. He leaned forward and picked up his cigarette packet from the coffee table, his hands shaking.

When he had leaned back again, Stephanie touched his arm: 'Roger, dear, I want you to do this for me. For us. I want a child; our child. You said you don't want to adopt; well, this way, the child will be yours.'

'Why should I have to pay someone to give me my own child? We can't afford to pay out money to this woman.' He lit his cigarette and shrugged Stephanie's hand away from his arm. He blew out a circle of smoke, then turned to face her, his dark eyes narrowed: 'If we could have had a child of our own, it would have been great. But we can't. Just face it. We can't do something like this, it's wrong.'

'No, you're wrong. It's the perfect solution.' Her voice came out high-pitched. She felt a frantic need to find a way to convince him. It was as if she was holding on to a fraying piece of rope, her dreams tied to the end; she had to pull in the rope before it snapped, and he had to help her. But his eyes were distant. There was no emotion in his gaze. It was as if he had given up and decided she was foolish.

He leaned back on the sofa and took a deep drag from his cigarette. She watched as he exhaled the smoke in front of him, staring blankly ahead, but she could see his mind ticking away trying to think of what he could say to her. Eventually he spoke, without looking at her.

'This is the maddest thing you've ever thought of. Sometimes I wonder what is going on in that head of yours. All you can think about is having a baby. Baby, baby, baby. Blah, blah, blah.' Then he turned towards her, irritation showing in his eyes. 'I didn't say anything before, because I know it was hard for you to hear that you can't have children. I thought in time you'd come to accept it, but no; you just keep wittering on and on and on like a broken record. Well, I'm sick of it.' He stood up as the ash from the end of his cigarette fell onto the cream carpet. He stubbed the cigarette out into an ashtray and folded his arms in front of him looking down his nose at her. 'You should know that if God had wanted you to have children, you wouldn't be bloody infertile!'

Stephanie gasped. 'How dare you! You... You... insensitive... bastard!'

Roger looked suitably embarrassed. 'Sorry,' he said, under his breath. 'I shouldn't have said that, but—'

'This is the most important thing to me, and all you can do is mock me,' she said through sniffs and tears. 'You just don't love me anymore; that's the real problem, isn't it?' She looked up at

him, her green eyes full of tears.

He handed her a tissue and sat down beside her: 'You're losing touch with the real issue here, Steph. You're losing your grip on reality.'

'What—'

'Let me finish,' he said, agitated. He looked at her and smiled a sad smile. 'You just said that having a baby is the most important thing to you. Shouldn't I be the most important thing to you? Think about it... you're the one who's putting a wall between us. You're more concerned about having a baby than you are about the way I feel.'

Stephanie sat in stunned silence. She knew what he said made sense, but her mind was not ready to hear that she had to give up her dream of having a child. She wanted to be with Roger, but she also wanted a child. 'Is it so bad that I want us to be a family?'

'Look, if it will mean I can get some peace, I will come with you to meet this woman, but I'm not promising anything. With any luck, you'll come to your senses and we can leave this in the past.'

'You'll come? You'll meet Miranda?' She smiled through her tears and shrugged away the doubts that were creeping into her mind. She wanted to focus on the positive. Roger seemed to be coming around to the idea. At least that's what she tried to tell herself.

'Don't get your hopes up, we haven't met her yet.' His voice was flat, emotionless.

Stephanie put her arms around him. 'Thank you, darling, thank you.' She put her head onto his chest and cried tears of joy as he shook his head, unable to understand how things had ever reached this point.

After meeting with Miranda, Stephanie and Roger discussed the matter again, and Roger's attitude seemed to have changed. It appeared that he had recovered some hope, and Stephanie felt that this would indeed be just the thing they needed to save their marriage: Roger would have a child of his own, and Miranda would be out of the picture once the baby was born; she'd said something about wanting to take a year off to travel abroad. Everything seemed to be coming together perfectly.

Miranda was twenty-two years old. She was quite ordinary looking; she had mousey-brown hair and was slightly on the plump side. She was pretty enough that Stephanie didn't have to be concerned about what the child might look like, but plain enough so she didn't have to worry about Roger taking a fancy to her.

She liked Miranda on first meeting her; she seemed sincere and very polite. When Stephanie questioned her about whether she'd given thought to how difficult it would be for her to give up her child, Miranda had replied: *'Some women are just not natural mothers, I suppose. The way I see it is, you want a baby and I can give that to you, in exchange for the money I need to travel. It's a fair swap. I don't really fancy sleepless nights and endless nappy changing at my age. I want to travel and see the world. My mum had six children and I'm the oldest; I was always being called upon to look after the younger ones. I made the decision a few years ago, when I was knee high in potty training and dirty nappies, that I don't want children of my own. Who knows, maybe when I'm older I'll change my views, but for now I want to be free to enjoy my life.'*

Miranda seemed like the perfect surrogate mother.

Once all the details had been agreed, Roger became more loving towards Stephanie; he began to pay much more attention to her, which seemed to be his way of assuring her that he loved her even though he would be having a child with another woman. He seemed much more considerate of her feelings and sensitive to her insecurity. It was a side of him that Stephanie had not seen for some time. Unfortunately, it didn't last long.

Almost as soon as Miranda announced she was pregnant, Roger became more distant. He spent most of his time at work, and would not return home until the early hours. Their relationship was once again failing, and Stephanie began to worry that they had made a big mistake in agreeing to the surrogacy. How could they bring up a child together if they hardly ever communicated? She spent most of her lonely nights crying.

When Alice was born, however, Roger's attitude seemed to change again, and they spent a few happy months together. Stephanie dared to believe that their marriage was back on track, but the happiness was short-lived. Roger began to stay out late more often. This led to arguments which became progressively worse. Finally, Roger left.

Stephanie thought back to the time of Alice's birth. The surrogacy arrangement now seemed like something murky and unspeakable, that was better forgotten. Even after all these years, she still could not get her head around how Miranda had so easily given up her child for a bit of money.

Stephanie wasn't present at Alice's birth, and neither was Roger. Miranda had insisted she didn't want them there. This made Stephanie jittery, worried that the girl could easily change her mind about giving them the baby. Her marriage seemed to be hanging by a thread at that stage, and her one hope was still that as soon as Roger saw his child he would become a loving husband again. She sighed at her naiveté whenever she thought back to that time. It was as if there were red flashing warning signs all over the place about the dire state of the marriage, but she chose to ignore them.

She had desperately wanted to take more of a role during the pregnancy, but Miranda had only agreed to meet with her and Roger twice in the nine months, and both times she had told them that she thought it was best if they kept their distance and treated it as more of a business arrangement so that emotions would not be involved. Miranda seemed to be acting rather neurotically, so Stephanie thought it best to go along with whatever she wanted.

When Alice was born, Miranda insisted that only Roger could attend to collect her from the hospital, as he could pretend to be her husband. She wanted things to look as normal as possible to the hospital staff.

Stephanie remembered how she had waited in anticipation for Roger to arrive back from the hospital with Alice, and how perfect Alice had looked. They told their friends that they had adopted her. Stephanie took comfort in knowing that this wasn't a complete lie as she did have to adopt her to make everything legal.

Looking up at the kitchen clock, as she ate her breakfast, her mind soon came back to the present day. She would have to meet Rita in less than half an hour. She finished her coffee and set off towards the Tube station.

Alice finished her shift at the bookstore at 1 p.m. She had lunch at a nearby café and then decided to visit her mother. Since yesterday, Alice had been feeling guilty about upsetting her by mentioning her father. Her mind battled between not wanting to hurt her mother's feelings, but at the same time wanting to acknowledge her own curiosity about the man who had abandoned her as a child.

On the way to her mother's flat, Alice saw a man selling flowers in the street. He had a few bunches of roses in his bucket, and when he saw Alice approach him, he picked out a bunch of yellow roses and held them towards her, smiling. His face looked dirty and weather worn, but his eyes were beautiful, an almost translucent blue. Alice remembered that Stephanie used to always buy yellow roses for the flat, saying that they reminded her of the sun and made her feel happy.

Alice reached into her handbag and took out her purse. The man smiled, revealing surprisingly white teeth. 'Thank you,' he said in an accent she did not recognise, as he handed her the bunch of roses.

The perfume from the flowers wafted up to Alice's nose as she walked along the street, the aroma reminding her of days when she was younger and more carefree, living with her mother. The flat always seemed to smell of roses in those days.

At 2 p.m., Alice arrived at Stephanie's front door. As she opened the door, she could hear laughter. Realising that her mother was not alone, Alice wondered whether she should leave and come back another time. She had only really wanted to make sure that her mother was okay, and not lonely, and she'd wanted to try to make up for upsetting her. From the sound of the chat and laughter emanating from the kitchen, she was fine. Alice smiled to herself. She decided she would leave the roses in the lounge with a note. As she was looking inside her bag for a pen, she heard a familiar voice. It was Rita's. The memory of the recent meeting with Rita in the café piqued Alice's curiosity. This woman knew about her father. Maybe it would be better to go into the kitchen and introduce herself. If she got to know Rita, she could find out all she wanted to know about her father, and she wouldn't have to bother Stephanie about it anymore.

Alice closed the front door slowly, trying not to make any noise; it occurred to her that maybe her mother and Rita would be discussing old times, which might include some stories about her father. It was hard to make out what the women were talking about, so she slowly crept towards the kitchen, glad she was wearing trainers as they didn't make too much noise on the wooden floor.

When Alice was standing outside the kitchen door, she heard Rita say: 'I still think you should tell Alice. She has a right to know.'

Alice raised her eyebrows.

'I can't. Well, at least not yet,' replied Stephanie.

Alice frowned. What was this secret that her mother was keeping from her? Just then, her keys fell from her hand onto the wooden floor, making a loud clanging sound as they landed.

'What was that?' said Stephanie.

In a panic, Alice quickly opened the kitchen door and said, 'Hi, Mum.'

Stephanie's eyes widened. 'Oh... er... hello, darling.' She was seated by the kitchen table opposite Rita.

'Hello,' said Rita, smiling.

'Hi,' said Alice, nodding at Rita.

She was kicking herself for dropping her keys. *What were they talking about?*

'Mum, I got you these roses.' She handed the flowers to Stephanie.

'Thank you, sweetie. They're lovely. My favourite.'

'What a thoughtful girl,' commented Rita.

Alice couldn't help feeling tension in the air. She had walked in when they were discussing something, and she had stopped them mid flow.

Stephanie began arranging the roses in a glass vase.

Alice sat down next to Rita, feeling slightly awkward.

'Er... would you like a cup of tea, Alice?' asked her mother.

'Um... okay.'

Her mother filled the glass vase with water and put it on the kitchen bench. She then took a cup from the cabinet and poured Alice some tea from the pot on the table.

Alice was only too aware of the silence in the room. Her mother and Rita had been chatting away together before she'd walked in. It was as if they were waiting for her to leave so they could continue; at least it felt that way to Alice.

'You were only a baby when I left London,' said Rita, breaking the silence.

'Yes, my mum told me,' said Alice, smiling.

'Your mother and I were just catching up on old times. We've been out of touch for over twenty years.'

'That's a long time,' said Alice.

'Darling, how's your arm? Did you go to the doctor?'

Alice was sure that her mother had interrupted to try to change the subject. She remembered Rita's words just before she'd dropped her keys: *'Alice... has a right to know.'*

'My arm's fine. Nothing to worry about.'

'Good.' Her mother smiled, then asked: 'So, have you been at work today?'

'Yes, I was there in the morning.'

'Have you had lunch?'

'Yes.'

'Good.'

Again there was silence. Then Stephanie looked at Rita. 'Have you kept in touch with Helen and Gordon?'

'No, I haven't seen them since I left London. What are they doing these days?'

'I'm not sure. I did hear they had three children and one of them became a doctor.'

'Oh, that's nice,' said Rita. 'I always liked Helen.'

Alice began to feel a bit out of place as her mother continued to discuss old times with her friend. When there was a break in the conversation, she stood up and said, 'I'd better be going. It was lovely to see you again, Rita.'

'I'll call you tonight, love,' said Stephanie.

'Okay.' With that, Alice left the room. She was tempted to hang around in the hallway to see whether her mother and Rita would continue the conversation they'd been having before she'd interrupted them, but as if able to read her mind, Stephanie followed her out of the kitchen and saw her out of the front door.

Stephanie returned to the kitchen table after seeing Alice out.

'She seems like such a lovely girl,' said Rita.

'Yes, she is.'

'So much like Roger. It was almost like having him in the room with us.'

'Hmm... not quite.' Stephanie laughed dryly. 'Roger is not a nice person, whereas my Alice is lovely.'

Rita frowned. After taking a sip of tea, she looked at Stephanie, and said, 'You seem to be harbouring a lot of hate towards him still.'

'I just don't like the way he left us and never kept in touch with Alice.'

'So, what are you going to do about the fact that she's now interested in finding him?'

'I'm going to try to dissuade her.'

'Is that wise?'

Stephanie broke a biscuit in two and began to nibble it. Then, sighing, she said, 'I don't know what else to do. If she finds him, he might tell her about the surrogacy. I wouldn't want her to find out about it from him.'

'That's why you should tell her.'

'But... No. I can't.' Stephanie fingered the lace tablecloth, nervously, looking towards the yellow roses as if they would hold the answer.

'What choice do you have? If Alice finds Roger and he tells her, she'll be upset that you've lied to her for so many years.'

'It wasn't lying.'

'Well, what else is it? She thinks you're her mum.'

'I am her mum. Miranda wasn't there to change her nappies, feed her, bath her, play with her, comfort her when she was crying—'

'I know, but Alice won't see it like that. She has a right to know who her real mother is.'

'Why? She never wanted her. Is she going to feel better if I tell her that her real mother wanted money in exchange for her child? Wouldn't she feel worse knowing that?'

'It's not going to be easy to explain it, but... If I recall rightly, didn't you and Roger say at the time that you were going to explain it all to her when she was old enough to understand?'

'Yes, we did.' Stephanie frowned. 'Things changed. If Roger and I had stayed together then maybe we would have told her. But when he left, I couldn't do it to her. How could I tell her that not only had her dad left her, but her mother had sold her at birth?'

'You and I know that the surrogacy agreement wasn't really like a sale. I mean, if you and Roger hadn't wanted a child, she wouldn't have been born. She *was* wanted. You and Roger wanted her. Miranda was just helping you to have the child you'd always wanted. If you explained it to her like that—'

'I can't.'

'All I'm saying is, it would be better coming from you than coming from Roger.'

'I just can't understand why she wants to find Roger now. She's hardly mentioned him before.'

'It was bound to happen, Steph.' Rita looked at the clock. 'I'm going to have to go, but if you need to talk about this again, let me know. You've got my number. I can help you tell Alice if you want.'

'No,' said Stephanie. 'I'm not planning on telling her. I'm just going to see what happens. Chances are, Roger won't want to know her anyway. I've warned her about that.'

'People change, Steph. He isn't necessarily the same person he was twenty years ago. He's older now. He might want to know his daughter. He might have other children.'

Stephanie stood up and started clearing away the tea cups and saucers. 'Thanks for coming over, Rita. It was great to see you after so many years.' She looked at the table as she spoke.

'Yes. Yes... it was good to meet up, and we must meet up again soon. Let's not lose touch now.'

Stephanie sighed and looked at her friend. 'I think it would be best if you didn't come here anymore. I don't want Alice to start asking you questions. She might ask you something about Roger.'

'I...'

'I'm not saying I don't want to keep in touch. We can meet at your house, or elsewhere, but just not here. I don't want to risk Alice making you feel uncomfortable.'

'I still think you should tell her everything. It's best out in the open.'

'I need to think about it,' said Stephanie, as she walked out of the kitchen towards the front door. She looked behind her, waiting for Rita to follow.

'Okay, you're the only one who can decide, Steph.' Rita smiled sympathetically as she left the flat.

Once alone, Stephanie sighed deeply as she realised how easy it would have been for Alice to have overheard them talking about her today. For years, she had planned to keep this information from Alice for ever, thinking it was for the best. Now, her control over the matter was slipping away bit by bit. Alice wanted to know about Roger, and Rita had come back into her life bringing with her memories of the surrogacy. As much as she wanted to ignore it, Stephanie could see that time was almost running out on her secret.

Ever since returning from her mother's flat, Alice had wandered around in a state of unease. *'You should tell Alice. She has a right to know,'* Rita had said. *Know what?* Alice had pondered that all day. It was definitely something about her father, she felt sure; after all, Rita had known her father.

Her mind would give her no peace. So, that evening, she

decided to phone her mother.

'Oh, hello darling,' said Stephanie. She hoped that Alice would not be able to tell from her voice that she had been crying.

'Mum, I couldn't really talk to you earlier because Rita was there, but the reason I came to see you was to say sorry about asking about my dad. I know I upset you. I was just curious.'

Stephanie could hardly contain her sense of relief. She covered the mouthpiece of the telephone and took a deep breath. Could this mean Alice would forget about trying to find Roger? 'Oh, I knew you'd see sense,' she said, on a sigh. 'You've made the right decision. It would have been foolish to try to find him after all these years, I'm so relieved.'

'But Mum—' Alice tried to interrupt.

Stephanie spoke over her: 'Thanks so much for those roses, darling. They brighten up the kitchen.'

'I know how much you like yellow roses.'

'We're happy together you and me, aren't we, darling? We don't need anyone else. Please try to understand that if I thought it would be a good idea for you to meet your father I would help you. I only want what's best for you.'

Alice's heart sank. Why was her mother so against the idea? Surely, it made sense that a girl would want to know who her father is, even if just to satisfy her curiosity? Alice still felt a desire to meet him, but now she knew that she would have to go behind her mother's back.

'How's your arm?' asked Stephanie, interrupting her musings.

'It's fine.'

'Have you been to see the doctor? What did he say?'

'He said it's nothing.'

'Hmm... maybe you should get a second opinion.'

'Mum?'

'Yes, dear.'

'About my dad, I still want to find him. I know you don't want to be involved, but it's important to me to meet him.'

Stephanie felt a familiar panic wash over her. 'But... Alice, think about it... If your father wanted to find you, he knows where we live; it would be easy for him. I don't want you to be disappointed.'

Alice thought about that for a moment and began to feel that her mother could have a point. What if she went to meet him and he shut the door in her face and totally rejected her? Would that be worse than this in-between place of not knowing? She sighed and said, 'I have questions about him, and I want to know if he has other children. I might have brothers or sisters that I don't know about.'

'It's just curiosity, darling. The grass is always greener on the other side. Even if he does have children, they might not want to know you. Rita and her brother had a falling out nearly twenty years ago and they never see each other. Family is not all it's cracked up to be. Me and you, we're happy. Why can't you just let sleeping dogs lie?' Frustration crept over Stephanie's brow and creased the lines closer together. She tried to hold in the anger that rose steadily and threatened to take over. The height of her emotions surprised her, but all she could recall in her mind was the cold way Roger had left her all those years ago and his indifference to Alice who was then a helpless child. Everything inside her was screaming at the injustice that he should be able to have a relationship with the daughter he so cruelly rejected, just because they had some overrated blood-tie.

Alice rolled her eyes. 'Mum, it's important to me. Okay, maybe I might meet him and be disappointed, but I don't want to live my life wondering "what if?". Remember that plane crash? When you saw the picture of the girl in the paper, you said she reminded you of me. Well, the next day, I saw her picture in the paper and I was shocked. She does look a lot like me. Her surname is Forester, just like my dad's. It has stirred up all these feelings. I've been feeling like there are missing pieces to my puzzle—like I'm incomplete—and all of this searching for my dad, it's to try to piece everything together.'

'Your father walked out on us both. He's a cold man. You should forget all of this.'

'Do you know something about my dad that you're not telling me?'

'Like what?'

'Well, do you know if that girl in the paper is related to him?'

'Oh, Alice, you're getting carried away with some fantasy. I have not seen or heard anything from your father for many years and I hope to never see or hear from him again.'

'If you could give me his last known address, I could take it from there. You don't have to be involved in the search.'

'You still want to go ahead with looking for him, even after all I've said?'

'Mum, just because I'm going to look for him, it doesn't mean I don't love you. This is just something I have to do for myself.'

'You're making a mistake.'

'I'm willing to make a mistake, I just don't want to be

wondering about it for ever and wishing I'd looked him up.'

'Take a bit of time, and think about it. I really don't think you should look for him.' Stephanie wondered whether the desperation in her voice was too obvious. Her mind was spinning. *What will happen if she finds him? What will he say about me? What if she finds out about the surrogacy?*

'Do you have his last known address?'

'No. I don't.'

'You're not just hiding it from me, are you? Please—'

'I didn't hear a thing from your father after he left, except when he contacted me through solicitors for a divorce. I have no idea where he was living and I really couldn't care less.'

'Does Rita know where he was living?'

'How would Rita know? She left London before your father and I split up.'

'It's just that when I came to the flat today, I heard her saying "Alice has a right to know". What was she talking about?'

Stephanie tensed, worrying whether Alice had heard anything about the surrogacy agreement; whether she had heard enough to put two and two together. 'Um... I think I mentioned that you wanted to find your father, and Rita just said you had a right to know him. I didn't agree, and I still don't agree with that. He messed up my life and he'd do the same to yours given half a chance.'

Alice could hear she was becoming upset. 'Okay, Mum, look, I'll think about what you've said.'

An audible sigh was heard from Stephanie.

'Thank you. You're a sensible girl. When you think it through, you'll understand what I mean.'

When Alice put down the phone she was left confused and began to wonder if she should just take her mother's advice and forget about her father.

Stephanie knew when she put down the phone, that she would have to make a decision now; either to tell the whole truth to Alice or somehow contact Roger. She hadn't been telling the truth to Rita or Alice when she'd told them that she had no idea where he'd moved to after they separated. The divorce petition had his address on it. For some reason, the address had stuck in her mind and she could remember it to this day: 25, Orchard's Mews, Witney, Oxford. She had read that divorce petition from cover to cover at least a hundred times.

She had not had any contact with Roger for about two years before she received the divorce petition, and it had come as quite a shock to her. She had never really missed him before she'd received the petition, and had often told herself she was glad to be living without him; without the constant arguments. For some reason, however, when he'd filed for divorce, it had made everything seem so final. It had saddened her, and she'd been almost reluctant to agree to the divorce.

As she pondered the past, she began to wonder whether Roger had another family now. It was very likely he did. He had been planning to remarry, and that was the reason he'd given for wanting the divorce. She knew it was possible he still lived at 25 Orchard's Mews, Oxford. After all, she still lived at the same flat that she'd been living in at the time of the divorce. Even if Roger didn't live at that address, she knew it would not be hard to find him. Roger's parents' address was in the old box that contained the photographs of Roger. She had not kept in contact with his parents, but she was almost certain that they would be living at the same address. When she had known them, they had always said that they would never leave that house. It had belonged to Roger's grandparents and he would inherit it one day. His parents would know where he lived now. Then, she found herself wondering whether they were still alive. Maggie Forester, Roger's mother, had been such a lovely woman. Alice reminded her of Maggie in the way she smiled, and her voice sounded very similar. When she'd been married to Roger, they'd often travelled to America to see his parents. Maggie and Ronald were very friendly and treated Stephanie as if she were their daughter. They said they'd always wanted a daughter, but Maggie had to have a hysterectomy shortly after Roger was born due to problems that ensued after the birth.

Stephanie felt sad thinking that she would never see them again, and then wondered why she was becoming so sentimental. She hadn't seen them since she'd split with Roger, although Maggie did still send gifts and cards for Alice on her birthday and Christmas until Alice was about ten years old.

It was possible Roger could have moved to America, she mused. He'd often spoken about relocating there for work. She'd often found it easier to think of him living in another country since their break-up. It had been hard for her to come to terms with. Her mind wondered about the plane crash. Alice had spoken of the young girl who looked like her, with the surname Forester. The plane had been flying from Boston. That's where Roger's parents lived.

She shook all of those thoughts from her mind and dearly clung on to the hope that she had made Alice think twice about contacting her father. But even as she thought that, she realised that the seed had been sown. Alice would want to meet with him sooner or later. If it wasn't now, she'd have to face it again in the future.

She thought about getting in touch with Roger. It would be so strange after all these years. But maybe it would be for the best. She would tell him that she had not told Alice about the surrogacy agreement, and ask him to keep it secret. It was the least he could do after leaving her to bring up Alice on her own.

Deep down, she knew that she would not be able to bring herself to contact Roger. She had built a wall to block out her memories of him, and kept it well maintained for years. Even the thought of having to talk to him or see him again was too much for her. She could not do it. That only left her with one option. She would have to tell Alice everything.

Chapter Six

Saturday 16th August 1997

Alice stood behind the counter in the bookstore and looked around her. It struck her that there seemed to be books on almost every subject imaginable. She wondered whether there were any books in the store that might help her to find her father.

She had racked her brain trying to think of ways to trace him. Living with her mother all her life, she'd not come into contact with any of her father's relatives. As he'd left home, she never found it odd that she didn't know them; after all, her mother wouldn't want to keep in touch with his family after the way he'd walked out on her leaving them both behind. Alice's family had always been just her and Stephanie. There was no one else to be able to help her put the pieces of the puzzle together. The only person she could think of asking was Rita, but she didn't want to upset her mother by getting her friend involved. It was going to be difficult trying to find her father alone, but she knew she had to try.

The bookstore was quite busy as it was Saturday, so Alice wasn't able to browse around looking for a book. She recalled seeing a book when she first started working at the store—a woman had bought it. It was called something like, "*The Ultimate Handbook: Researching Your Family Tree.*" The title had intrigued her, but as she had been busy with her studies at the time, it had slipped her mind.

Late in the afternoon, when only one customer was browsing the store—a middle-aged woman who seemed to be trying to find a novel to read—Alice began to wander around. She began by checking the "General Reference" section; that seemed like the best place to start her search. She couldn't see any books about family trees, or tracing missing people.

Rob, the manager walked out of the kitchen area at the back of the shop, holding a cup of coffee. 'How are things going,

Alice?'

'Um... fine thanks.' She tried not to look too startled. Oddly, she felt guilty, as if she had been caught stealing.

'Sold many books?' he asked, his eyes searching the store and then resting on the lone customer who was still thumbing through the latest best-sellers seemingly trying to make up her mind as to which one to purchase.

'We've been quite busy today,' said Alice, walking back behind the counter, realising she would not be able to continue her search. 'We've sold quite a few books.'

'That's what I like to hear,' said Rob, taking a sip of coffee.

'Um... do you know whether we have any books about tracing missing people or long lost relatives? Er... it's just, a customer was asking about it earlier.' Alice felt her cheeks redden.

Rob frowned and rubbed his chin. 'Hmm... I'm not sure. Have you checked the computer records?'

Why didn't I think of that before? she wondered, feeling stupid. 'Oh... er... I'll do that.'

'I don't actually think we stock those types of books,' said Rob, placing his coffee cup on the counter and walking around towards Alice. 'Excuse me,' he said, pointing at the computer next to the till.

Alice moved to the side so he could get past.

He began to type something, but after a couple of minutes he shook his head and told her that they didn't have any books specifically on those subjects; only reference books with chapters containing snippets of information. He said it would be a good idea to order something like that for the store, and he would do so when he next put in an order with his suppliers.

She smiled at him but felt frustrated inside, wondering how on earth she would be able to begin her search.

Alice arrived back at her flat at 6 p.m. She was just about to start preparing her evening meal when the phone rang. It was Jenny.

'Hi, Jen, how are you?'

'Fine. I'm just calling to let you know the details for the party on Tuesday. We'll collect you at about eight from yours. The party starts at seven-thirty, but we don't want to turn up too early; we'll let it get started before we arrive. Frank's friend—the one whose birthday it is—is called Tony, and it's going to be at his house. It's in Kensington somewhere. Have you decided what you're going to wear?'

'Er... No, I'd almost forgotten about the party,' she lied. It had been at the back of her mind throughout the past few days, and she'd been worrying about what she should wear. Although nervous, she couldn't wait to see Andrew again. 'Um... I'll probably wear jeans with a dressy top.'

'You should wear a dress; you look great in dresses but you hardly ever wear them. How about that black dress you wore when we went to Sheri's birthday party?'

'Yeah, maybe...'

'You sound a bit down, are you okay?'

'I had a bit of a disagreement with my mum.' Alice frowned as she remembered their last conversation.

'Oh? What about? It'll probably blow over.'

Alice played with the curly wire attached to the phone, twisting it around her finger as she spoke: 'It was about my dad.'

'I thought you never knew your dad.'

'Yeah, that's what the argument was about... Well, it wasn't really an argument, but my mum got upset when I told her that I wanted to find my dad—'

'You want to find him?' The shock and surprise in Jenny's voice was audible.

'Well... I want to meet him. It's curiosity I suppose. I want to know if I have any brothers or sisters. You've got a brother and a sister, I've always envied that.'

'You can have my brother if you want. He's mad. And my sister is always stealing my clothes. It's not all it's cracked up to be, Allie.'

'You know what I mean, though?' Alice sighed.

'Yes, I suppose so. If I were in your shoes, I'd probably be curious too.'

'My mum won't help me look for him. She hates him for leaving us.'

'Well, that's understandable. He might be a horrible man. There are a lot of them out there.'

'Yes, but he's my dad and I want to meet him.'

'Well... isn't there someone else you can ask? A relative? One of your mum's friends?'

Alice thought of Rita and shook her head. 'I don't want to involve any of my mum's friends. It'll just upset her. And, I don't have any close relatives.'

'Hmm... well, have you tried looking up his name in the telephone directory?'

'That's a good idea, but I don't know if he still lives in London... or even in England.'

'Well, it's worth a try,' said Jenny. 'I'll help you if you like. We'll talk about it on Tuesday when I see you. In the meantime, try not to worry. Just think of Andrew!'

Alice giggled and felt pleased that her friend was on the other end of the phone line and couldn't see her blushes. 'Okay,' she said. 'See you on Tuesday.'

When Alice put down the phone, her first thought was whether she had any telephone directories in the flat. She was pleased that she'd spoken to Jenny about it; Jenny was always so practical and positive about things. Over the past few days the confusion in Alice's mind had made it hard for her to concentrate on anything and she hadn't even considered the possibility that her father's telephone number could be sitting there in a telephone directory waiting for her to call it.

She looked around her flat, sure that she'd had a telephone directory at some time, but all she could find was the Yellow Pages. Her mother had some telephone directories at home, so she decided she would visit her tomorrow and try to have a look through them. Feeling more optimistic, she settled down to supper with her mind firmly set on the party, images of Andrew illuminated in her mind.

Chapter Seven

Sunday 17th August 1997

Alice woke up at ten o'clock. She had dreamt about Andrew. It didn't surprise her because she had spent so much time the evening before thinking about him. Jenny's phone call had brought the party to the forefront of her mind and it was a welcome change for her to think about something other than her family problems.

She had thought about Andrew quite a lot over the past few months. They had never really spoken to each other but she had admired him from afar. She met him at the beginning of her second year at university. One of her friends, Selina, had introduced them. She had been having lunch with Selina...

'I'm just going to the toilet,' said Alice, 'Can you watch my food?'

Selina smiled and nodded. Alice walked away towards the toilets and as she did so, a young man walked towards her; he smiled at her when she looked at him and she noticed how blue his eyes were. They reminded her of a cloudless sky on a summer's day. She bowed her head as she walked past him, feeling her cheeks redden, wondering whether she had stared into those eyes just a little too long. She was kicking herself as she walked into the toilets realising that she hadn't even returned his smile, as she'd been so distracted by his beautiful eyes. She felt silly. How could she just fall for someone like that without even knowing him? But she couldn't get him out of her mind. She checked her appearance as she washed her hands and wished she was one of those girls who wore make-up. She had never really been a girlie girl when she was growing up and had never experimented with make-up; now she didn't know where to start, so she didn't wear any at all, fearing that she'd end up looking like a clown if she applied it.

She found herself hoping she would see that boy again as she walked back into the canteen. Sure enough, as if her prayers had been answered, the boy was standing next to Selina, chatting with her.

Alice felt her flushed cheeks become hotter as she approached. She tried to pretend she hadn't noticed the boy standing there and sat down opposite Selina.

'Oh, this is Alice,' said Selina, to the boy, who smiled that killer smile again and reached out a hand to shake hers. Alice looked up at him and felt as if she was floating on air. She could hardly control any of her movements. Somehow, she managed to shake his hand.

'I'm Andrew, nice to meet you.'

'You too,' Alice said, almost inaudibly. She then went back to eating her lunch.

Alice watched as Selina chatted freely with Andrew, and wished she could too, but words eluded her. Anything she did think of saying, she dismissed as being silly.

Shortly, Andrew announced that he had to leave. 'It was nice to meet you, Alice. I'm sure we'll see each other around.'

'Yes,' she managed to say, feeling that it was too little too late, as he turned on his heels and walked out of the room.

Selina explained that she and Andrew used to go to the same secondary school, and she'd only just found out he was at the same university. After that, the subject changed to talk of the latest happenings in EastEnders, and thoughts of Andrew had to remain a fantasy teasing Alice's mind as she tried to concentrate on what Selina was saying.

From the first day she met him, Alice became slightly obsessive in her feelings for Andrew. She would look out for him in the university, but he was on a different course so their paths hardly ever crossed. She did manage to see him a few times but had never really had a proper conversation with him. That same tongue-tied feeling would overwhelm her when he stopped to greet her, so the most there had really been between them was a "hello" or a "how are you?" as they passed each other in the corridors. Other times, they had smiled or waved from a distance.

It excited Alice to think that Andrew liked her too. She had convinced herself that they would get together at some stage and felt it was just a matter of time. She was always hopeful, wishing that she and Andrew would get the chance to meet and talk properly. Her mind drifted to thoughts of the upcoming party; perhaps that would be the opportunity she had been waiting for.

She got out of bed and looked through her wardrobe trying

to decide what she would wear to the party. She didn't want to dress up. She never felt comfortable in anything too fancy. Thinking back to Jenny's suggestion, she decided she would take her advice and wear her favourite black dress; it was made of crushed velvet, and she liked the feel of the soft fabric against her skin.

As she held the dress in front of her, looking in the mirror, she began to daydream about what she would say to Andrew and what he would say to her. She improvised an imagined conversation that she would have with him at the party. Her mood lifted as she fantasised about their meeting.

Soon, she realised it was getting late and she still hadn't had any breakfast. She made her way into the kitchen and prepared a boiled egg and some toast. As she crunched the toast, she remembered that she had meant to visit her mother, to try to look for the telephone directories.

After breakfast she got dressed and ready to leave. As she walked towards the front door, she noticed the newspaper lying on the living room table; the one with the photograph of Jane Forester. She decided to take it with her.

Alice arrived at her mother's flat at 12 noon. 'Hi, Mum,' she said, as she walked into the kitchen.

'Oh, hello, dear. It's nice to see you. How are you?' Her mother had been cleaning the kitchen cupboards but was now looking at Alice, dishcloth in hand.

'I'm fine.' She couldn't help noticing that her mother's face looked tired. This reminded her that the last time they'd spoken, she had upset her by talking about her father.

'Have you had breakfast, Alice?'

'Yes.'

The conversation seemed to stop there. Her mother turned around and continued cleaning the cupboards. Neither Alice nor Stephanie could think of anything to say. Alice desperately wanted to break the silence, but the only thing she could think of saying was, 'Mum, where do you keep your telephone directories?' She didn't think that would be a good idea. Her mother would ask why she wanted them, and she would have to lie. She had never been very good at lying to her mother.

Stephanie also wanted to say something, but she was on edge, expecting Alice to start talking about her father again. Stephanie ran all possible topics of conversation through her mind, but they all seemed to come back to the same thing; somewhere along the line, Alice would mention her father. It seemed that they had reached a point of no return here. Alice had opened the can of worms and they were now wriggling to get out.

She found Alice's sudden interest in her father difficult to bear, it had torn open old wounds, rekindling distant memories that she had kept locked away at the back of her mind, thinking them long forgotten. Things had moved so fast. Alice had given her no warning that she would want to find her father, so Stephanie had not been able to adjust or find a way around it. She filled a bucket with water and began to mop the floor, trying in vain to wash away the thoughts in her mind at the same time.

The silence became too much to bear, with the undertone of thought that hovered around the room. Stephanie didn't know if she was just being paranoid, but she was sure Alice wanted to ask more about her father. She wondered whether if she showed Alice a photograph of Roger, it would somehow satisfy her curiosity. Maybe she just wanted to know what he looked like. Feeling desperate, she had to ask: 'Alice, darling,' she began.

Alice had her back to her mother, sitting by the kitchen table pretending to read the *Sunday Mirror Magazine.*

'Alice, I have a confession to make.'

'That sounds interesting.' Alice turned around in her chair to face her.

'When you asked me the other day if I had photos of your father, I said I didn't. Well, I do have a couple of old photos of him. I was hoping you'd decide not to look for him; trying to stop you.' She paused, holding onto the mop handle as if for support. 'For your own good,' she added. 'I know that I probably can't stop you if you've made up your mind, but...' She was having difficulty looking Alice in the eyes, 'I was hoping that maybe if I show you the photos, that would be enough for you. Maybe you are just curious to see what he looks like? Anyway, I'll try anything if you'll stop this nonsense about wanting to find him.'

This surprised Alice. Her mother seemed almost afraid at the thought that she might find her father. What was so terrible that she didn't want her to have any contact with him? What deep, dark secret would she uncover if she found him? There seemed to be something her mother wasn't telling her; something that would maybe affect their relationship. Did her mother have an affair? Was that the reason her father had left? All sorts of thoughts were parading around Alice's mind. Now, rather than being persuaded to stop looking for her father, she felt even more fuelled.

'I don't know what happened between you two all those years ago. I mean, you've never told me the details; and maybe I don't really need to know the details, but he is still my dad. He *is* my dad, isn't he?' she asked, as another stray thought taunted her brain.

'Yes, of course he is!' said her mother, agitated.

'I just feel like I'm climbing a mountain trying to explain this to you. It's like you don't think I'm capable of making my own decisions. You had a mum and dad, and you knew who they were. You've never been through what I'm going through at the moment. Try to put yourself in my position for one minute. What if you didn't know who your dad was? Would you want to find out? It's not just a picture of him I want. I want to meet him, speak to him, find out about him.'

Stephanie sighed. She stood next to the sink and folded her arms in front of her. 'I have already realised I can't stop you doing this. I just needed to try because I am your mother and I know what's best for you.' Again, she did not appear able to look Alice in the eyes.

'Okay, will you tell me the real reason you are trying to stop me seeing him? There's some big secret, isn't there?'

Stephanie's mouth fell open. Then, she shook her head and shrugged. Twisting around, she turned on the tap and began putting on her washing up gloves. 'I just don't want to see you get hurt. He might have a new wife, a new family.'

There was silence for a moment, then Alice said, 'I'm sorry, Mum, I can see how it would be hard for you to find out that he is married again, maybe with other children. I've been selfish only thinking of me.'

Stephanie turned around on the spot to face Alice. 'I couldn't care less if he's remarried with ten kids and as happy as Larry. I am only thinking of you. What if he doesn't want to know you? What if he has a new family and he hasn't told them about you? If you turn up out of the blue it could do more harm than good.'

'Well, I wasn't intending to turn up out of the blue. I was going to phone first. That's why I came today to find his number in your telephone directories.'

Stephanie frowned. 'Oh, there was me thinking you've come

to visit me, and all along you're just thinking about finding your father.' She took off her gloves and stormed out of the kitchen.

Stephanie could feel her head spinning. It was all out of her control now. Alice had made up her mind. She wondered whether she should just tell her everything now. She took a deep breath and walked towards her wardrobe in her bedroom. Reaching inside, she took out the old shoe-box. When she removed the lid, the first thing she saw was the picture of Roger holding Alice in his arms, smiling. His smile seemed so genuine. He had been so happy. *They* had been so happy. How could she have imagined, when she was taking this photograph on that bright sunny day all those years ago, that within a few months her life would be change completely? She would never have imagined that she would be holding this photograph in her hands almost twenty years on not with happy memories but with memories of pain.

She took the photograph out of the box along with the other two photographs of Roger. As she did so, she wondered how long it would be before the other secret she had kept hidden for years would have to be revealed.

Alice stood in the kitchen after her mother had walked out, wondering whether she should follow her to the bedroom. Her eyes had seemed sad, and Alice felt bad for upsetting her. Just then, she saw her returning along the hallway holding what looked like bits of paper in her hand.

Stephanie held out the photographs to Alice as she re-entered the kitchen and after handing them over, she sat at the kitchen table, her head in her hands.

Alice placed the photographs on the table and sat down next to her. 'This is my dad?'

'Yes.'

Alice stared at the black-and-white photographs that were quite faded now. She recognised herself as a baby as she had seen many photographs over the years that her mother had shown her. Her father was holding her in his arms in one of the photographs, smiling. His smile seemed so sincere. He was happy. She felt warmth and pride as she looked at the picture, and couldn't help smiling back. Then she looked at each of the other photographs in turn, noticing how she had the same almond-shaped eyes and wavy fair hair as her father.

'These are nice,' she said, turning to smile at Stephanie. She noticed her eyes were red as if she were about to cry.

Stephanie avoided her eyes and looked at the kitchen table.

'They were taken in happier times,' was all she said.

'What's the story behind this picture,' asked Alice, holding up the one where her father was holding her.

'Oh, Alice, I would really rather forget,' Stephanie said bluntly, and stood up. 'You can keep them.'

'Mum, I just want you to know that even though I'm looking for my dad, this won't change anything between us. You brought me up, he was never around. None of that is going to suddenly change.'

'But things *will* change.' She sat opposite Alice and tears formed in her eyes. 'There are things I haven't told you.'

Alice leaned forward, interested. 'Go on,' she urged.

Stephanie sighed. She shook her head and stood up, feeling suddenly out of control; she had almost started to tell Alice everything. But how could she?

'Mum, what haven't you told me?' She twisted around in her chair to see her mother wiping a tear from her eye, as she stood at the kitchen sink.

'I don't think this is the right time to talk about everything. Let's just say I don't want you to look for your father. Aren't you happy the way we are, just me and you? We don't need anyone else.'

'Oh, Mum. We've been through this.'

'He's a stranger to you,' continued Stephanie, looking out of the kitchen window, as if lost in thought.

'I don't want my own dad to be a stranger. And I might have brothers or sisters that I don't know about.' She reached into her bag, which was hanging from her chair, and pulled out the newspaper she had brought with her.

'This is Wednesday's newspaper. I brought it around to show you. Remember I told you about the photograph in the newspaper of the girl who was in the plane crash? She has the same surname as my dad. Look, this is the picture.' She placed the newspaper close to her mother, so she could see the picture of Jane Forester.

'What about it?' asked her mother, but Alice could see she felt uncomfortable.

'She looks like me. You have to admit.'

'Well, yes, she does look a bit like you. A lot of people look like other people, it doesn't mean they're related. One of my clients told me I look like Angela Rippon, that doesn't mean we're related!'

'Okay, listen to this.' Alice felt she had to try to convince her mother to take her seriously. 'This girl,' she pointed to the picture of Jane Forester, 'was in the plane crash last Sunday night. I woke up at exactly quarter past twelve on that night, and I thought I heard a loud bang. I'd had a bad dream. I felt really scared and couldn't sleep for ages. The next night, I had a dream about a plane crashing and me drowning, then I saw the picture of Jane, and well... I became more convinced that maybe the dream and the plane crash were linked in some way. If we're related, maybe I could sense something was wrong? Remember how you told me that your mum used to know when people in the family were going to die because she used to dream about them?'

'You're getting carried away.'

'No. What if I've inherited something from Nan, and I can sense these things?'

'Really, Alice, you're making too much of this. If you woke up in the middle of the night and thought you heard a bang, of course you'd be scared, living alone. Maybe it's about time you moved back here. I hate to think of you on your own and frightened.'

'It was because of the dream that I was frightened, Mum. I like living alone.'

'Living alone isn't that great. It's lonely sometimes. It would make more sense if you moved back home with me. You have too much time to think when you're alone, and you've always had a vivid imagination; no wonder you're creating all these fantasies in your head.'

'Fantasies? You're not listening to me!' Alice stood up. 'I don't know why I even bother to tell you anything.'

Stephanie looked at her and she shook her head slowly; her eyes appeared sad. 'This is all my fault, Alice. Please sit down.'

Alice felt concerned that her mother may now start to cry. She sat down and fiddled with the edge of the newspaper nervously.

'You're lonely. Of course you are. You're an only child. I was lonely. Do you know, I used to tell people I had a sister. I always told myself that I would have more than one child, or none at all. I thought my parents were cruel not to have given me a sister or a brother.' She reached out and took Alice's hand. 'You have to understand, darling, it's just the way things turned out. I would have loved to have had a lot of children. But I couldn't.' She took a deep breath, feeling that now may be the time to reveal all. 'I couldn't have children, Alice... I...' She pulled her hand away, tears of frustration filling her eyes. She felt unable to go through with telling Alice. It seemed like an impossible task.

Alice stood up and walked over to her, putting a hand on her back to comfort her. 'Mum, don't cry. This isn't about me being lonely, or wanting a brother or sister. It's not your fault.'

'But I've failed you,' said Stephanie, holding on to Alice's arm as she looked up at her. Mascara had run down Stephanie's face, making two, uneven black lines on each of her cheeks. Alice sighed and handed her a tissue.

Stephanie blew her nose and wiped her face. 'Not only are you an only child, but you've only got one parent. I never meant for that to happen.'

'None of that matters,' said Alice, playing with the sleeve of Stephanie's blouse as she spoke. 'I'm not looking for a new life. I just want to know more about my background.'

'But... But, this is a dream. The plane crash; the girl in the paper... it's all a fantasy.' Stephanie had put on her gloves again and now began mopping the floor as she continued to speak: 'I've heard about this. Children, like you—'

'I'm not a child,' interjected Alice.

'Well, okay *young people* like you, who don't know one or other of their parents; they often fantasise about who their parent might be. It was on one of those shows—Oprah or Ricki Lake. It's quite common for someone like you to create weird and wonderful connections between themselves and their absent parent. I mean, some believe that their parent must be rich or famous, or something like that.'

'What has that got to do with me? I haven't fantasised about anything.'

'The girl in the paper,' said Stephanie as she kept her eyes down whilst mopping the floor, hoping this conversation would soon be over. 'The vivid dream,' she went on. 'This is some sort of fantasy you've created. You saw the picture of the girl in the paper and you've somehow made the connection between that and your dream about the plane crash... Which may or may not have been a dream about a plane crash... You might have imagined that after you read the paper—'

'I did dream about the plane crash. That's what's so weird about all of this. That's why I'm trying to make sense of it. I haven't imagined anything,' said Alice, sitting down, arms folded in front of her, feeling furious with her mother.

'Oh, Alice... you've tried to make it all fit together so that your imaginary half-sister is this person you've seen in the newspaper.

Anyway, there's no point going over and over it. You have to try to find something else to occupy your mind. I blame these universities with their long summer breaks. Your mind has been working so hard all year and then suddenly you have nothing to occupy it. You've always had a wild imagination. Something like this was bound to happen eventually.'

'You can be so condescending at times!' said Alice, pouting. 'I've decided to look for my dad. That will clear this up. Then we'll see whether this is fantasy or not.' She stood up and picked up her bag from the kitchen table. As she placed the newspaper back in the bag, she shook her head.

Stephanie stopped mopping and stood staring at her. 'Darling, please forget about this. You need to concentrate on your studies. You'll be going back to university in a few weeks; you don't have time for anything else. Please be sensible.'

Alice looked again at the photographs of her father. 'Can I have this photo?' she asked, picking up the one in which her father was holding her.

Stephanie looked at the floor, her face reddened. 'Yes, of course.' Then, looking up at Alice, tears in the corners of her eyes, she continued: 'Now, promise me you'll forget about looking for your father. You can't rush in and do something like that just because you've had a silly dream. It was just a coincidence, darling, nothing more than that. Plane crashes happen all the time; it just happened that you dreamt of one on the same night. I mean, think about it: you've had dreams of plane crashes at other times—'

'No, I haven't as far as I can remember. And, I don't believe in coincidences. Things happen for a reason.'

'This girl,' continued Stephanie, as if she hadn't heard her, 'she doesn't even look that much... Well, just forget about her.'

'I've got to go now,' said Alice walking out of the kitchen door. As she stormed through the hallway, she spotted the pile of telephone directories under the telephone stand. Bending down, she picked up the one that had "A-N" on the spine and took it with her.

Stephanie was trembling as she heard the door slam shut. *She's*

going to look for Roger. The thought stunned her. It had been years since she'd had any contact with him; and now, suddenly, he was going to be back in her life.

The idea of seeing Roger again almost frightened her; and the fact that Alice might see him before she did was even more of a concern. *What will he say to her?* She feared he could lie and turn Alice against her. And he might think she already knew about the surrogacy agreement. Stephanie felt her throat tighten. She gulped for air. *What can I do?* She paced the kitchen, then saw the telephone from the corner of her eye. *Maybe Rita will know what to do?*

She dialled her friend's number with shaky fingers, hardly able to keep control over them. The numbers on the telephone appeared blurry through her tears.

'Hello,' said Rita, sounding in high spirits.

'Oh... hello, Rita... it's me, er... Stephanie...' she said between sniffles.

'Steph, you sound upset. Are you all right?'

'I'm in such a panic. I don't know what to do. I've... I've just seen Alice... She wants to find Roger.' She spoke quickly, almost stumbling over her own tongue trying to get the words out.

'Calm down, Steph. Do you want me to come over?'

'No. Yes... Oh, I don't know.'

'Listen, I'll come over to your place. I'll be there in about an hour. In the meantime, please try to relax... Everything will be okay.'

Everything will be okay. The words resounded in Stephanie's head when she put down the phone. She turned around and the first thing she saw were the photographs lying on the kitchen table. She ran over and grabbed them, not looking at them, not wanting to see them again; then she rushed over to her bedroom and opened the wardrobe taking out the old shoe-box. She stuffed the photographs back in there and began to cry again.

Sitting on her knees next to the old box that contained the remains of her life with Roger, she began to ponder how she could stop Alice. *I need to get to him first,* she thought. She rooted through the box and found some of the correspondence she had kept from the divorce. Roger's address was on one of the documents. She held it up and took a closer look to make sure she'd remembered it correctly. She felt sick to the stomach thinking that she would have to speak to him; but something told her that was the only option she had left if she didn't want to lose Alice's trust for good.

When Rita arrived at Stephanie's flat at 2 p.m., she could see the remains of her tears strewn across her face; like blemishes scarring her make-up.

'Steph, I came as soon as I could. Are you okay? Listen, let me make you a cup of tea and we will talk about everything.'

Stephanie's eyes seemed distant, and she stood unmoving, almost as if she were in a catatonic stupor.

Rita took her arm and led her through the hallway into the kitchen.

'I don't want any tea,' said Stephanie, pulling away from her grip and making her way into the living room. She slumped down onto the sofa. 'I think I'm going to have to contact Roger. It's the last thing I want to do, but if Alice finds out I've been lying to her all these years—' She looked up at Rita, who was standing at the entrance to the living room. 'That's what I've been doing, isn't it? Lying to her. I'm not her mother. She still thinks I'm her mother. Oh, what have I done?' She began to cry again.

Rita took off her jacket and threw it over the armchair nearest the door. 'Oh, Steph... don't be so hard on yourself.' She sat next to her friend on the sofa and hugged her. 'You're the only mother Alice has ever known. Even if she found out the truth, she would still see you as her mother. You were only doing what you thought best.'

'But I lied. I was too much of a coward to tell the truth,' said Stephanie, reaching for a tissue to wipe her nose.

'Perhaps you should explain everything to Alice before she meets Roger. That way, you won't have to worry about contacting him yourself.'

'But... If there's a way... If I can... I want to keep this from her. I wanted to tell Roger that she doesn't know about the surrogacy.' She looked into Rita's eyes to try to find some indication that she agreed with her. 'That would be the right thing to do, in the circumstances... wouldn't it?' She nodded, hoping that Rita would do the same.

Rita sighed and turned away. When she looked back at Stephanie, her forehead was creased into a frown. She reached over to the box of tissues on the coffee table and handed another tissue to Stephanie. 'Of course it's up to you,' she began, 'but in my opinion, this is your opportunity to tell Alice the truth. It must have been hard keeping it secret from her all these years. She should be told.'

'But she'll hate me for not telling her before, won't she?' Stephanie blew her nose and wiped her eyes.

'It might come as a shock to her, but she won't hate you. I mean, at the end of the day, her real mother never wanted her, did she? Why would Alice want to know her?'

'But I've been keeping the truth from her...'

'She'll understand.'

'I only did it for *her*... I thought it was in her best interests. I...'

'I'm sure you've been a wonderful mother, Steph. Alice seems like such a lovely girl; she goes to university. You must be so proud of her.'

Stephanie nodded. 'I am proud... but even though I brought her up, I'm not her mother, am I? The whole idea of the surrogacy agreement was that I would be able to have a child of my own. Her real mother never wanted her. If I didn't want her, she would never have been born. If Roger and I hadn't split up... who knows? Would we have told her? I'm so confused, Rita.'

'This is definitely a situation where you couldn't really have planned anything. You should just explain to Alice that you never saw a reason to tell her, because her real mother didn't want her.'

'But that sounds so cruel.' Stephanie stood up. 'My poor little Alice. She's always been my princess. I... I wanted to be her real mother. It wasn't my fault I couldn't have children. She's more than a daughter to me. I couldn't have loved her more if she was my own. I don't want to lose her.'

'You won't lose her—'

'But how can you be so sure?' She looked down at Rita on the sofa.

Rita couldn't meet her eyes.

'I just can't imagine telling her. I can't imagine it.' Stephanie's eyes had become distant again. She sighed deeply.

'It would be better coming from you than from Roger,' said Rita. She stood up and approached Stephanie. 'Listen, why don't you invite her for a meal and tell her you have something important to tell her.'

Stephanie looked at her with wide eyes. 'Are you sure I should do this? I'm still not sure—'

'Only you can make that decision, Steph, but in my honest

opinion, I think you should have told her years ago... Sorry, I know that's not what you want to hear. I was surprised when you first told me that Alice didn't know the truth. It's no good to have secrets.'

Stephanie sat on the sofa and sighed. 'I've been alone, and I've had to make all the decisions about Alice on my own. No one ever helped me. I only did what I thought was best.' She looked up at Rita, who smiled sympathetically.

'I know that. I don't doubt that for a minute. But all I'm saying is, you have an opportunity now to tell her. It's time.'

'You make it sound so easy; it's not easy.'

'I'm sure it's not. But it will probably be easier than you think. Most things usually are. Look, I can help you tell her, if you like?'

'No,' Stephanie shook her head gloomily. 'This is something I have to do myself.'

Alice sat on the sofa in the front room of her flat. Tears of frustration filled her eyes as she thought back to the conversation she'd had with her mother. She lifted her bag from the floor and took out the telephone directory; as she did so, the photograph her mother had given her fell to the floor. She lifted it up and stared at it for a while.

If only there were a simple solution to her problem, she mused. If she kept her mother happy by not contacting her father, she would remain in this constant limbo of not knowing about him. She longed to know what he was like as a person, and whether she had inherited any of his personality traits. She knew she looked like him; that had been obvious from a young age as she had never really looked like her mother. Alice's eyes were dark brown, whereas Stephanie's were green; Alice's hair was wavy and blonde whereas Stephanie's hair was dark brown and straight. When she was younger, she'd wanted to look more like her mother, and had even gone through a stage where she'd insisted on dyeing her hair the same colour as her mother's just so there would be something they had in common. Looking back, she realised that may have been her way of dealing with her father's rejection; wanting to side more with her mother against the man who had left her.

Somehow, seeing his photograph today, made her more

curious to meet him. Hearing people say that she looked like him was one thing, but actually seeing the proof with her own eyes was something else. It was almost as if she felt more drawn to him now that she could see the family resemblance.

Her excitement at the prospect of getting in touch with her father was hampered by Stephanie's insistence that she shouldn't contact him. She'd been looking forward to finding not only her father but maybe a sister; the picture of Jane Forester in the paper had spurred her on. But the way her mother had behaved had left niggling doubts in her mind. She knew her mother would be upset if she did find her father, but as far as she could tell there was no real reason why, except the fact that she didn't want Alice to be hurt or disappointed. Alice already felt hurt and disappointed and doubted that she could feel any worse, even if he did refuse to meet her. All she did know was that she had to try, and she hoped her mother would understand.

Picking up the telephone directory, she wiped away the tears that were forming in her eyes so she could see the writing more clearly. She turned to the section for surnames beginning with "F". She flicked through the pages until she came to "Forester". Then, it occurred to her that she didn't know if her father spelt his name with one "r" or two. Was it "Forester" or "Forrester"? There were three listings for "R. Forester", and one "R. Forrester." All the addresses were quite local. Alice was struck by the thought that she could have been living so close to her father for so long, without knowing him.

She couldn't bring herself to dial any of the telephone numbers. She could hear her mother's voice in her head, telling her that she didn't think she should contact him; that he probably wouldn't want to know her. Alice decided she would wait until Tuesday and talk to Jenny about it. Jenny always knew what to do.

Placing the telephone directory on the coffee table, she went to make a cup of tea. As she was sitting at the kitchen table, holding her mug and staring at the wall, the telephone rang. She didn't want to answer it, not feeling up to talking to anyone. Eventually the phone stopped ringing. Alice stood up and went into the front room. She switched on the TV and sat down on the sofa. The telephone began to ring again. Sighing at the irritating noise, she wished she'd taken the phone off the hook. Picking up the handset to stop the ringing, she reluctantly said, 'Hello.'

'Darling, hello, it's me.'

'Hi,' said Alice, quickly, trying to sound upbeat. From the sound of her voice, Alice could tell that Stephanie had been crying, and that made her feel bad again for upsetting her.

'Listen, Alice, are you busy tomorrow evening?'

'No, not really.'

'Good.' There was a pause and then her mother continued: 'I'd like to cook dinner for you. There's something I have to tell you; something I can't tell you over the phone.'

Alice felt suddenly nervous. 'Is it about my dad?' she said, hopefully.

'Please don't ask me now, dear. We'll talk tomorrow. About seven?'

She could hear disappointment in her mother's voice, as if whatever she was going to tell her was something she would rather not tell.

'Okay, I'll come over after work tomorrow,' said Alice.

'I'll see you tomorrow then, dear. Bye.'

Alice was left confused. Whilst it was possible that her mother had finally realised how important it was for her to see her father; she couldn't help thinking that there was more to this. The way her voice had sounded—almost as if she were being forced to tell her something against her will—was unsettling.

An unwelcome thought invaded Alice's mind then: *what if he's dead? Is that what all this is about? Maybe that's why she's trying to stop me looking for him...* She shook her head as if to rid it of her suspicions. *I'll find out tomorrow,* she thought.

Gloom descended, and she suddenly felt foolish for not considering all the potential outcomes of her search; she had never once entertained the notion that her father may have died.

When Stephanie put the phone down, she felt as if she was on the edge of a cliff being urged to go forward. She wondered whether she would be able to go through with telling Alice; after all, she was already putting it off until tomorrow...

She felt a lump forming in her throat. She knew the real reason she was delaying telling Alice: she knew that after she told her, their lives would all be changed for ever. There was no way to escape that. Her reason for not telling Alice was simple; it was the same reason as it had always been and it tore at her heart. Her reason was that she wanted—no, she *needed* to be Alice's real mother. By keeping the truth from Alice, she had succeeded for some time in fulfilling that need. Now it was clear, she was only going to be Alice's mother for one more day. She could feel the time ticking away furiously, marking the end of her dream.

Chapter Eight
Monday 18th August 1997

As Alice was getting dressed for work, she heard the familiar sound of the post arriving. On the front doormat, she found a brown envelope and a postcard. Flipping over the pretty beach scene, she smiled as she read the postcard:

Having fun in Spain! Wish you were here, Alice! It's sooo hot. I'm very brown! See you in uni! love, Sonia xx

Sonia was one of her best friends at university. Alice flipped the card back over and stared at the photograph of a beach, with a crystal clear blue sea, foaming waves beating against the white sand on the shore, the sun reflecting over the perfect scene from a cloudless sky. For a moment, Alice felt as though she were there, and wished she could be somewhere far away.

Alice's attention then turned to the brown envelope that bore the frank of the local health authority. She realised at once that it was probably the appointment letter Dr. Small had said she would receive for tests at the local hospital. Since last Wednesday, Alice had felt no further pain in her arm, so as she opened the envelope she wondered whether she had overreacted about the pain. She didn't really feel that she needed any tests done. Looking at the letter, she saw that there was an appointment for her to attend the hospital next Tuesday, 26th August. She put the letter on the kitchen table and attached the postcard to her fridge with one of the magnets that was on there, then she returned to her bedroom to finish getting ready for work.

Whilst stacking some books in the General Reference section of the bookstore that afternoon, Alice spotted one of the books that Rob Bairns had told her about on Saturday: *Private Investigations*. She felt curious and wanted to look through the book right then and there, but she looked about her and saw that the bookstore was quite busy, and as her eyes met those of one of the customers who was standing nearby, Alice blushed, feeling sure that the customer had seen the title of the book and put two and two together. It was absurd, but Alice felt paranoid, as though if she looked through the book, all the customers would know it was because she was looking for her father.

'Alice!' Charlotte's voice rang out above the quiet chatter in the bookstore.

Tearing her eyes away from the customer, Alice looked towards the cash desk. There was quite a queue forming.

'Alice! Are you free?' came Charlotte's voice. 'Can you come and serve a couple of customers, please?'

Alice took the book with her, and made her way to the counter.

She placed the book face down on the counter, feeling self-conscious and not wanting anyone to see the title.

'Phew, that was busy for a Monday afternoon!' said Charlotte, looking flushed, after she'd served the last customer in the queue. 'I need some water... you?'

'Er... yes, please,' said Alice, one eye on the book she had placed on the counter. When Charlotte disappeared into the staff kitchen to get the water, Alice saw a chance to look through the book.

As she was looking through the contents page, Charlotte came up behind her. 'Here you go, a refreshing glass of water.'

Alice placed the book back on the counter, knowing she would have to wait until later to look at it again. She took a glass from Charlotte and sat down.

Charlotte drank her water quickly, hardly taking a breath, and then wiped her mouth with her hand. 'That was what I needed,' she said, smiling. As she put the glass on the counter, her eyes rested on the book. It was a large A4 hardback book. As Alice held her breath, Charlotte picked it up. '*Private Investigations*,' she said, reading the title out loud. 'Sounds interesting. I wonder what it's doing here?'

'Oh, one of the customers decided not to buy it,' said Alice jumping to her feet. 'I'll put it back on the shelf.' She reached out her hand to take the book from Charlotte.

'No, wait,' said Charlotte, flicking through the book. 'This has got some interesting stories in it, look,' she said, pointing a gold-painted fingernail at one of the chapter headings that said: "Locating Missing People". 'The film I'm starring in at the moment is about this boy who's been adopted, and he traces his mother. It's a real tear-jerker. I have a few lines in the film. I play the woman at the adoption agency who helps him find the right room where he can search their records. You know, I'm sure this will be the film that launches my career.' Charlotte's eyes twinkled with thoughts of stardom. Then she smiled at Alice, but her demeanour quickly changed and she looked as though she was about to relate something important. 'My ex-boyfriend was adopted. His name was Peter. He traced his mum. I went with him when he was going to meet her. He went into the house by himself and I waited outside. He was in tears when he came out... but he was happy... Really happy. I hadn't seen him that happy in ages. He was usually so miserable, which was part of the reason we broke up. I mean, who wants to go out with a misery guts, hey?' She laughed, but there was a sadness in her eyes, an almost wistful gleam. 'Oh, well. I sometimes wonder what he's doing.'

'But if he was happy after he met her, why didn't you stay together?' Alice felt confused.

Charlotte seemed to snap out of her reverie. 'I wasn't going out with him at the time he found his mum. He just needed someone to drive him to her house. He never learnt to drive. That was probably another reason we broke up, come to think of it. I used to have to drive us everywhere, and that usually meant driving him home from pubs when he was drunk. He only ever seemed to be happy when he had a few drinks. Of course, the next day he'd be miserable again.' Charlotte rolled her eyes.

'Um... Charlotte. How did Peter find his mother?' Alice looked at her hands as she spoke.

'Through the adoption agency.'

'Oh.'

'You're adopted, aren't you?' said Charlotte.

Alice blushed. 'Er... no.'

'Oh, sorry. I must be mixing you up with someone else. But didn't you tell me once that you've never met your father?'

'Yes.' Alice stood up and took the book from the counter hoping she could get lost between the bookshelves and not have to talk about this now.

'Have you ever tried looking for him?' asked Charlotte.

'No.' Alice forced a smile and shook her head.

'You should,' said Charlotte, smiling back at her.

'Well, I have been thinking about it recently.' She held the book closer to her as she spoke as if for reassurance. 'My mum's invited me to dinner tonight and I think she might have some news about my dad, because I mentioned to her that I wanted to look for him.'

'Oh, wow! That's exciting! Your life is just like a Hollywood movie. Mine's boring... no divorced parents, no long lost father. Wow! I envy you, Alice.'

Alice felt the adrenaline course through her as she noticed the time on the clock. In less than three hours she would know what her mother wanted to tell her.

Stephanie looked at her face in the hallway mirror. Her eyes were sunken and black around as if she had been crying for ever. She reached for her handbag that was dangling over her coat on the coat-hanger behind the front door. She fished around until she found her concealer. *I really need to clear out the mess in this bag,* she thought, as a stray receipt fell onto the floor. She absent-mindedly picked it up and looked at it. The top of the receipt showed that it was from the café across the road from her salon, where she had taken Alice for lunch on the day they'd bumped into Rita. She scrunched up the receipt and placed it in the pocket of her cardigan, thinking she would throw it away when she went into the kitchen.

Placing her bag on the side table, she took off the lid of her concealer and carefully covered up the signs of the sleepless night before. She had tossed and turned knowing that she would be seeing Alice and telling her about Miranda, and about the surrogacy agreement. As she struggled to get some sleep she couldn't shift the fears that were at the forefront of her mind: *If only I'd told Alice all of this when she was a little girl; when she needed me. She doesn't need me now. She could easily walk away and leave me.*

It seemed logical that as Alice was determined to find her father, she would also want to find her real mother when she knew the truth. The more Stephanie turned things over in her mind the more she felt that she had been selfish by keeping this secret from Alice. And lately, it was as though every word she uttered to Alice was a lie. Rita was right. It was time to reveal all. She would have to live with the consequences.

Telling Alice the truth would, Stephanie knew, be one of the hardest things she had ever done in her life. Most of her sleepless night was used up trying to think of the best way to tell her. She finally decided that she would start from the beginning; explain that she could not have children, and that Miranda was a last resort. Surely, Alice would work out that it was Stephanie and not Miranda who had loved her from the start. Miranda had sold her own child. But then, Stephanie realised that she had bought her; she was just as much to blame for treating Alice like a commodity. How would Alice take the news that she was bought and sold? The night had left Stephanie in a state of exhaustion. By the time the morning sun had begun to peep through the gaps in the curtains, her head felt like it could explode. The brightness did nothing to lighten her mood, instead it began to wind her up even more knowing that not only would she have to reveal a painful secret, but she would have to do so after a fitful night when she had been unable to rest.

Her alarm clock sounded at 7 a.m. She had been due to go to the salon, but she did not feel up to it. She phoned in and left a message on the answer-phone to explain that she would not be going to work; she felt guilty momentarily, because that meant her clients would be disappointed having to have their appointments re-scheduled. Sighing, she turned over in bed pulling the duvet over her head to block out the light, and tried to get some sleep. It was 8 a.m. when she finally fell asleep.

She awoke at 2 o'clock in the afternoon, in a cold sweat. She had been screaming in her dream, calling after Alice who was running away from her. It was becoming darker and darker, until she couldn't see her anymore. 'Come back, Alice! I love you!' she had screamed, and then woken up to find herself in bed, as the midday sun battled to get through her curtains into the room.

Alice had been a child in Stephanie's dream, about eight years old. The child-Alice had shouted at her: 'You're not my real mum!' Roger had also been in the dream. Alice had said to her: 'I don't love you anymore. You lied to me. I'm going to live with my daddy.'

Roger had taken Alice by the hand and said: 'Miranda is her real mother, not you.'

When Stephanie opened her eyes, at first she had felt relieved that it had been a dream, but then she worried in case it was some kind of warning against telling Alice. But she put that to the back of her mind. She would have to tell her. There was no alternative.

Stephanie took the home-made Lasagne out of the oven; Alice's favourite meal. She sighed deeply. She had prepared the dish in the hope of putting Alice in a good mood, but deep down, she knew that food would be the last thing on Alice's mind when she heard the truth.

She almost dropped the hot dish on the kitchen floor when she heard a key turn in the front door.

'Hi, Mum! It's me!'

Stephanie's heart jumped. She carefully placed the Lasagne on the kitchen bench and turned around to greet Alice.

'Darling, so good to see you,' she said, her voice sounding very high pitched. She coughed, hardly able to meet Alice's eye.

'Mmm, dinner smells good.' Alice's lips curved into a smile.

'I made it specially,' said Stephanie, busying herself by reaching into the cupboard for plates. 'Er... would you like anything to drink?'

'What have you got?'

'I have some wine; it's white. Or, you could have fruit juice; I have orange or cranberry.' Stephanie had walked over to the fridge and although she had the door open, she was not really looking inside. *This is going to be harder than I thought.* She could hardly bear to look at Alice, for fear that her guilt would show on her face.

'I'll have some wine,' said Alice.

Alice sat at the kitchen table. 'How was your day, Mum?'

'I didn't go to work today,' she replied, taking two wine glasses out of the cupboard and placing them on the kitchen table.

'Oh?'

'Took the day off.' She brushed it aside, with a wave of her hand.

'Lucky for some,' said Alice. 'I was at the bookstore today.'

'Oh, that's nice,' Stephanie replied, absent-mindedly, not really having heard what Alice said. She finally took the oven dish to the table and began to serve the food, feeling oddly as if she were in the company of a stranger.

Alice began eating as soon as the food was put in her plate. 'Mmm, this is delicious.'

Stephanie sat down opposite her, frowning, but trying to smile. She took a sip of wine, hoping that the alcohol would steady her nerves.

'So, what did you want to talk to me about?'

Stephanie almost choked on the mouthful of food she had just taken. She had wanted to wait for the right moment to discuss everything. Washing down the food in her mouth with some wine, she looked at Alice with a concerned frown.

'It's about my dad isn't it?' Alice mirrored her frown.

Stephanie nodded.

'I was thinking about this all day,' said Alice, now fingering the table cloth.

Stephanie feared she might make a hole in the delicate lace, because of the way she was holding the fabric between her fingers. The tablecloth had been a gift from Rita when Stephanie and Roger had married. She only brought it out on special occasions. She had put it on the table today, without thinking; wanting the place to look nice. Now, she regretted using this tablecloth; it held so many memories.

Thankfully, Alice stopped touching the tablecloth and picked up her wine glass. 'I think I know what you're going to tell me. I think I've worked out why you were so against me trying to find him. You kept saying I'd get hurt.' She sipped her wine and then placed the glass on the table.

Stephanie's cheeks reddened. Had Rita said something to her? Had Alice heard more than she let on the last time she was here when Rita was visiting?

'He's dead, isn't he?' said Alice, quite unexpectedly.

Stephanie shook her head and stood up. 'No. He's not dead. Well... not as far as I know.' She could not bear to be sitting at that table. Suddenly the room seemed to have no air. She walked over to the window, opened it slightly and stood staring out at the dwindling sunshine over the backs of houses and small square gardens that made up the terraced row where her flat was situated.

Alice stood up. The meal at the table was forgotten it seemed, as both women stood, almost lifeless, like mannequins, not knowing what to say next.

'You said you had something to tell me that you couldn't tell me on the phone.' Alice broke the silence.

Stephanie twirled around towards her. Her face was still flushed despite the cool air that was now circulating in the kitchen. 'Let's finish our meal. Then we can talk.'

'I'm not hungry.'

'But it's Lasagne; your favourite.'

'I'll eat it after. I need to know what you were going to say.' Alice gestured for her mother to sit at the table, and sat back down. She stared at the food now going cold in her plate.

Stephanie took a tissue from the box on the kitchen bench, preparing herself for the tears that she knew would come. She sat opposite Alice and cleared her throat. 'There's something you should know. Maybe I should have told you years ago, but you must understand I was trying to do what was best.' Her eyes began to fill with tears.

'Okay, what is it?' Alice shrugged.

'You know I love you, don't you, Alice?'

Alice felt embarrassed. She wasn't used to seeing her mother like this, and although she loved her dearly, it wasn't something that she ever really said out loud. It was just something that was understood between them. She looked at the small roses on the tablecloth that brought back memories of her youth, when her mother would entertain guests and always insist on using the lace tablecloth. 'Of course,' she replied, feeling herself blush.

Stephanie wiped her eyes with the tissue.

'Why are you crying, Mum?'

Stephanie stood up again and walked back to the kitchen window. *What shall I say?* Her mind was whirring.

'Look, whatever you tell me, it won't make a difference, okay? You're the one who brought me up, I know that. I'm not suddenly going to leave you for my dad if that's what you're worried about.'

Stephanie turned to face her, leaning on the kitchen bench for support. 'I always wanted to have children. I wanted lots of children. Three or four would have been ideal,' she began. 'Your father and I tried to have children for so long. Nothing worked. I went for years hoping and praying for a child, and as I got older it seemed that my dream would pass me by. Alice, please don't h... hate me,' her voice broke and she began to cry. She walked over to the kitchen table, taking a few more tissues from the box on the way. When she sat down, she took a deep breath and tried to compose herself.

'What are you trying to tell me?' Alice stood up, her brow furrowed. She shrugged her shoulders, shaking her head. 'Why are you crying? What could be so bad? And... And... why would I hate you? You're not making any sense.'

'Okay,' Stephanie began. 'Look, sit down, please, and I'll tell you.' She closed her eyes.

Alice sat down hesitantly, unsure if she really wanted to hear what she was about to be told.

'I'm not your mother.'

'What?' Alice frowned. Then she smiled. 'This is a joke, right?' But, looking at Stephanie's face she knew it was not a joke.

'I'm so sorry, darling. I had to tell you in case you found your father and he might have—'

Alice stood up, and then felt light-headed. 'I don't understand.'

'I know. I wanted to tell you when you were younger, but your father had left, and there never seemed to be the right moment.'

'You're not my mum?'

Stephanie stood up. 'Well, not biologically. But I brought you up. I was the one who—'

'Who's my mum?'

'That's not important.'

'Huh!' Alice's face became red. 'Not important?'

'You don't have to know—'

'I want to know!' shouted Alice.

'Please calm down, darling. Oh, I knew this would happen. This is why I never told you before.'

'You don't think I have a right to know who my own mum is? Who do you think you are to decide that?'

Stephanie's mouth fell open.

'You've lied to me for so many years, making me think you're my mum.' Confusion swarmed Alice's brain; it was a surreal conversation, one she'd never have imagined she would ever have. *Is this really happening?* She held her forehead, and tried to calm down.

'It wasn't like that, Alice. The woman who gave birth to you didn't want you. It was a surrogacy agreement. I paid her to have a baby for me because I couldn't have a baby. Do you understand that? I was the one who wanted you. It was only because I wanted a child that you came into the world.'

'But she's my mum, not you,' said Alice, feeling as if the space around her had now become hollow, as if she were floating in a dream. She sat down; the light-headedness was unnerving.

'Alice, are you okay?' Stephanie ran towards her and put an arm around her.

She looked at Stephanie, the woman she had called "Mum" for so long. *How can she not be my mum?* She began to cry, unable to stop the flow.

'Oh, Alice, don't cry, I love you. I'll always love you.' She stroked Alice's hair and gave her a tissue to dry her eyes. 'Sweetheart, go into the front room, and I'll make us both a cup of tea. We'll talk about this properly. I'll explain everything.'

Alice stood up and walked out of the kitchen door, wanting to carry on walking out of the front door and to wherever the road would lead. The shattered pieces of her world remained on the kitchen floor where they had fallen, and she felt that she was trampling on the fragments of hope that lay under her feet. The unexpected revelation had left a bullet hole in her soul. There had been no warning; she had not been able to prepare. How could things ever be the same again?

Stephanie walked into the living room carrying two cups of tea. Her hands shook. Alice was on the sofa staring straight ahead. The news had hit her like a thunderbolt. Nothing could have prepared her for hearing that Stephanie was not her real mother. Stephanie was all she had known. Having no father, Alice had felt that the bond between herself and Stephanie was even greater, as they had both been abandoned. But now nothing made sense. There were so many questions in her mind. *Why didn't she ever tell me this before? If I didn't ask her about my dad, I would never have known.*

Stephanie placed the cups of tea on the table in front of Alice. Alice leaned back on the sofa. She didn't want tea. She looked at Stephanie from the corner of her eye. Stephanie's eyes were red. She was wiping the corners with a tissue, sniffling. Alice remembered what she had said to her; words floated back into her mind: *Your father and I tried to have children for so long.... as I got older it seemed that my dream would pass me by... don't h... hate me... The woman who gave birth to you didn't want you. It was a surrogacy agreement. I paid her to have a baby for me... It was only because I wanted a child that you came into the world.*

'How much money did you pay?' asked Alice.

'Wh... What, dear?' Stephanie twisted around on the armchair to face her.

Alice played with the tassels on the cushion that sat beside her on the sofa. 'You said you paid my mum to have me. How much?'

Stephanie sighed. 'Why... Why would you want—'

'Just tell me!' said Alice, annoyed.

'One thousand pounds, I think it was...'

'That's all? That's all I was worth? One thousand pounds—'

'That was a lot of money in those days.'

'Was it common to buy and sell babies in those days, too?'

'No.' Stephanie reached towards the table to get her cup of tea. She didn't want to drink it and felt sure that even a sip would cause her to throw up, but she felt nervous. It was a distraction. Alice was not taking this well. Stephanie felt almost frightened of what she would do next.

Alice picked up her own tea cup, not knowing why. Then she put it back down on the table abruptly, spilling some of the contents onto the clean white tablecloth below.

Stephanie gasped almost inaudibly.

Alice watched as Stephanie held her cup of tea in her hands; she was visibly trembling. *It can't be easy for her.* The thought came into Alice's mind as she felt a pull of empathy towards Stephanie, but immediately she pushed the emotion aside. Her feelings battled inside her. She loved Stephanie; she had brought her up as her own—but the other side of that story was that Stephanie had lied to her; kept the truth from her. The trust was broken.

'I am really having a hard time understanding all of this,' said Alice, holding her forehead.

Stephanie put her cup down on the table. 'I know. Can you understand why I didn't tell you before?'

'No!' screamed Alice.

'Alice, please. What I meant to say was... this is why I didn't tell you. It's such a hard thing to have to tell someone.'

'I just feel so unwanted,' said Alice, standing up. 'Not only did my dad leave me, but my own mum sold me.'

'Well, it wasn't quite like that—'

'Well, what was it like then?' She looked down at Stephanie, who appeared small suddenly; sitting there on the armchair, her arms crossed in front of her. 'You bought me. I was born to be sold!' She walked towards the window as if in need of air.

'Alice, you were born because I wanted a child. I love you

with all my heart. I couldn't have children of my own.'

'Surely there were other ways! Adoption. Did you consider that?'

'Your father didn't want to adopt.'

'But he had a child with a stranger... Wait... was she a stranger? Did you know my mum? What's her name?'

Stephanie stared at her hands, picking at the corner of her nails where some of her red nail varnish had begun to peel. 'Her name is Miranda Carey.'

'Miranda Carey,' repeated Alice. 'Where is she now?'

'I don't know,' said Stephanie, holding her breath. This was one of her fears; now Alice would want to find *her* too. She sighed. 'Miranda was a student, I met her through Rita. One of Rita's friends knew her.'

'Rita knows about this? I thought there was something odd about the way she looks at me.'

'Rita convinced me to tell you the truth,' said Stephanie. 'I was all alone all these years, bringing you up. I didn't know what to do for the best. If I'd thought it was the right thing to do, I would have told you sooner.'

Alice walked over to the sofa and sat down.

'Drink your tea, dear; it'll make you feel better.'

Alice looked at the two cups of tea on the coffee table. She wanted to scream.

'So, why did Miranda agree to have a baby for money? Why would someone do that?'

'She was young... A student. She wanted to travel the world, so she needed money.'

'What was she like?'

Stephanie thought back to when she had first met Miranda. 'I can't really remember much about her.'

'Do I look like her in any way?'

'No. You look like your father.'

'Does Rita still know her?'

'I don't think so. She hasn't mentioned anything to me. But it was one of Rita's friends who knew Miranda.'

'You must have got to know Miranda.'

'I didn't. She kept herself to herself.'

'Did you keep in touch with her after I was born?'

'No. That wouldn't have been right. Anyway, she went off to travel the world with the money we paid her... at least that's what I heard from Rita.'

'Do you think Rita still keeps in touch with the friend that knew Miranda?'

Stephanie closed her eyes briefly. 'Why do you want to know that?'

'Well, maybe that friend would know where Miranda is.'

Stephanie pursed her lips. She lowered her eyelids, and once again began to pick at her flaking nail varnish. 'So, do you want to look for her too, as well as your father?' she said, not looking at Alice. She could almost feel Alice slipping away from her. She had been her whole world for so long; now it felt like she may lose her for ever. Her eyes filled with tears.

'I think I'd like to meet her,' said Alice. 'If only to find out if we've got anything in common.'

Stephanie nodded and forced a weak smile.

'You really should have told me all this before,' said Alice, shaking her head.

'Maybe.' Stephanie held back her tears.

Alice stood up. 'I have to go. I need to get my head around all this.'

'Darling, why don't you stay here tonight? You can sleep in your old room. I don't want to think of you alone when you're in this state.'

'No, Mum, I'll be fine.' She paused and looked at Stephanie, realising she had called her "Mum". But she wasn't her mum. 'Oh, I don't know what's real and what's not anymore,' she said, thinking out loud. 'I'll call you tomorrow. I have to go.'

Stephanie stood at her front door and watched as Alice walked along the street towards the Tube station. Her heart felt torn apart inside. The cold look in Alice's eyes as if she were looking at a stranger when she left the house—that was the worst part. Something of the trust between them had been whittled away tonight.

Jumbled thoughts floated around Alice's mind as she lay in bed staring at the ceiling. The tears kept up a constant flow, but she hardly noticed them anymore. Thoughts of her early childhood haunted her mind; Stephanie was always there in every memory, but now that had all been tainted. She had never doubted for one moment that Stephanie was her mother. Now a faceless individual, Miranda, took her place. A woman who had sold a child.

Alice recalled how she had once thought she looked a bit like Stephanie's mother. Stephanie had mentioned to her one day that her own mother's hair had been blonde and she had shown Alice a photograph of her. It was a black and white photograph. Upon looking at it, Alice remembered saying: 'I look a bit like her, don't I?' She also remembered her mother saying: 'Hmm... you look like your father, Alice.' But Alice had gone away with a feeling that she had inherited some features from her maternal grandmother. Now, that was all dissolved. There was no way she could have inherited anything from Stephanie's mother.

This thought stirred up other feelings that were bubbling below the surface. She began to wonder whether Stephanie had ever really loved her. After all, she was not her real mother. She had seemed sincere when she told her she loved her, but somehow Alice felt a detachment, as if she no longer belonged with Stephanie. It was almost as if an invisible wall had taken away the closeness they had once shared; the closeness that Alice believed could only exist between a mother and her real daughter.

She pondered as to whether she would have stayed with Stephanie if she'd found out at a younger age that she was not her mother. Then she recalled that her father had left *her* as well as Stephanie. She would not have been able to go to him. She didn't want to think about that, it made her feel as though she didn't belong anywhere.

She lay awake for hours, unable to close her eyes; almost as if she thought that by closing her eyes she would be losing control of an already turbulent situation. She wanted to keep a tight grip so that nothing else would change.

Alice wished that she had never thought about looking for her father. Her life had been so much easier before. She had opened a door into a world which had been left abandoned for years. There were secrets, dark shadows and uncertainties behind the door. Alice was gripped by fear. She knew she could not go back now. She needed to find out about her father. It had changed from a want to a need. She would have to face her fears...

Chapter Nine

Tuesday 19th August 1997

When Alice awoke, her thoughts immediately went back to the night before. She could not escape the memory that entered her mind, like a heavy weight landing on top of her. The strongest emotion she could feel was helplessness as if she were floating in a vast empty space with no control over where her life was going. Anxiety consumed her, and she felt afraid to face the day.

I'm not your mother... I'm not your mother... the finality of those words, the absurdity of the words; they circled around in her mind, taunting her. *But how could that be?* Surely it had been a dream?

Forcing herself out of bed, she went to the wardrobe and opened it trying to concentrate her mind on doing the normal things; getting dressed, having breakfast—but those words were still there. Stephanie's eyes, red from crying, were clear in her mind. *Maybe it was a dream,* hope battled against hope. *Maybe I'm still dreaming?* Turmoil raged through her mind. *What is real? Who am I?*

Looking through her wardrobe, but not really looking, her hand touched the soft velvet of her favourite black dress, and suddenly a memory sprang to mind, waking her from her semiconscious state. She remembered that she had agreed to go to Frank's friend's birthday party this evening; she had planned to wear this dress. Walking over to her dressing table mirror, the only thing she could think of was that she had hardly slept... *I'll look terrible.* Thoughts of Andrew appeared in her mind—perfect, handsome Andrew. She sat in front of the mirror and saw that she looked pale and tired. Her eyes were red and puffy with dark circles surrounding them.

Up until yesterday evening, she had been looking forward to the party... to seeing Andrew again. Now, she wanted to hide away. *He can't see me like this.* Depression overwhelmed her.

Through her eyes, the ghosts of her feelings were transparently gazing out at the world. The shock, disillusionment and disappointment were obvious and etched into her face. She was a portrait of her anguish.

She stood up and approached the phone at her bedside table. She resolved to call Jenny and tell her she was too ill to attend the party. It would help that she had been crying so much; her voice would sound suitably croaky.

'Hello.' Jenny answered the phone in her jovial voice.

'Oh, hello, Jen, it's me.'

'Alice, hi! Have you just woken up? Your voice sounds different!'

'Er... I'm not feeling well—'

'Oh, no! You're not phoning to say you can't come to the party, are you? Please, don't say that!'

Alice felt weak, as though she would cry if she spoke further. Staying in this flat would not help her get over the pain. She wanted to see Jenny. Jenny always had a way of lifting her spirits.

'Allie?'

Alice took a deep breath. 'Um... I'll come to the party.'

'Great! So, are you looking forward to seeing Andrew again?'

'Yeah!' said Alice, trying to sound enthusiastic.

'So, what were you phoning about?'

'Er... just wanted to check what time you'd be picking me up.'

'Oh. I think we agreed about eight, didn't we?'

'Oh, yeah, I forgot.'

'Okay, well, I'll see you tonight! And remember to dress up!'

'Yeah, see you later.'

Alice hung up the phone and walked back to the dressing table. Taking another look at her reflection, she began to cry.

Trying to focus her mind on the upcoming party, she told herself: *It's what I need; to take my mind off everything.* She spent the rest of the day tidying up her flat, whilst listening to loud music, in an attempt to stop herself thinking too much.

As the time came closer for Jenny and Frank to collect her, she began to feel increasingly nervous. She worried that if she had a few too many to drink, she might accidentally tell Jenny—or even someone else at the party—what Stephanie had revealed to her. The last thing she wanted to do was to tell anyone; it felt like a dark, embarrassing secret that she wanted to keep locked away.

At 8.05 p.m., the doorbell rang. Jenny was standing outside.

As soon as she saw Alice she jumped forward and gave her a hug: 'Hi Allie! Wow! You look great!'

'Thanks,' said Alice, surprised at the compliment. When she'd looked in the mirror a few moments before, she'd let out a sigh and wished she owned some make-up so she could try to cover up the signs of her sorrow.

'Come on!' said Jenny, 'Frank's waiting in the car.'

'I'll just get my jacket.' Alice played nervously with the string of fake pearls she wore around her neck. Walking towards the coat rack, she took one last look in the mirror by the door and noticed the sadness in her eyes. Frowning, she smoothed her hand along a crinkle that had formed in her velvet dress when she'd been sitting down, pulled on her jacket and ran out of the door, trying not to think.

Once inside the car, Jenny began to talk enthusiastically about the party and the people they would be likely to see there. Surprising herself, Alice joined in with the chatter and began to feel almost normal again.

They arrived at the party at about 9 p.m. There were already many people at the house, and loud music was blaring from large speakers in the front room. The atmosphere was smoky in the living room. Alice looked around her at the people who were laughing and dancing. There were a few faces she recognised from university.

A tall, attractive dark-haired boy approached them. 'Frank! Glad you made it, mate! Jen! Hi, how are you?' He leaned forward and kissed Jenny on the cheek.

'I'm great!' shouted Jenny, over the music.

'Tony,' said Frank, to the boy who had greeted them, 'this is Alice; Jen's friend.' He put an arm around Alice.

'Hello, Alice, pleased to meet you,' said Tony extending a hand to shake hers. 'I'm Tony! It's my party—'

'And I'll cry if I want to,' said Frank, teasing.

'Oh, shut up, Frank,' said Tony, laughing.

'Nice to meet you,' said Alice, shaking his hand, although she was not sure her voice was heard above the sound of the music blaring. 'Happy Birthday!' she said, almost shouting the words.

'Thanks!' Tony smiled, then he looked into her eyes as if trying to remember something. 'Have we met before?'

'Um... I don't think so,' said Alice, unsure.

'You old charmer,' said Frank, laughing.

'No, seriously, Frank; I thought I recognised her.' He paused.

Then it was as if a light bulb sparked in his eyes. 'Oh! I know! You look like one of my sister's friends: Jane. She'll be at the party. You might see her; then you'll know what I mean. Blimey, you two could be sisters!'

Alice froze. *Jane? Jane Forester? Is she coming to the party?* She watched as Frank handed Tony the bottle of wine they had brought with them, and the two boys disappeared into the crowd of people dancing in the middle of the room. Alice looked around the room, frantically searching for the girl who looked like her. Then, she sighed; the whole point of coming to this party had been to try to stop thinking about everything her mother had said, and about looking for her father. All she had wanted to do was enjoy herself. She felt someone poke her in the arm. It was Jenny.

'Look,' said Jenny.

Alice had to read her lips because the music was now even louder. Then Jenny said something else, which Alice didn't catch.

'What?' she said, leaning closer to her. 'I can't hear a thing.'

She then saw Jenny pointing towards the door. Andrew had arrived. Alice smiled at Jenny, but when she looked back at Andrew, she saw that he hadn't arrived alone. He was with a very attractive girl: she was tall and slim with long, wavy brown hair. Andrew said something to the girl and they both laughed. They seemed happy. Alice frowned. When she looked back at Jenny, she could see the disappointment in Jenny's eyes. Alice could not help taking one more look at Andrew. When she looked again, she saw him kiss the beautiful girl on the cheek, and then gave up hope of anything happening between herself and Andrew.

In the past, she had wondered whether Andrew had a girlfriend. Somehow, she'd imagined she would be devastated if she found out he was already in a relationship. She began to wonder why she didn't feel more disappointed now; after all, she had spent the past few months thinking about him and what it would be like if they were together. It was a dream that she had hoped would come true; but right now she felt nothing. It didn't seem to bother her.

'I'll get us a drink,' said Jenny, during a rare quiet time between songs. 'The night is still young. There are lots of boys at this party. Forget about Andrew.'

Alice smiled at her friend as she watched her walk away. She began to ponder the reasons why she no longer seemed to care about finding love. Perhaps what Stephanie had told her had affected her in more ways than she had suspected. It was as though her feelings and emotions were switched off. Maybe last night's revelation had turned a page in her life, so she was now a different person. The old Alice had been in love with Andrew, she had been Stephanie's daughter, she knew who she was. The new Alice had no identity; this new Alice had never known Andrew or had any dreams about him. Her past life had been wiped away and now she had entered an undiscovered world where she would have to find her way alone.

Jenny returned with the drinks. She handed Alice a plastic cup of red wine. 'Drink up, and forget!' she said smiling. 'Andrew's not that great anyway. There are plenty more fish in the sea!'

Alice sipped on her wine. Somehow, she could not agree with Jenny's statement. She had never seen Andrew look better than he did tonight.

Jenny leaned closer to her and said: 'What do you think of Tony? He's nice, isn't he? And, he's single.'

Alice smiled, whilst thinking that she didn't really want a relationship at the moment.

'Oh, I can see Frank calling me. I won't be long,' said Jenny, disappearing off to the other side of the room.

Alice stood alone feeling like an alien as she watched the crowd of partygoers. Everyone here seemed so happy; she didn't feel that she belonged. She drank her cup of wine quickly and went to get another drink. Perhaps with a few more drinks inside her, she would be able to stop thinking so much. She found a table at the side of the room that displayed bowls of crisps and other snacks, along with bottles of wine, cheap champagne, beer cans, etc. She found a bottle of wine that was almost full and poured some into her cup. After drinking it all in one go, she felt foolish, realising that she was in no fit state to get drunk. What if she then started to tell everyone about what Stephanie had told her? It was on the tip of her tongue as it was; all the thoughts flooded her mind, until it felt that they could almost fall out if she didn't keep her mouth shut. She placed the bottle of wine on the table, but then decided to fill up her cup again as the warm feeling of daze began to fall upon her after the first couple of cups of wine. Her mind was beginning to feel hazy, just as she wanted it to feel. She needed more wine, to keep up that trancelike state. This time, she promised herself she would sip the wine, rather than downing it at once. She turned around on her heels and that small movement made her worry that perhaps she had already had enough alcohol. It had gone straight to her head as she had hardly eaten a thing all day. She tried to focus on the crowd of dancers, and steadied herself by holding on to the table top. She almost spilt her cup of wine. A few drops found there way onto her skirt. As she wiped them away with her hand she felt glad she was dressed in black; hopefully the stains would not be so obvious.

She looked around the room that was still slightly spinning from the effects of the alcohol. She couldn't see Jenny anywhere. Then, from the corner of her eye she noticed a face she thought she recognised. She turned around ignoring the dizzy feeling, and saw Jane Forester. *Am I actually drunk, already? I must be hallucinating,* she thought. Then, she remembered something Tony had said about a girl called Jane being his sister's friend. She could not help staring at Jane. She felt pleased that at least Jane was not facing in her direction, so she couldn't see her stare.

Jane was talking to another girl, they seemed to be having fun. Alice decided to drink the rest of her wine, for courage, and then to go and speak to Jane. She wanted to find out more about her; find out if her suspicions were correct. She downed her wine and placed the cup on the table behind her.

Just then, she felt a hand on her arm. It was Jenny. 'Oh, hi, Jen.'

'Hi, I was just coming to get you.' She pointed to somewhere on the other side of the room. 'I'm over there with Frank and Tony, come and join us.' She took Alice by the hand.

'Er... wait, Jen.' Alice stood still. 'Do you know many people at this party?'

'No, not really; they're mainly Tony's friends.' Then, smiling, she said: 'Oh, I like this song,' as the intro to a dance track began to play. She shook her hips. 'Let's dance, Allie!'

'Wait. Do you know that girl over there with the red dress?' She turned around to point at Jane, but she could not see her.

'Which girl?' Jenny looked at her blankly when she turned back to face her. 'Look, are you coming to dance or what?'

Alice looked around frantically, trying to find Jane in the crowd. She began to walk towards the living room door. 'Where are you going?' shouted Jenny over the music. She followed Alice, frowning.

When Alice reached the door to the living room she noticed that Jane was standing by the front door. She was taking her jacket from a coat hook. Alice turned around sensing Jenny behind her. 'Look!' she said, 'That girl. Do you know who she is?'

Jenny leaned over her to get a better look. 'Blimey, Allie, she looks just like you!' Jenny's eyes were wide.

That reaction was all Alice needed to spur her on; knowing she wasn't the only one who thought Jane looked like her. Before she knew it, she was walking towards Jane. She felt sure that the alcohol had something to do with it because she doubted she would have been so confident otherwise. There was something else though; an overwhelming feeling that she couldn't let Jane get away without making some sort of contact—as if there were an invisible force between them, drawing her towards Jane like a magnet.

Jane glanced at her as she approached, then her eyes widened as if she were surprised.

'Excuse me,' said Alice. 'Are you Jane Forester?'

'Um... yes.' Jane was now staring at her. 'Wh... Who are you?'

Alice only now noticed that Jane had a plaster cast on her right arm, from her elbow to her wrist; then she remembered the plane crash. 'I'm Alice Turnbull.' She said, looking back at Jane, whose stare had now turned into a frown.

The short, plump girl who had been talking to Jane, said: 'Are you two related?'

'No,' said Jane to the girl. 'I've never met her before.' Then, turning to Alice, she frowned again and said: 'We haven't met before, have we?' Confusion was clear in her eyes.

'No.' Alice shook her head.

'You look so alike!' said the other girl. 'Like sisters!' She laughed.

Alice laughed nervously. Jane looked embarrassed. 'Um... anyway,' she said. 'I was just leaving. Can you help me with my jacket?' she asked her friend.

'Did you hurt your arm in the plane crash?' asked Alice.

Jane eyed her suspiciously: 'How did you know about that?'

'It was in the papers.'

Jane blushed.

'Is your dad called Roger?'

'No.'

'No?' Alice's face dropped. 'Roger Forester is my dad, I thought...'

'Thanks, Susie,' said Jane when her friend finished helping her put on her jacket. 'Bye... uh, sorry I've forgotten your name...'

'Alice.'

'Alice,' she repeated, nodding as she turned to leave.

'Wait, Jane.'

Jane span around quickly to face her, but appeared irritated.

'It's just that... well, we look so alike. My parents divorced when

I was a baby. I thought, because your surname is Forester... he might be your dad...' As she spoke, Alice felt increasing weird, as if she were revealing secrets to a room of strangers for no reason. Jane was looking at her, blankly. She appeared more embarrassed by than interested in what Alice was saying.

'I don't know what you're talking about,' said Jane, finally. 'My father was never married before, and his name is Ken.' She walked towards the door and then turned back. 'You are obviously mistaken. Sorry.'

Alice felt her face flush red. *How could I have got it so wrong?* She regretted drinking that wine. If she hadn't, she would never have approached Jane. She was actually glad for the loud music now; at least there were only a couple of people who had heard her speak.

'Sorry,' said Alice. But Jane had already walked out of the door.

'Are you all right, Allie?'

Alice turned around and when she saw Jenny, felt instantly mortified. She hadn't known that Jenny was standing behind her. 'You... Did you hear all that?' she asked, pensively.

'Um... most of it. Er... look, why don't we get another drink?'

'No.' Alice shook her head. 'I don't feel well. I think I'll go home.'

'You can't go home alone, especially if you don't feel well—'

'I'll get a taxi,' she said, agitated.

'No... No, listen, we'll be leaving soon. Wait for us. I'll go in and talk to Frank.'

Jenny disappeared back into the living room. Alice felt as if she might faint. Susie, Jane's friend, walked past her, eyeing her with what appeared to be sympathy or perhaps concern for Alice's state of mind.

Alice's perception was hazy, and in a way she was now pleased she had drunk so much wine; at least she wasn't able to think about much. She felt tired and wanted to sit down. She looked behind her to see whether she could sit on the stairs, but there was a couple kissing, sitting at the bottom of the stairs. So, she wouldn't even be able to get past them to go upstairs and find a quiet room in which to lie down.

As she walked back into the living room, the loudness of the music overwhelmed her for a few moments; she had to stand still, trying to get her bearings. When she finally felt as though she had control of herself again, she looked up and surveyed the room, trying to find somewhere to sit. The sofa at the far end of the room was free. There were bags and coats on it, but no one was sitting there. She made her way over, and cleared a bit of space so she could sit down. She sat there for what seemed like an hour or so, but was probably less time. People were slowly starting to leave the party. The room became less crowded and the music had been turned down so that it was now possible to hear people talking. She could see Jenny, Frank, Tony and a couple of other boys chatting and dancing. Jenny waved at her to join them, but Alice didn't feel like talking to anyone. She thought about dancing. Sometimes at parties, she would often lose herself in the music and spend hours on the dance floor. Those were always her best memories. She loved dancing. But now that the people in the room were few and the music had been turned down, she didn't really want to get up and dance. She would feel too conspicuous.

As she looked over at Jenny, she wondered when they would be leaving. She looked at her watch, it was nearly 11 p.m. She thought about calling a taxi. The telephone on the side table next to the sofa seemed to beckon her for a moment. She decided that if Jenny and Frank didn't make a move to leave within the next half hour, she would call a taxi and go. As she leaned back on the sofa, she caught sight of Andrew who was standing on the opposite side of the room... alone. He seemed to be looking directly at her, and when she looked at him, he smiled, appearing almost embarrassed that she had noticed him looking at her; then he turned away and she saw that he was pouring himself a drink.

He smiled at me, she thought wistfully. Her eyes remained fixed on him, and she wondered where that girl was—the one who had accompanied him to the party. Maybe she'd gone to the toilet? *Maybe she isn't his girlfriend*, she dared to think. Then, she saw Andrew pick up two cups from the table and her heart sank again. He'd obviously poured a drink for his girlfriend as well. She hung her head and considered once again calling for a taxi. But then she realised she didn't have any telephone numbers for local cab firms.

Just then, someone said: 'Hi Alice.' It was a voice she recognised. Looking up, she saw Andrew. *He remembered my name.* He smiled at her again and held out one of the cups towards her. 'It's only orange juice, I'm afraid; they've run out of booze.'

She took the cup from him and smiled awkwardly. She thought of all the times she had longed for a moment like this—to be alone with Andrew, to have a chance to talk to him.

Andrew moved a couple of coats onto the back of the sofa and sat next to her. 'I'm Andrew,' he said.

'Yes... Yes, I remember we met once,' said Alice, tripping over her tongue.

'Selina introduced us.' He sipped his drink.

Alice smiled to herself whimsically. *He remembered meeting me.*

'I noticed you've been sitting alone on this sofa for a while,' he said. 'Are you okay?'

She blushed and was glad that it was dark in the room; the only light coming from the wall sconces—three or four on each wall—and candles scattered erratically on tables and sideboards.

'I... I wasn't feeling well,' she said, looking at her hands. 'I'm just a bit tired, I think.' She turned to look at him and tried to smile, but her face felt stiff as if smiling was something she had never done. She wanted to be excited by this moment, and there was excitement bubbling beneath the surface, but she was also not able to shrug off her feelings of anguish at the events of the past few days.

He smiled at her again and she noticed his eyes just as she had done when they'd first met. She found herself staring at him. For a short time—it could not have been longer than a few seconds—they looked at each other, locked in each other's gaze.

'Well,' he said eventually, looking at his hands, 'it's not long before we have to go back to uni.'

'I know,' was all she could think of saying. She looked across the room and saw Jenny and Frank were still dancing. For an instant, when looking in Andrew's eyes, she had felt as though she was far away, in another place; but now she remembered everything she had been trying to forget.

'What are you studying?' he asked. He seemed genuinely interested—his look no longer intense but friendly.

'Law,' she replied, forcing a smile.

'Ah! So, one day you'll be a hotshot lawyer!' He grinned.

'Hmm... I'm not sure,' she giggled. For a moment, again, she had forgotten her pain, but now it was back. She really wanted to enjoy this moment, but she couldn't help her mind going back to her meeting with Jane and everything Stephanie had said to her.

She looked across the room and her eyes met with Jenny's. Jenny gave her a broad smile and a wink, noticing that Andrew was sitting next to her. Alice smiled back, but was really wishing that Jenny would tell her they were going to leave. She didn't feel very sociable, and couldn't think of a thing to say to Andrew. *He probably thinks I'm not interested in him.*

She turned towards him just as he was getting up off the sofa.

'I'll be going now,' he said.

'Okay,' she said, knowing she had not been very good company. It felt as though her dreams were slipping from her hands as Andrew walked away. He turned around before he left and said, 'I'll see you at uni.' He then went to say good-bye to Tony. Alice wanted to reach out and stop him leaving, but she had a sinking feeling that it was too late.

Finally, Jenny and Frank approached her. 'Come on, Allie,' said Jenny, 'we're off.'

Alice felt relieved.

'Bye, Tony. Great party,' said Frank as they headed for the door.

As Frank opened the front door, Susie—the girl who had been talking to Jane earlier—said: 'Bye, Frank.'

'Oh, bye, Susie,' he said, waving at her.

As they got into the car, Alice's curiosity got the better of her. 'Frank, who was that girl you just said bye to?'

'Tony's sister, Susie. Why?'

'Oh, I just thought I recognised her from somewhere.'

'Well, she is a law student,' he said as he settled himself in the driver's seat, 'but I think she goes to a different university than you.'

'Do you know her friend—Jane?' Alice was glad it was dark in the car as her face reddened when she recalled that Jenny had heard her talking to Jane earlier. Thankfully, Alice was sitting behind the front passenger seat where Jenny was seated.

'No,' said Frank, answering her question.

Alice leaned back in the car seat and looked out of the window wondering how she was ever going to get to know more about the mysterious Jane.

'Tony kept going on about how much you look like someone called Jane, all evening,' said Frank, breaking her train of thought.

'Oh, what happened with you and the gorgeous Andrew? I saw you chatting to him,' said Jenny, changing the subject.

'Yeah, I saw that,' said Frank. 'You two were very cosy on the sofa. I thought I might have to get the fire extinguisher out.' He laughed.

'Really?' Jenny's voice was tinged with excitement. 'Did you kiss? I didn't see that.'

'No, we didn't,' blurted Alice, embarrassed.

'I was just kidding.' Frank laughed again.

'Oh,' Jenny sounded disappointed. She twisted around as far as she could in the front seat to look back at Alice. 'Allie, when I saw you two chatting, I asked Tony if Andrew had a girlfriend, 'cos you know we saw him arrive with that girl; well, apparently she's just a friend. Andrew's unattached.' Jenny was grinning.

Alice forced a smile at her friend. She didn't say anything, feeling sure she had spoilt any chance of a relationship with him. She had behaved so coldly towards him and hated herself for it. After all the months of waiting for a chance to talk to him, she had let herself down; she didn't want to think about it. The opportunity had passed her by.

Jenny and Frank began to argue about which tape they would play in the car: 'But you were listening to that on the way here. It's my turn to choose,' said Jenny, annoyed.

'I don't want to listen to U2,' said Frank. 'I'm the one driving. I should be able to choose.'

'I prefer Radiohead's other album; so if you want to listen to them, let's listen to that.'

'No, I want to hear the new one; I haven't had a chance to listen to it properly.'

'Huh! It's always on in the car when I get in here.'

'Well, I don't drive that much...'

Alice had tuned out of their conversation and was staring out of the window looking at the rain and the streetlights. Uppermost on her mind was the conversation she'd had with Jane.

The drive took about half an hour. By the time they arrived at Alice's flat, Jenny and Frank were chatting happily. Alice's thoughts consumed her.

'Are you asleep back there?' asked Frank as the car came to a halt.

'No,' said Alice, her mind tuning back to the present with the change in motion of the vehicle.

'You've hardly said a word since we left Tony's,' he said, twisting in his seat to look at her.

She unfastened her seat belt and forced a smile at him. 'I'm fine.'

'She's been too busy dreaming about Andrew, haven't you?' Jenny giggled.

'Yeah, someone will be having sweet dreams tonight,' said Frank, laughing.

Alice put on her best fake laugh and opened the back door

of the car.

'Thanks for the lift,' she said as she exited. 'It was a great evening.'

'I'll just come to the door with you and make sure you get in safely,' said Jenny stepping out of the car.

Alice knew that Jenny had heard what she'd said to Jane, and she knew that she was probably going to ask her about it. She wished she could just go into the house and disappear under her bed sheets until morning.

'Are you all right, Allie?' asked Jenny when they reached her front door.

'Yeah, fine.'

Jenny spoke in a lowered voice, even though Frank wouldn't be able to hear them from that distance, as if she were relaying a secret: 'It's just, you know I heard everything you said to Jane earlier.'

'I know,' Alice brushed it aside with a wave of her hand. 'I must have been mistaken.'

'Jane does look like you. It was an easy mistake to make.'

'Thanks, Jen.' Alice smiled at her as she fumbled with her key ring trying to find the front door key. 'She has the same surname as my dad, so I thought she might be related to him... Well, you know... you heard...'

'Yeah. Listen, just because her dad has a different first name, doesn't mean you're not related. Does your dad have a brother? You might be Jane's cousin. Me and my first cousin, Harriett, look almost like twins.'

Alice sighed. 'That's true, I hadn't thought of that. Hmm... But I don't know much about my dad... I'm not sure if he's got a brother.'

'Well, I'm here for you if you need to talk. And don't feel bad about what happened, okay?'

'Thanks, Jen.' Alice put her key in the lock, then she paused. 'Jen... do you think Frank could find out more about Jane through Tony? I mean, his sister seems to be good friends with her.'

'That's a good idea, Sherlock. I'll talk to Frank about it.' Jenny smiled.

'Thanks.'

Just then, Frank tooted the car horn.

'Oh, I'd better go, Allie. I'll phone you.' Jenny walked away towards the car.

Alice lay in bed unable to sleep. She could still hear the music from the party pulsating in her head. So much had happened since the plane crash—since her dream. Her life had been turned upside down, changed beyond recognition. It had only been a week, but it seemed much longer.

She kept replaying the conversation she'd had with Jane, over and over in her mind. Could Jenny be right? Could she be her cousin? It was certainly possible. Stephanie would know if her father had a brother.

Her thoughts turned to Stephanie, who was now "Stephanie" in her mind when she thought of her, rather than "Mum". Alice remembered she had told her she would call her today. Looking at her alarm clock, she saw that it was 11:45 p.m. It was too late to phone her now; she would be asleep. She felt a twinge of guilt for not phoning her, aware that Stephanie had been very upset after their last meeting.

Having had time to think it over, Alice was no longer angry with her for not telling her about the surrogacy agreement. In truth, she wished she had never told her. *Ignorance is bliss*, she thought. *I wish I didn't know. I wish Stephanie was my mum.*

She thought about Miranda, and momentarily wondered about whether she could find her. But then she felt foolish, realising that Miranda had never wanted her: she had sold her; given her away. Why would she want anything to do with her now? But she wondered whether Miranda may have regretted giving her away. Did she ever think about her and wish she could find her? Pushing the thought from her mind, she decided to concentrate on finding her father first and deal with everything else later.

A tear came to her eye as she thought of the way she had spoken to Stephanie. She had been angry when she found out, but now she knew that none of it was Stephanie's fault; not the fact that she was unable to have children of her own, the fact of her husband leaving her to bring up a small child on her own, or the fact that she had been so afraid of losing Alice that she hadn't told her the truth. She resolved to phone Stephanie in the morning and tell her that she understood and that she had forgiven her.

She tried to think of something else and her mind went back to the party. She remembered Andrew and felt sad again. She cried frustrated tears. She felt sure that he would have got the impression that she wasn't interested in him. *Why is everything going wrong at once?*

As Stephanie lay in bed that night, she wondered how she had managed to get through the day. The salon had been very busy in the morning and she had hardly had the time to sit down. She put on a happy face and had managed to fool some people, but many of her regular clients commented that she seemed "tired" or "quiet". A couple of times, she made the excuse that she needed to go to the toilet, but in fact had taken a few minutes to cry bitter tears and take deep breaths to calm her mind.

At lunchtime, she told Rosie she had a migraine and would be taking the afternoon off. She asked her to phone her clients and rearrange her appointments. She could tell that Rosie didn't believe her. Stephanie had never suffered from migraines. But even though they'd been friends for a long time, she could not bring herself to tell Rosie what was really wrong. There was only one person she could speak to about this.

She phoned Rita and had been unable to say much on the phone as she could not hold back the tears. Rita had met her at the café where they had first met each other again after almost twenty years.

She spent two hours with Rita in the café, not eating but trying to come to terms with everything that had happened.

'You look pale, Steph. You should eat some lunch, you've been working all morning.'

'I think I've lost Alice. I think she hates me. The way she looked at me. How can she ever forgive me? I lied to her.' Her tears began to spill, and the waitress who was passing by their table tried to pretend she hadn't seen, busying herself with wiping a nearby table.

The café was buzzing with the lunchtime crowd, many of the customers queuing up to buy a take-away sandwich. All the tables were occupied. Stephanie was hardly aware that there was anyone else around, and if she had been, she would not have cared. Her world had fallen apart. After a sleepless night, no breakfast and a busy morning at the salon, she didn't really care what she looked like, what she said, or who witnessed it.

'Steph, you're not wearing any make-up. I hardly recognised you,' said Rita. 'You really should try to put things into perspective. Don't let this bring you down. Alice is shocked, but when she's had time to digest it, she will understand.'

'She said she'd call me today. I've been waiting for her call all morning. Every time the phone rang in the salon, I went to pick it up, even when I was in the middle of doing someone's hair. I'm desperate to talk to her.'

'Well, why don't you call her?'

'No, I can't.' Stephanie's face blanched and for a moment Rita thought she would faint.

'Oh, this is ridiculous. You haven't slept, and you haven't eaten anything all day; you're not thinking straight.' Rita stood up. 'I'm going to get you a sandwich and then we'll talk some more.' Her forehead creased into a frown.

Stephanie sat alone at the table and now noticed a few people looking at her, but when she looked at them they turned away. She had caught sight of her reflection a couple of times in the salon mirrors, mostly avoiding looking at herself, but when she had, she saw that the bags under her eyes gave away the fact that she hadn't slept, and her hair was unkempt as she had hardly bothered to brush it that morning. She had got dressed quickly, after having difficulty getting out of bed because she had not slept, then she had splashed some water on her face and ran a brush through her hair once or twice. Her appearance was the last thing on her mind when she left the house that morning.

Feeling self-conscious now, she wiped her eyes with a tissue from her handbag and tried to compose herself. Rita brought her a sandwich and a cup of tea. Stephanie smiled at her friend.

'I'm so sorry, Rita,' she said.

'No need to apologise.'

'I've been behaving so selfishly, dragging you here and then not listening to you.'

'Look, Steph, I understand. It's okay. Eat your lunch.'

She took a bite of the sandwich and washed it down with a sip of tea. She looked beyond the people seated at the tables, out at the street and towards the sky. There were hardly any clouds and the sun was out. She tried to concentrate on the brightness of the day, to pull herself out of the mire of her thoughts. 'Do you think Alice will ever talk to me again?' she said almost to the sky beyond the window.

'Oh, of course she will,' said Rita, sipping her coffee and

frowning at Stephanie.

Stephanie pulled her eyes away from the view outside and looked at her friend. 'Thanks for coming, Rita. You're such a good friend.'

'It's okay. I just wanted to make sure you're all right. I personally think you did the right thing telling Alice. She'll thank you in the end.'

'Do you think so?' A shred of hope for Stephanie to grasp onto. Her eyes brightened for a fraction of a second.

'I'm sure of it,' said Rita, nodding and smiling.

'It's just the way she looked at me; it was like she was looking at a stranger,' said Stephanie, her eyes distant again.

Stephanie's mind snapped back to the present and she looked at her alarm clock as she lay in bed. It was 11:45 p.m. *She didn't call, she said she would phone today. Maybe she forgot, maybe she'll call tomorrow.* Trying to block out her thoughts, she fell into a deep exhausted, dreamless sleep.

Chapter Ten

Wednesday 20th August 1997

Alice arrived at *Bairns' Books* at 8:45 a.m.

'Hi,' said Charlotte, brightly. 'How are you?'

'Oh, fine,' she replied, unconvincingly.

'So, tell all.' Charlotte grinned at her as she made her way behind the counter. 'How was the party? It was yesterday, wasn't it? I want to know everything!'

'It was a great party.' She turned her face away from Charlotte.

'Did you get to talk to that boy you fancy?'

'Yes.' She felt herself blush, not so much from romantic thoughts of Andrew, but more from embarrassment at how their conversation had turned out.

'Come on then, I want all the sordid details.' Charlotte leaned in towards her, so that it was impossible for Alice to avoid her eyes.

'Um... there's nothing to tell, really.'

'You're so cool!' said Charlotte, smiling at her. 'You've fancied this boy for ages and now you get to chat to him and you're just so calm about it. I would have literally been tearing his clothes off if it had been me.' She laughed.

Alice couldn't help joining in with the laughter.

'So, when are you gonna see him again?'

'We swapped numbers,' she lied. 'I'll probably call him next week.'

'You ice queen. I wish I could be more like you, Alice!'

She forced a smile at Charlotte, wishing they could change the subject.

'Now, let me tell you all about *my* evening!' Looking much more comfortable being in the spotlight once again, Charlotte sat down on the stool behind the counter and began to relate details about her evening out with her new boyfriend, Dave; an actor she had met on a recent film set. As Alice listened to her, she couldn't help thinking about Andrew. She dearly wanted another chance to talk to him.

When Alice returned from lunch, Charlotte greeted her with: 'Oh yeah, I've been meaning to ask you how your search for your dad is going. Did your mum tell you where he lives?'

It came as a surprise to Alice that Charlotte had asked her this; she had always assumed that Charlotte was more interested in herself than anyone else, and had taken it for granted that anything she said to her would be forgotten after a few minutes. That's one of the reasons she had told Charlotte about her father in the first place, or indeed about Andrew; believing that she was someone she could talk to but not worry about having her judge her or ask too many questions.

Alice's initial reaction was just to stare in disbelief at Charlotte.

'Well?' asked Charlotte, snapping her out of her reverie.

'Um... no. My mum doesn't know where he lives,' she said finally.

'Oh. Never mind,' said Charlotte.

A customer came along and Alice was glad that at least it would distract her from asking anything else.

That evening, on the way home from the bookstore, Alice decided to visit Stephanie. She wanted things to go back to normal... Well, as normal as they could, considering that she now knew Stephanie wasn't her real mother. It was undeniable that things were different now, but she knew she still wanted Stephanie to be a part of her life. She had always been there for her.

When Alice arrived at Stephanie's flat, she found that she had not yet returned from work. Alice decided to surprise her by cooking a meal. She looked in the kitchen cupboards and decided to make a risotto. She had just finished cooking when Stephanie arrived home.

'Hi, Mum,' she said. She had said "Mum" instinctively, without thinking about it, then realised that she felt strange saying it. It seemed like the wrong thing to call her.

Stephanie did not miss the fact that, firstly, Alice had called her "Mum" and secondly, judging by the smell emanating from the kitchen, she had cooked a meal. It felt like a weight had been lifted off her shoulders. For the first time in almost two days, she felt she could breathe again. She had been thinking that Alice hated her and that was the worst feeling in the world.

Alice noticed that Stephanie seemed pleased to see her. She was smiling, but she looked tired; older somehow. She looked as though she hadn't slept. Alice knew that she had been the cause of her anguish, and felt momentarily guilty.

'Darling! This is a surprise! How lovely to see you,' said Stephanie, somewhat over enthusiastically, as if she were greeting an acquaintance in whose company she felt nervous. She was unsure how Alice would behave and was trying to placate her in advance.

'Did you have a good day at the salon?' asked Alice as Stephanie entered the kitchen.

'Yes, sweetie. How about you? How was work?'

It seemed that Stephanie was having a hard time maintaining eye contact with her.

'Oh, it was quiet,' said Alice. 'I've cooked a risotto. I don't know if it's any good. I didn't have the recipe with me. But it's the thought that counts, right?' She faked a laugh, while frowning.

'Yes,' said Stephanie. 'It smells lovely; I'm sure it'll be delicious.' She could see that Alice was tense. She, herself, felt nervous. At some stage it was obvious that Alice would talk about Monday night's conversation, and she was bracing herself for that, unsure what else she could say.

Alice took out two plates from the cupboard and began serving the dish.

She placed both plates on the table in silence.

'What would you like to drink—' She was about to say "Mum" again, but she stopped herself just in time; she still felt uneasy about using the word.

Stephanie watched her place the two plates on the kitchen table with the steaming rice dish. 'Er... I think I have some white wine in the fridge that would go well with this,' she said.

'Okay.' Alice walked over to the fridge and took out the wine, then she took two wine glasses out of the glass fronted cupboard.

Stephanie could feel the tension in the air. *Perhaps she's cooked this meal, because she's planning to ask me more about Roger.* The thought unnerved her. She would prefer to be the one to bring up the subject. Alice walked over to the table and placed the wine glasses there. She then returned to the cutlery drawer to take out some forks and spoons.

'Alice, darling.'

Alice looked at her as she placed a spoon and fork next to her plate.

Stephanie knew she was taking a risk, not really knowing if Alice had intended to talk about Roger again, but she wanted to clear the air before they sat down to eat and to get an idea as to what Alice was thinking. 'Please sit down, dear.' She took a deep breath as Alice sat opposite her. 'I... I've been worried about how you've been since... Well, I know it came as a shock to you on Monday when I told you... Well, I've been feeling really bad about—'

'Don't,' interrupted Alice, 'I'm okay about it. In fact, that's why I came over today—to say that I think I understand why you didn't tell me.'

They were both looking at their plates of food, not eating. Stephanie breathed an audible sigh of relief.

'I think I would have preferred it if you told me when I was younger. It would have been easier,' continued Alice.

'I know.' Stephanie picked up her fork. 'I was wrong. But I can't go back and change that. When you were growing up, you hardly ever mentioned your father. I didn't think you were interested in looking for him. It was easier to carry on as we were.'

'It may have been easier, but it wasn't necessarily right,' said Alice. She raised her head and saw that Stephanie was looking at her. Their eyes met momentarily, then Alice looked back at her plate.

'I'm sorry, Alice.' Stephanie took a mouthful of food. 'The risotto is lovely,' she said, hoping they could now change the subject. It was painful for her to accept that Alice had not really forgiven her. 'You'd better start eating your food or it will get cold.'

Alice began to eat. Silence hung between them.

'This is very tasty. Where did you learn to cook like this? It certainly wasn't from me.'

'Oh, it's just a recipe that was on the back of a packet of rice.'

Silence again.

Stephanie could not think of a thing to say. In the past, the two women had happily eaten a meal together in relative silence, not feeling the need to talk much. But somehow today was different; it was like there was a barrier that had to be broken down so that they could get back to their previous relationship. The only thing that could break it down was interaction. Stephanie tried again to initiate a conversation. 'You're going back to university soon, aren't you?'

'Yes.'

'Have you seen many of your friends during the summer break?'

'Yes, I went to a party yesterday,' said Alice, thinking of Andrew.

'A party? That's nice.'

'Yes, it was okay.' She frowned as she recalled the disastrous chat with Jane, the time she'd spent alone on the sofa, and then the failed conversation with Andrew.

They finished their meal in silence.

Stephanie stood up and cleared away the plates. 'Alice, I have some ice cream in the freezer if you'd like.'

'No thanks.'

'A cup of tea?'

'Okay. I'll make it,' said Alice, standing up.

'No, don't worry. I'll make it. You cooked the meal,' said Stephanie. 'Why don't you go and sit in the front room and I'll bring the tea in. I think I have some of those chocolate biscuits that you like, too.'

She felt relieved when Alice left the kitchen. It had been so hard to talk to her. They used to be able to chat freely about everything; Stephanie couldn't get used to the icy feeling in the air between them.

Stacking the dishes in the dishwasher, she caught sight of the childhood photographs of Alice that were displayed in the glass fronted cabinet. In one of the photographs, Roger's arm could be seen behind Alice. She recalled that he'd been in a bad mood that day, snapping angrily at her when she tried to take a picture of him with Alice. He had refused to be in the shot. Years ago, when Alice was still a child, Stephanie would look at that photograph and instantly remember Roger. That photograph had always served as a reminder of him. Thinking about it now, she couldn't understand why she kept it displayed. Perhaps, she mused, she wanted to prove to herself that she could get by without him and that the memory of him didn't faze her. After all, he had been the one who had left. He had broken the family apart; leaving his only child who was completely innocent, and never even trying to contact her. Only a cold hearted man could do something so callous. The photograph served as a reminder of what he had left behind; and in a strange way, it helped Stephanie get through the hardest years.

She found Alice sitting on the sofa in the living room, slightly hunched over and staring at her hands. Stephanie forced a smile as she handed a cup of tea to her and sat down.

'Does my dad have any brothers?' Alice's question was unexpected.

Stephanie shifted in her seat and frowned. 'No. He was an only child, like me,' she said. 'What's on TV, Alice?' She tried to change the subject. Picking up the remote control, she switched on the television and began to flick through the channels.

'I met Jane at the party I went to yesterday.'

'Oh? Is she a friend of yours?' asked Stephanie.

Alice looked at her as if she had said something stupid. 'No, Jane is the girl who was in the newspaper; the one who looks like me. Her surname is Forester. That's why I thought we might be related.'

'Alice, I've already told you where I stand on this. You can look for your father, against my wishes, but I don't want to be a part of it.' She leaned back on the sofa, taking a sip of tea and looking at the TV.

'I will need your help with some things. You haven't told me anything about him.'

'Have you been watching *Coronation Street* recently?' asked Stephanie, ignoring her. 'It's very good.'

Alice looked towards the television and sighed. 'We have to talk about this,' she said.

'Shush, I'm watching this.'

Alice reached out and took the remote control, turning off the television.

'Alice!' Stephanie looked at her, her eyebrows raised.

'Who else can tell me about my dad? Maybe I should ask Rita?'

Stephanie reddened. 'You have to understand, darling, talking about that time in my life brings back bad memories.' Leaning forward, she placed her tea cup on the coffee table and picked up the *TV Times* magazine that was lying there. She began flicking through it, obviously not reading it.

'I can understand that. I just need a few answers and then I'll look for him on my own, I promise.'

Stephanie sighed and put the magazine on her lap. 'What do you want to know?'

'Jane said that her dad's name is Ken. Does my dad have any cousins called Ken, maybe?'

Stephanie looked at her hands and then into Alice's eyes. She closed her eyes briefly as if what she was about to say was momentous. 'Your father's name is Ken.'

'What?' Alice's mouth fell open.

'His name is Ken—'

'So who is Roger Forester? You mean, he's not my dad? Why did you say—'

'Wait, let me explain—'

'Explain? Explain? You were supposed to explain everything to me on Monday but then you told me that Roger is my dad—but now it's Ken.' Alice stood up quickly, almost knocking the coffee table over. Her tea cup tipped over and the contents spilt onto the tablecloth, painting the white fabric a dull beige colour. Neither woman appeared to notice the tea which was dripping from the edge of the table onto the cream-coloured carpet. Alice stood opposite Stephanie, who was still seated on the sofa. 'So, not only are you not my mum, but the man who I thought was my dad is not even my dad!' Alice's face was red, and tears brimmed in her eyes. 'Who is the man in the photographs you showed me? Is he my dad? Is he Ken?'

'Please, Alice, if you'd only let me get a word in edgeways. Ken Forester is your dad; or to be more precise: Ken Roger Forester. He always used his middle name as his first name. He didn't like the name "Ken". I only found out that his first name was Ken a few weeks before we married. Everyone knew him as Roger.'

Alice wiped her tears on her sleeve, and looked visibly relaxed. 'So, he *is* the same man.' She sat back down on the sofa. 'I knew it.'

Stephanie shook her head and shrugged her shoulders.

'Jane must be related to me. My dad must have other children. She must be my half-sister.'

'You don't know that for sure—'

'Oh, come on, Mum; even you have to agree there are far too many coincidences here. She must be my sister.' Alice smiled.

Stephanie did not miss the fact that Alice had called her "Mum" and she momentarily felt more secure. 'I just don't want you to be disappointed.'

'It's exciting,' said Alice, her eyes full of joy. 'I've got this whole new family that I didn't know about.'

Stephanie frowned. 'Alice; you said you spoke to Jane at the party. Did she say anything else?'

'Only that her dad wasn't married before.' Her smile faded slightly. 'So, Jane doesn't know about us. I suppose that explains why she looked at me as if I was strange. But I just know she'll be as excited as I am, to find out she has a sister. Who knows? Maybe there are more of us... Dad might have other children.'

'You're getting carried away. Even if Jane's father is your father—'

'He is.'

'Hmm... even if he is; he has obviously not told his new family that he has another child. He left us. You already know what rejection feels like, I don't want you to go through it again.'

'I'm old enough to deal with it.' Alice shrugged. 'Besides, my friend Jenny is going to try to find out more about Jane. Jen's boyfriend knows one of Jane's friends; well, one of his friend's sisters knows her. So, I'll soon find out where she lives. Then I can get in touch with my dad.'

'Just don't set your heart on a happy ending. I don't want you to get hurt.'

Alice smiled at Stephanie. 'Look, whatever happens, I still have you and that's enough for me.'

Tears formed in Stephanie's eyes and she hugged Alice tightly as her mind clung on to the words she'd just spoken. 'You'll always have me, darling.'

As Stephanie watched Alice leave the flat that evening, aside from the sense of trepidation about her new determination to find Roger, she also felt a sense of renewed hope, like the faintest hint of the sun trying to break out from behind a sky thick with clouds. One thing that Roger and Miranda could never take away was the fact that she had been Alice's mother for the past twenty-one years. She would always have that, no matter what.

Chapter Eleven

Thursday 21st August 1997

Alice arrived home from the bookstore at 6.30 p.m., and went straight into the kitchen to put her take-away fried chicken onto a plate. The past few days had taken their toll and she felt tired; almost jet-lagged. It seemed that she had been existing in a different time zone to everyone else, unable to sleep at night.

Just as she switched on the television and settled herself on the sofa to eat, the telephone rang. It was Jenny.

'Hi Allie. Listen, me and Frank are meeting up with Tony and his sister, Susie, for a meal tonight. Do you wanna come?'

Alice remembered that Susie had witnessed her conversation at the party with Jane. She felt herself blush. How could she face meeting up with Susie again after that? But at the same time, she knew it would be an opportunity to try to find out more about Jane.

'Maybe,' said Alice, still mulling it over.

'Oh, come on. You know what Frank and Tony are like when they get together; I'll be bored.'

'But you can talk to Susie,' said Alice.

Jenny replied, lowering her voice as if to prevent anyone overhearing: 'But I thought it would be an opportunity for *you* to talk to Susie; you know, about Jane.'

'It would—'

'Great,' interrupted Jenny. 'We'll be over to pick you up in about half an hour.'

'But...' Alice eyed her fried chicken dinner, growing cold on the table in front of her. Jenny had already put down the phone.

Alice put her dinner in the fridge and waited tensely for Jenny and Frank to arrive.

At 7.15 the doorbell rang. Jenny stood outside smiling. 'Ready?' she said, jovially.

'Yes, I'll just grab a jacket.'

As Alice stepped out of her flat she saw that Tony and Susie were in Frank's car with him.

'Hello, Alice,' said Frank as she got into the back of the car. 'How are you? Had any good dreams about Andrew recently?' He laughed.

'Frank, stop it,' said Jenny, pushing him from behind.

'Just kidding, Alice,' he said.

'You've met Tony and Susie already, haven't you?' said Jenny.

'Yes.' Alice nodded towards Susie who was sitting in the middle of the back seat. Frank was driving, and Tony sat beside him in the front passenger seat.

Alice was glad that it was dark in the car, as she could feel her face was flushed. She couldn't help but recall the way Susie had looked at her after she'd witnessed her conversation with Jane.

Alice faced the window, giving the appearance that she was enjoying the view, when really she was just hoping that she didn't feel this nervous when they got to the restaurant.

'Pizza all right for everyone?' asked Tony.

'Yes,' the others said in unison.

Once inside the restaurant, they waited for a table to become available. Tony and Frank were chatting about a mutual friend they knew, and Susie had said something to Jenny which Alice didn't quite catch, as she was being distracted by her thoughts.

'I totally agree,' said Jenny. 'Alice and I say that every time we're out, don't we?'

Alice's eyes widened and she forced a smile. 'Yes, we do,' she said, hoping there would be no further discussion on that particular subject.

A waitress approached them and Alice breathed a sigh of relief.

They were shown to their table. Alice chose the seat closest to Jenny, and furthest from Susie. She wasn't sure if she was imagining it, but Susie seemed to be looking at her awkwardly. Flashbacks to the conversation with Jane kept flaring up in Alice's mind every time she looked at her.

After they had chosen where to sit, Jenny turned towards Alice: 'I need to go to the toilet. You?' She seemed to be hinting that she wanted to speak to her.'

'Er... yes, I'll come with you.'

When they entered the ladies' toilets, Jenny said: 'On the way to your flat, I was trying to convince Susie to give you Jane's address, but she seemed reluctant. I thought maybe you should try asking her.'

'I'm not sure... If she doesn't want to—'

'I think it will be better coming from you,' interjected Jenny. 'You can explain better why you want the address.'

'I'm embarrassed, Jen. I'm sure Susie thinks I'm weird. She heard everything I said to Jane, and God knows what Jane has said to her since.'

'I don't think she thinks you're weird. Maybe she finds it all a bit strange. But even she admitted that you and Jane look so alike. At the end of the day, this is your only chance—while we're out with her.'

'I know you're right. Let's just see how it goes.'

The two girls returned to the table. The food had already arrived.

'We ordered for you. Hope you don't mind,' said Frank. 'You always order the same pizza, anyway,' he said grinning.

'That's okay,' said Alice.

Jenny made a face at Frank, sticking her tongue out.

All five began to eat and there was silence for a few moments.

'Everyone's hungry then,' said Tony, smiling.

They all giggled.

After a brief discussion about how good the food was, Jenny turned towards Susie. 'Susie? Alice wants to ask you a favour.'

Alice's face blanched.

'I know,' said Susie. 'It's about Jane, isn't it?' She looked at Alice, not seeming to notice the strange colour Alice was sure she had turned.

'Um, yes.'

'You want her address,' said Susie, whilst using her fork to remove the olives from the top of her pizza slice.

Alice was pleased she was no longer looking directly at her. She could now feel the blood rush to her face, and her mind went blank.

'I've thought about it,' continued Susie, taking a bite from her pizza slice. 'I really think I should ask her first,' she said, whilst chewing. 'Does anyone want the olives from my pizza? I don't want them.'

'Yeah, I'll have 'em,' said Frank.

'Wait,' said Alice. 'We haven't finished discussing this.' She surprised herself by saying that, but something inside her could not let it lie. She could feel all the eyes at the table were on her. Taking a deep breath, she continued: 'Listen, I know Jane is your friend, and you don't have to help me if you don't want to; but I think it would do more harm than good if you told her that I want her address. You see, I've had a chat with my mum, and I'm almost sure that Jane is my half-sister. She doesn't know, though, judging by her reaction at the party. Her dad... Our dad, obviously hasn't told her. The reason I want her address is so that I can get in touch with my dad. He should be the one to tell Jane.'

'Come on, Sue, what difference would it make if you give her Jane's address? Don't be so stubborn,' said Tony picking up his glass of beer.

'I'm not being stubborn.' Susie pouted. 'It's like I'm going behind her back.' She picked at the salad bowl with her fork, frowning.

'I'm sure she'll thank you when she finds out why you did it,' said Tony.

'Yeah,' said Frank.

'I'm not so sure.' Susie sighed.

'Look,' said Alice, twisting around in her chair so that she could face Susie. 'I could look for my dad by myself, but it would take ages. I wouldn't be asking you if I wasn't desperate.'

'Sue, it's obvious she's related to Jane; I mean, look at her! It's not as if you'd be giving her address to a stranger,' said Tony. He smiled at Alice and took another swig of his beer.

'I have to think about it,' said Susie, frowning. 'I need the toilet.' She left the table.

Tony and Frank began to talk about football. Jenny tried to reassure Alice that Susie would come round to the idea. They began to talk about university and other things. When Susie returned to the table, she still looked glum. Alice felt too nervous to try asking her again.

Alice was the first to be dropped off home. She waved good-bye to the others in the car.

As she was watching the evening news, the telephone rang. It was Jenny.

'Allie, I've got some great news!' she said brightly.

'Really? What?' Alice was still looking at the TV screen even though she had turned down the volume.

'I've got the address you wanted!'

Alice quickly lost interest in the TV. 'How? I mean, how did you persuade her?'

'When we dropped you off in the car, Tony kept going on at her about it. He pretended he knew you really well through Frank, and told her that you're really nice and honest—which you are. Anyway, he said he would take the blame if anything went wrong. So she caved in.'

'Wow! That's amazing,' said Alice.

'Yeah, the only condition is that you can't tell Jane where you got the address; you mustn't mention anything about Susie or Tony.'

'That's fine, I'll think of something.'

Jenny read out the address and a telephone number, and Alice wrote them down. Her mouth fell open as the realisation hit her that she had her father's address and telephone number and he lived in London, so close to where she was living.

'This is so weird,' she said to Jenny. 'Finchley. That's only a few miles away. Imagine—all this time I might have passed my dad on the street and not even known it was him.'

'That's true,' said Jenny. 'So, what are you gonna do now?' she asked excitedly.

'Well, I suppose I should visit him. I'm not sure. If I'm honest, this has come as a surprise; I wasn't expecting to get the address so quickly. I want to meet him, don't get me wrong, but I thought it would be sometime in the future... but now... well, I could literally go and see him tomorrow, couldn't I?'

'I'm a bit confused, though. At the party, you said something about your dad having a different name, or something.'

'I spoke to my mum last night and she explained some things. I always thought his name was Roger, but apparently Roger is his middle name. He'd been using it as his first name. Now, it seems that he's gone back to using "Ken"; his proper first name.'

'Oh, right,' said Jenny.

'Well, put it this way: I'm ninety-nine per cent sure it's him.'

'That's pretty sure.'

'Do you think I should just turn up at his house? What should I say? "Hi, Dad, I'm your long lost daughter"?' She laughed and Jenny joined in.

'I'm sure you'll think of something to say to him... But aren't you going to phone him first?'

'I don't know. Do you think I should?'

'I don't know.'

'Oh, Jen, I'm getting really nervous about this, already.'

'You'll be fine,' said Jenny. 'Oh, and before you hang up, I have some really exciting news for you!'

Alice's mind was so preoccupied with thinking about the impending meeting with her father that she didn't really pay attention, and was hoping she could just get Jenny off the phone so she could think about what to do. 'What?' she said, sounding disinterested.

'Andrew wants your phone number!'

Alice now forgot about her other troubles. 'Andrew?' she gushed. 'How? I mean... why?'

'He likes you, you idiot!' Jenny giggled.

Alice's mind went back to their brief conversation at the party and she smiled to herself, hardly aware that she was smiling, so caught up in the moment. Then, she frowned. She began to feel jittery: what if Andrew phoned her, and they went out somewhere and she behaved the same way she had done at the party? *That would definitely put him off.* She didn't feel ready to see him again. 'I can't see him... Well, not yet.'

'What are you on about?' Jenny's voiced was laced with incomprehension. 'You've been waiting for this chance.'

'I know. I do like him, but I have got so much going on, I don't think I would make very good company.'

'Oh, you mean finding your dad? Well, you can just arrange to see Andrew after you've seen your dad,' suggested Jenny.

'It's not just that,' said Alice, speaking her thoughts: 'I was really gloomy at the party; I don't want to be like that again when I see Andrew. It's just... I'm not myself at the moment. I can't think straight. When he was talking to me at the party, I was practically ignoring him. I couldn't help thinking about Jane, my dad, and my mum. It really threw me when she told me she's not my real mum.'

'What?' Jenny sounded alarmed.

Alice suddenly remembered that she hadn't told her about that. She always told Jenny everything, but this was different; she hadn't wanted to tell anyone.

'Allie?' Jenny's voice rang in her ear.

'Sorry, I wasn't going to tell you that... See? I can't even control my own mouth. I was going to keep it a secret until I had time to come to terms with it... Not that I ever will,' she said, sullen.

'You mean to say that your mum is not your real mum?' Jenny sounded as if she was having trouble keeping up with all the revelations.

'I only found out on Monday evening. That's part of the reason I was so moody at the party.'

'You should have told me.'

'Maybe.'

'Do you want to talk about it? Maybe it'll make you feel better?'

'No,' said Alice. 'I'm not ready.' Her voice broke.

'Okay, sorry.'

'So, Andrew asked for my number?'

'Yeah. Well, Tony asked me for it so he could give it to Andrew. Hey, maybe Andrew has a thing about moody girls who ignore him.' Jenny laughed trying to ease the tension.

Alice giggled.

'Tony actually said that Andrew has fancied you for a while.'

Alice's eyes widened in disbelief. 'What should I do, Jen?'

'Maybe meeting Andrew again will cheer you up.'

'Maybe, but I think you're right: I will go and see my dad first and then when I'm feeling more up to it, I'll arrange to meet Andrew.'

'Are you going to try to find your real mum too?' asked Jenny, curious.

'Not yet... I don't really want to think about that.'

'Sorry,' said Jenny.

'Listen, Jen, don't give Tony my number.'

'But—'

'I can't speak to Andrew when I'm feeling like this.'

'Hmm... okay. Well, why don't I ask Tony to give me Andrew's number? Then you can call him when you're ready,' suggested Jenny.

Alice blushed, wondering whether she would have the nerve to call Andrew. 'Um... yes. Okay. Maybe.'

'I'll do that,' said Jenny.

When Alice put down the phone she felt cold. She had told Jenny about Stephanie not being her real mum; and somehow, saying it out loud to someone had made it seem all the more real. She had been trying to forget about it, but now here it was again, uppermost in her mind. Standing up, she walked to the window and stared outside without really looking at anything. Her thoughts went back to her childhood; there was such security and love in the home Stephanie had built for them after Roger left. She had never doubted even for one moment that Stephanie's world revolved around her.

She walked over to the sofa and sat down, thoughts of the telephone conversation spinning through her mind. She grabbed onto the one positive thing that had come out of it: Andrew liked her. Andrew! She smiled; the memory of Jenny telling her that, was like the sun coming out from behind the clouds. Suddenly, she felt special and she felt loved. Someone loved her. She knew she would have to hold onto that feeling while she was navigating her way through the other matters that she had to somehow accept: Stephanie was not her mother, and her father may not want to know her.

As that thought found its way to her conscious mind, she noticed she was still holding the pen in her hand—the pen she had used to write down her father's address and telephone number.

Insecurity reared its head, and as she looked at the words and numbers she had written on the paper, she began to wonder whether it was in fact her father's address. Had she, as Stephanie had suggested, just been carried away by a dream? She remembered how Jane had looked at her at the party; she'd had no knowledge of her father being married before. So maybe it was true; maybe this was a different Ken Forester. It could all have been a long line of strange coincidences. Had she been fooled into thinking that she had found her father?

She stared at the piece of paper. On the one hand, she wanted to throw it in the bin and carry on her old life as best she could; but on the other hand, she desperately needed to know.

Without thinking, she picked up the phone. The handset shook against her ear as she dialled. The phone began to ring, once, twice, three times, four times. She was beginning to feel relieved that no one answered; she wouldn't have to speak to him yet. But, just as she was about to put down the phone, a voice said: 'Hello'. It was a man's voice. Deep and loud. Could it be her father?

'Hello,' repeated the voice, a little agitated now.

'Hello,' said Alice quickly. But she had no idea how to continue.

'Who is this?' he asked, brusquely.

Alice forced the words from her mouth: 'Um... can I speak to Mr. Forester, please?'

'Speaking,' said the voice.

Alice's mouth fell open.

'Who is this?' he said.

'Um, I'm Alice,' she said, finally finding her tongue.

'Who?'

Her name didn't have the effect on him that she had secretly hoped it would. He did not remember her. He had not been waiting for her to call him all these years. She felt disappointed, somehow, but then realised that she was expecting too much... *Alice is quite a common name, I suppose,* she thought.

'I'm Alice Turnbull. Your daughter.' There, she had said it. That would leave no room for doubt.

There was silence on the other end of the phone line.

'Well, I'm not really sure what to say,' came the eventual response.

'I've been looking for you for a while,' she said, daring to hope that he cared, and holding on to the belief that this was her father she was speaking to.

'Alice, I think this is quite inappropriate. Why have you contacted me after all this time? Wait... is Stephanie okay?'

'Yes,' said Alice, surprised at his question. The last fragment of doubt was now erased. *It's him. It's my dad.* A shiver left her with goose bumps.

'Well then, why are you calling?'

Why? Alice frowned. 'Well, I'd like to meet you,' she said in a small voice.

'Meet me? Why?'

He wasn't making this easy for her. She had hoped he would take over the conversation, invite her over, ask her how she was. There was none of that.

'I should think that's obvious,' she said, offended.

'Why? What is obvious? Alice.... you're twenty-one years old, and we've never kept in touch. Why on earth would you want to meet me? It's absurd. I have a different life now; a new family. I don't want to upset them by raking up the past. I'm pleased to have heard from you, so I can now rest easy that you're okay, but I really don't see any point in us meeting.'

Alice felt the tears in her eyes. She held them back. 'I... I know about your new family. I've met Jane. Do you have any other children?'

'Oh my God! What have you said to Jane?'

His response came as a shock to her. *Stephanie was right. He doesn't want to know me.* A tear trickled down her cheek and she covered the mouthpiece on the phone momentarily as she sniffed back the flood that was due to arrive.

'I haven't said anything to Jane,' said Alice morosely. 'Well, when I met her, I said that I thought we had the same dad; but I thought your name was Roger, and she said her dad was called Ken, and... well, she thought I was crazy. You... You've never told her you were married before—'

'Why would I? That's part of history as far as I'm concerned.'

'And me?' said Alice, feeling unable to stop her words. 'What about me? Am I part of history, too?'

'Please believe me, I never meant to hurt you. When I left Stephanie, I left that part of my life behind; and yes, that included you. I've never been a father to you. You're grown up now. You don't need me. It would hurt too many people if we met up now. Please stay away.'

'But what about Jane?'

'What about her?'

'She might get curious now that she's met me. I mean, we look alike.'

'Well, of course you look alike, you're—'

'Sisters. Yes. And I think Jane has the right to know she has an older sister, and I'd like to know her.'

'What? Look... Okay, you're sisters, but that's all. You're strangers. Face it, Alice. You grew up apart. You'd have nothing in common.'

'Actually, both me and Jane are studying law; so we're not that different.'

'I mean it, Alice. Stay away.'

'Why are you being like this?'

'Have you spoken to Stephanie about contacting me?' he said.

'She doesn't approve of me getting in touch. In fact, she told me you probably wouldn't want to know me.'

'There you go, then. You should take her advice. Just pretend I don't exist. Pretend I'm dead. I don't care. Believe me, it's for the best.' With that he hung up the phone.

Alice looked at the phone in her hand as the buzzing sound took the place of her father's voice. She frowned. There were still so many questions in her head. Why had he been so cruel? He didn't care about her at all. Were there even more secrets? Perhaps he didn't know that she knew about the surrogacy. Maybe that was why he didn't want to meet her—he didn't want to have to be the one to tell her. Eventually, Alice replaced the handset onto the phone and shook her head. She had started the phone call with such hope.

She felt as though a door had been closed in her face and she was left out in the cold, tired and scared, with no one to turn to. The icy greyness of her new environment was too much to bear. She had reached out but had been rejected. She could hold back her tears no more. They began to flow.

Chapter Twelve

Friday 22nd August 1997

As Alice sat eating her corn flakes the next morning, after a sleepless night, she mulled over the conversation she'd had with her father the night before. It was as if it were a recording being constantly replayed in her mind, over and over again. She remembered every word and was desperately trying to analyse why he didn't want to see her. Could it really be as simple as him not wanting to tell her about the surrogacy agreement? Or maybe he had been shocked at hearing the voice of the child he had abandoned some twenty years before. His reaction would not have been thought through. Perhaps he was just feeling guilty about deserting her and Stephanie, and he did not want to be confronted about it, so he preferred to cut ties rather than face up to the wrong he had done. Alice went over and over the possible reasons as she tossed and turned in bed, and now as she sat at the kitchen table she was again thinking the same things. She had not reached a conclusion, and the incessant repetition in her head was threatening to drive her crazy.

She finished her breakfast and went over to the fridge to pour a glass of orange juice. Then she saw the photograph that Stephanie had given her, the one where her father was holding her in his arms and smiling. Alice's eyes were transfixed on the photograph that now hung from a magnet on the fridge. He seemed happy to be a father in that picture. What had gone wrong?

Maybe if he saw me? The thought entered her mind. *Maybe if he saw how similar I look to Jane... He couldn't turn his back on his own flesh and blood, could he?* She decided that the best thing to do would be to go and see him. A phone call was so impersonal. It was also possible, she thought, that he may be regretting telling her to stay away. She refused to believe that her own father just didn't want to know her.

Alice went into her bedroom to get her handbag. She looked out of the window; it seemed like a warm day, but she decided to take her denim jacket and umbrella, just in case. Exiting her bedroom, she took a deep breath and walked over to the side-table next to the sofa. There it was: his address. She could not believe that she was actually going to do this—going to visit her father. Lingering doubts crept in again as she recalled the way he had spoken to her, but she tried to put that to the back of her mind. She would give him the benefit of the doubt. He had not been expecting her call; maybe he would be nicer to her now he had had time to think about it.

As she stepped outside, her thoughts turned to Stephanie. Stephanie had always been there for her in the important times; this was one of those times. She felt she owed it to Stephanie to let her know that she was going to visit her father. She recalled their last few conversations and how Stephanie had tried to warn her about him. *She was right about him,* thought Alice, but again she pushed the thought away. *I have to meet him, at least once.*

She arrived at the hairdressing salon at 12 noon. Stephanie was busy blow-drying a client's hair, so she suggested that Alice wait for her and they would go to lunch when she finished.

Alice went into the kitchen area at the back of the salon to get a glass of water. Rosie, one of the hairdressers, was in there. The staff at the salon knew Alice quite well as she often visited. When she was younger, she used to go there to help with sweeping the floor, making tea for clients, etc.

Rosie Jones had been working at the salon for as long as Alice could remember. She was about Stephanie's age, but always appeared to be trying to look younger than her years. Rosie wore short skirts and lots of brightly coloured make-up. Today her bleached-blonde hair had streaks of purple running through it. The last time Alice had seen her, her hair had been black; and once, Alice had hardly recognised her when she'd walked into the salon—Rosie had completely straightened her naturally curly hair and dyed it bright red.

Rosie and Stephanie were good friends. Even though they worked together all day, Rosie would often visit Stephanie at home, and Stephanie and Alice had been to Rosie's house a few times. Rosie always seemed to be up to date with what Alice was doing even when she hadn't seen her for ages.

'You'll be going back to university soon, won't you?' said Rosie, after they'd said hello. She spoke as if she wasn't really expecting an answer, then continued: 'My Sandra will be going to university soon. She's studying French. She wants to be a teacher. I don't know if teaching is such a great job these days. Children don't respect teachers like they did when I was young. Well, even in my day some of the teachers used to have a hard time. But Sandra's made up her mind. Are you enjoying your law degree?'

'Um... yes. It's quite interesting. There's a lot of reading involved.'

'You'll probably end up being a famous lawyer. Your mum is always going on about how clever you are.' Rosie smiled and dunked a biscuit in her tea, losing half of it in the cup. 'Oops,' she said, as she desperately tried to retrieve the biscuit with a teaspoon.

Alice smiled, trying to pretend she hadn't noticed. 'Oh, my mum always exaggerates.' The words "my mum" resounded in Alice's head, and her face flushed with colour. Her mind was invaded by the unwelcome thought that Rosie might know about the surrogacy. Alice wondered whether all of Stephanie's friends knew.

'Oh, well, I'd better get back to work,' said Rosie.

Alice smiled at her and breathed a sigh of relief.

She followed Rosie out into the reception area of the salon.

Rosie greeted her next client, an elderly woman who wanted her hair dyed.

Sitting in the reception area, Alice flicked through some magazines. She would have to talk to Stephanie about getting some new magazines for the salon, she mused; all the ones on the table were at least a year old, and there was one battered copy of *She* that was dated May 1992.

Finally, Stephanie finished with her client and approached Alice. 'Hello, darling,' she said, a half-smile on her face. Her brow furrowed, as if she were unsure how Alice would treat her. Or perhaps, she was picking up a feeling that Alice wanted to talk to her about her father again. Stephanie always seemed to know what Alice was thinking.

They went to a café close to the salon. As it was a sunny day, they sat outside.

'So, how have you been, Alice?' asked Stephanie after they settled down to eat their lunch.

'Fine,' said Alice. 'I've found my dad,' she said, thinking now was as good a time as any to break the news. She braced herself for the response.

'You've found him?' Stephanie almost screamed the words,

startling a pigeon that had approached their table looking for crumbs.

Alice closed her eyes briefly and then continued: 'I've got his address and telephone number. It's amazing because he only lives in Finchley. It's so close, isn't it? I couldn't believe it.' She hoped that if she kept talking, it would be easier for Stephanie to digest the information.

Stephanie was looking at her with wide eyes and an open mouth as if she had been frozen in time. When Alice fell silent, Stephanie shook her head slightly as if she didn't really believe what she was hearing. 'Um...' she began, 'so, he's moved back to London, then.' She appeared nervous; fidgety. She put the sandwich she was holding onto her plate as if she had lost her appetite. 'When we got divorced he was living in Oxford. I thought he'd still be there.'

'No, he lives in Oakview Road, number twenty-seven.'

'Oakview Road,' said Stephanie, automatically repeating the words.

'Yes, it's quite close to Finchley Central Station.'

Stephanie nodded and picked up her sandwich again. Alice wasn't sure, but she thought she could see tears in her eyes.

She watched as Stephanie took a bite of her sandwich.

'I spoke to him on the phone last night,' she said, hoping it wasn't too soon to tell her that.

Stephanie blinked and her eyes widened in surprise. 'Y... You spoke to him?'

'Yes, he was a bit surprised to hear from me.' Alice's fingers played with the napkin in front of her on the table as she spoke. 'Well, he would be, wouldn't he?' she added, faking a laugh.

Narrowing her eyes, Stephanie frowned. 'Wh... What did he say?'

'I'm going to visit him today,' said Alice, evading the question.

'That is surprising!' Stephanie's eyes were wide. 'You mean he's invited you?'

'Well, no, he hasn't exactly invited me. But as I say, it was a shock for him to hear from me like that, so he didn't offer for me to visit. But I think it would be the right thing to do—to go and visit him. I mean, it's much easier to talk to someone face to face rather than over the phone... I'm sure he'll be pleased to see me if I go.' She knew she was rambling, but she was trying to convince herself as much as Stephanie.

'What... What did he say exactly... when you phoned?'

'It was unexpected. He didn't really know what to say. He

didn't really have much to say. I think it'll be better in person, face to face,' said Alice, rambling again.

'What did he say, Alice?'

She avoided Stephanie's eyes, knowing that she would see straight through her; Stephanie always could tell when she was lying.

'Okay then; he said he didn't think it would be a good idea for us to meet.' Alice shrugged.

'I knew it. Didn't I warn you?' Stephanie closed her eyes briefly, then picked up her cup of coffee and took a sip.

'But I'm still going to see him,' said Alice resolutely.

'You've always been stubborn, Alice. I knew I wouldn't be able to stop you once you got it into your head you wanted to see him. But, darling, I was always only thinking of you when I said I didn't think it was a good idea.' She wiped her mouth with the napkin that had been in her lap and looked Alice in the eye. 'Your father has always been a selfish man. It sounds to me as if he hasn't changed. He left us, without a thought of what would happen to us. Just disappeared. Do you know,' she narrowed her eyes, 'it would serve him right if you did just turn up at his door and shock his new family. He probably hasn't told them about us... um... about you, has he?'

'No,' admitted Alice.

Stephanie shook her head and turned to look at the traffic along the busy high street.

'So... you agree with me then? You think I should go and see him?'

'I didn't say that. I'm just saying that maybe it would teach him a thing or two about disregarding other people's feelings. But, darling, I don't want you to get hurt. I know I've said this before, but it will more than likely end in tears. He'll disappoint you, just like he did all those years ago when he deserted us. He has no feelings.'

Alice saw a bitter look on Stephanie's face that she had never seen before.

'Alice, dear, you can't really expect him to want to know you now, after all this time, when he hasn't even bothered to contact you.'

Alice didn't want to accept what she was hearing. She wanted to believe that if her father saw her, he would want to get to know her. She took a sip of coffee. 'I've made up my mind, I am going to see him.' She did not look at Stephanie, but instead looked into the distance trying to concentrate on something other than the nagging doubts in her mind.

'I hope I'm wrong, for your sake. I hope he's changed now that he has another family and children. Does he have any other children?'

'I only know about Jane.'

They walked back to the salon in silence.

'Alice,' Stephanie called out, as Alice turned around to leave. 'Please just don't expect too much. Don't get your hopes up.'

Alice smiled and waved good-bye.

Alice felt excited, but nervous, as she stepped off the Tube train at Finchley Central Station. She stood at the station entrance for a few minutes before walking in the direction of her father's street.

She wondered whether she was doing the right thing. Thinking back to the telephone conversation she'd had with him, the persistent doubt crept in to her mind again. He hadn't wanted to meet her; had told her to stay away. When she reached Oakview Road—*his* road—something made her stop at the corner, and for a short while, she felt rooted to the spot, unable to move any further forward. She felt stupid. *What will I say?* She tensed, and creased her brow as she also worried what *he* would say to *her*. Would he be as rude as he had been on the phone? *Does he really not want me in his life?* The questions ran through her mind until she lost the courage and confidence she'd had when she'd first set out on the journey.

Turning around, she looked back in the direction of the underground station, and wondered whether the best thing would be to just go back home. She could go home and think about it; maybe come back another day and try again. That sounded like a better plan. She looked at her watch. It was nearly 3 p.m. *He's probably at work, anyway*, she thought to herself. She began walking back towards the Tube station, but when she reached the station entrance, she stopped walking and looked behind her in the direction of her father's street. She had really wanted to meet him today, and that feeling was still there drawing her back towards the house. She knew that she would regret getting back onto the train and going back home. *I've come this far; what harm would it do to have a look at the house?* she thought.

Walking along Oakview Road, she thought of Jane and her father and how they must have walked along this street thousands of times. As she walked, she kept an eye on the door numbers. Very soon she was standing outside the house. Number twenty-seven. She took a deep breath. Standing outside the house, she realised that it looked much the same as the other houses in the street—grey bricks, wooden door. Somehow, irrationally, she had expected the house to look different, to stand out in some way. But, there was nothing special or distinctive about it at all.

Noticing the well-kept front garden, with a neat hedge surrounding a display of various flowers, she began to imagine her father must like gardening. Nervously, she looked at the iron gate and the three steps leading up to the front door.

The image of her father as a young man (from the photographs she had seen) came into her head. She wondered what he looked like now.

She stared at the house for a while longer, in an almost trancelike state, aware that her father and Jane walked in and out of that door every day. The thought filled her with a sense of loss. She had missed so much of their lives.

Just then, a woman called out to a young boy, who was running along the street. The small boy ran past Alice. The woman followed some feet behind, pushing a pram. Alice came back down to earth as the woman approached her. The woman smiled at her as she hurried past, trying to keep up with the small boy. 'Alex! Stop running!' the woman called out, as she continued on down the street. Alice then began to feel conspicuous, wondering how long she had been standing in the same spot, looking at the house. *I should leave,* she thought; imagining neighbours looking through their net curtains wondering who the strange girl was.

She was about to turn away, when she saw the next-door neighbour's door opening. An elderly woman stepped out, and looked straight at her. She had a shopping trolley with her. Waving at Alice, she cried out: 'Hello, love!'

Alice felt embarrassed. 'Hello,' she replied, waving back at the woman. She then turned to walk away, hoping to avoid any awkward questions, like 'why have you been staring at this house for so long?'. She felt paranoid, as she had no idea how long she had been staring at the house, and imagined it may have been a long time, so mesmerised was she by this place; the place where her father lived.

'Wait, Jane, wait!' called the woman.

Alice felt nervous. *Jane's here?* She wished there was somewhere she could hide, but all the gardens in this road were well maintained, with trimmed back hedges. She turned around towards where the woman was standing, dreading having to talk to Jane again and explain what she was doing here.

'Jane,' the old woman stood right in front of her and smiled.

It was only then that Alice realised: *She thinks I'm Jane!*

'Um... I'm in a bit of a hurry,' said Alice. 'I'll see you later.' She then turned around and started to walk away quickly, not wanting to explain to the woman what she was doing there. However, it soon became apparent that the woman was following her.

'It won't take a minute, love.' The woman had somehow caught up with her and was now standing quite close behind her.

Alice turned to face her. She was amazed to find that the woman continued to talk to her as if she still thought she was Jane.

'Jane, dear,' she said, seeming a little out of breath after chasing Alice along the street. She pulled a brown package out of her shopping trolley. 'This came for your mum this morning.' She held it towards Alice. 'The postman left it with me, because there was no answer at your house when he knocked. Anyway, I don't want to hold you up, but it's probably easier for me to give it to you because you can just take it straight in. Well, I'm going shopping now. See you later.'

Alice reluctantly took the parcel from the woman, fearing that if she didn't she would have to explain that she wasn't Jane and that would lead to a whole conversation that she wasn't prepared to have.

She watched the woman walk away. Staring at the parcel in her hands, she wasn't sure what to do. Before the neighbour had interrupted her thoughts, she had more or less decided that she would go home and come back another day. But what could she do with the parcel? It was too big to fit through the letter box, and she couldn't just leave it outside: the old woman would see it when she returned from the shops; or worse still, someone would steal it.

In a panic, unable to think straight, she thought about taking the parcel home with her and began walking back to the Tube station. The only thing she could think of was that she had to get away from the house. How many other neighbours had seen her standing outside?

As she walked, she considered just dumping the parcel

somewhere, or putting it in someone's dustbin; but she knew it wouldn't be that simple. The old woman would most probably mention to Jane's mother that she had handed it to Jane.

She looked down at the brown package and started to read the name. The addressee was "Mrs. Miranda Forester". *What? It doesn't make sense.* She stopped walking and shook her head. Could it be possible that her real parents had married and were living together in that house? No, it couldn't be true. She didn't want to think about it. Her real mother and father, together. For how long? She felt betrayed. They had abandoned her. She meant nothing to them. It wasn't possible. *This must be a different Miranda.*

She walked back towards number twenty-seven and opened the front gate. Her arms were shaking so much that she was afraid she would drop the parcel, and hoped there was nothing breakable inside. Before she reached the front door, it opened. Jane Forester stepped out and looked at her suspiciously.

'Hello,' said Alice, blushing, aware that Jane must have seen her through the window. She wondered how long she had been looking at her.

'Hello,' said Jane, frowning, 'what are you doing here?'

'I... I...' said Alice. Her mind went blank.

'Well?' asked Jane.

Alice noticed that Jane still had the plaster cast on her right arm. She shuffled her feet, trying to think of an answer for Jane. She couldn't tell her why she'd come. She remembered her father's harsh words on the telephone and how he did not want Jane to know anything about her. 'Um, I just...' Alice shrugged her shoulders and started to turn around.

'Excuse me!' Jane's voice was suddenly louder.

Startled, Alice turned back around to face her and saw that her features were now twisted into a grimace.

'It's to do with what you said at the party, isn't it?' asked Jane, her tone of voice seemed a little calmer now, although her eyes were still boring a hole into Alice.

'Y... y... yes,' Alice stuttered.

'What you said about my dad being married before... to your mum—it's been bothering me. You must have had some reason to suspect... Well, I mean, do you have any proof of what you're saying?'

Alice's mouth fell open. Could she tell her? 'Only what my mum has told me,' she said, cautiously. She could almost hear her father screaming at her not to tell Jane, but then something switched inside her. *Why should I protect him? I don't owe him anything.* She remembered she had the photograph of her dad in her bag; she put it in there that morning—she didn't know why, except that when she'd seen it again, and seen his smiling face, it made her wonder how he could have changed so completely. She was bringing the photograph with her in case the opportunity arose for her to show it to him; thinking that perhaps the image would help to remind him that he had once loved her.

Reaching into her bag, she fished it out. 'I have this. That's me with my dad,' she said, holding out the photograph towards Jane.

Jane took the photograph and her eyes widened. 'Um...' she said, 'th... that's my dad.' She handed the photograph back to Alice, and then stared at her, open-mouthed.

Alice began to feel slightly guilty, and looked down to avoid Jane's eyes. It was only then that she remembered she was still holding the package that the old woman had given her. 'Oh,' she said, holding it out towards Jane. 'I met your neighbour, the old woman. She thought I was you, so she gave me this for your mum.'

Jane took the parcel in her left hand, and cradled it under her arm. 'Oh, Mrs. Hutchins, she's a bit short-sighted!' Jane giggled nervously. 'Thank you,' she said, looking at the parcel. Then, she continued to stare at Alice.

'Well, I'd better be off,' said Alice.

'But... why did you come? You must have wanted to see my dad,' said Jane.

'I don't know. I don't...'

'He's not in at the moment,' said Jane. 'You could come back this evening; he's usually home at about seven o'clock. Or he's home at weekends. Tomorrow or Sunday.' Although she appeared slightly dazed and confused, Jane was being helpful, and Alice began to feel more at ease.

'Did he say anything about speaking to me on the phone last night?'

'No,' said Jane. Turning back towards the front door, she carefully placed the parcel inside. After closing the door, she said: 'Anyway, I have to go.' She appeared suddenly nervous. 'I've got some shopping to do. It was nice to see you again.' She began to walk towards the gate.

Alice followed her. 'I didn't mean to shock you,' she said. 'I came to see my dad; I just wanted to meet him. I didn't know you would be here. Maybe I shouldn't have told you about this.'

'No, I'm glad you did,' said Jane turning around. 'I mean, you're right about me being shocked, but I'm glad I know.'

'It's just that, your dad... I mean, *our* dad... well, he didn't want you to know... yet. He thought it would be for the best if you didn't know. I suppose he has his reasons,' said Alice.

'Yeah,' said Jane.

'Listen, Jane. I'd prefer it if you didn't say anything to him about this meeting. I think he'd be upset if he knew you'd found all of this out from me. He probably would have preferred to tell you about me in his own time.'

'Okay,' said Jane, nodding. 'Anyway, I suppose you'll be visiting him soon, and then we can get it all out in the open.'

Alice felt tense again, imagining a meeting with her father, but she was glad that at least Jane seemed to be taking it so well; maybe that would make it easier for her to approach him. 'Yes, soon,' said Alice.

Jane smiled at her as she walked out of the gate.

As she walked away, Alice suddenly remembered the name on the package, "Miranda Forester". She followed Jane.

'Jane? Can I just ask you one question before you go?'

Jane hesitantly turned to face her.

'It might sound a bit strange, but I'm just curious to know. It's just that I think your mum might know my mum. Do you know what your mum's surname was before she married your dad?'

'Um, yes... It was Carey.' Jane smiled.

'Thank you,' said Alice, quickly, catching her breath.

'Well, bye, then,' said Jane, eyeing Alice curiously.

'Yes, bye.'

Alice watched as Jane walked away from her along the street: Jane Forester, who she now knew was her sister. Not just half-sister, but sister. She watched as she turned the corner of the street and disappeared into the High Road. Then Alice turned around and headed back to the Tube station. Her mind was full of unanswered questions.

Alice couldn't believe the events of the day. She couldn't really remember anything after saying good-bye to Jane and watching her walk away. Somehow, she had made her way back to her flat but she didn't know how. Her mind was full of confusion. She thought back over the past two weeks. Things seemed to be happening, everything was changing, but she had no control.

She could not believe it was possible that she had lived for twenty-one years not really knowing anything about where she came from. Everything that she had believed in had been a lie. The hardest part to accept was that Stephanie was not her real mother. She knew now that up until this moment, she had been almost in denial. Now, she could not deny the truth. She had found out beyond doubt, that her real mother actually existed. Miranda was no longer just a fictional character. She had seen the proof of her existence clearly, with her own two eyes; parcels do not arrive addressed to people who do not exist.

She could not shake the feeling of betrayal that permeated her mind each time she remembered the name on the parcel. It was a feeling that came from the pit of her stomach. She found it hard to accept that for all these years, her real mother and father had been living together only a few miles away, with her sister, and yet they had never once contacted Stephanie to find out about her. She had not mattered to them. They had abandoned her. They had never wanted her.

Why did they leave her with Stephanie? It didn't make sense. They obviously wanted children. They had Jane. Was it possible, that in all these years, they had never thought about her or wondered how she had turned out? She was sure there must be more to the story; something that would answer her questions.

She began to wonder what sort of reaction she would get from her parents if she went to visit them now. Her father had been so unkind on the phone. How would Miranda react? She began to question what she really hoped to get out of seeing them. Wasn't it better if she just accepted that Stephanie was the only mother she had ever known? Shouldn't she just carry on as she was? At least Stephanie cared about her; she was sure of that. The more she thought about her real parents, the more she began to imagine them as uncaring, unfeeling people, who had abandoned their baby daughter, and had never given a thought to her welfare.

Maybe she was expecting too much. Shouldn't she just get on with her life with the satisfaction that she now knew who her real mother and father were? But, somehow, she felt unable to do that. She had gone too far now. She could not turn back. It was as if her mind was on a one way street.

She thought about Jane. Jane had seemed nice. She had

seemed interested that she had a sister she hadn't known about. Alice knew that what her father had said was true—she and Jane were strangers. They had grown up apart. She felt sad about that. She wished that she'd had the opportunity to grow up with Jane. She remembered the look of shock on Jane's face when she had seen the photograph of her dad.

Suddenly, she felt nervous. She had not thought about the consequences of anything. What if Jane said something to her parents? It could just slip out. Would it even be possible for Jane to *not* say something? After all, finding out that she had a sister she never knew about must have affected her too. Would it lead to an argument? Would there be more lies, to cover up the lies? Her father had been so anxious that Jane should not be told. Maybe he would make Alice out to be the liar.

She regretted rushing in. She had been so determined to find out the truth that she had ignored the advice Stephanie had given her, and she had also ignored her father's request that she should not tell Jane anything. What would happen now? Perhaps her parents would not want to have anything more to do with her now that she had shattered their little family unit. What would Jane do? Would she thank Alice for letting her know, or in the end would she come to hate her and see her as an outsider; the person who had come into her life after so many years just to tip the scales?

But, then, she remembered something that Jane had said. She had said that she was glad she knew that Alice was her sister. Alice felt warm inside, remembering this. A calmness came over her, and she didn't feel so upset about everything. She felt glad that she had discovered the truth. As she became aware of that, she felt more in control of the situation: she could decide the next move. If she wanted to see her parents, she could. If she decided to carry on with her life as before, she could. It was her choice.

She recalled that Jane had seemed happy at the thought that Alice would be visiting her father, but no sooner had the thought come into her head, Alice began to appreciate that things were not so simple. The feeling of gloom, which had been with her for the past two weeks, returned. She could not get past the fact that her parents had abandoned her and that she had never had the opportunity to be a part of their family. There was still so much that needed explaining.

The telephone rang. Alice lifted the handset. 'Hello,' she said.

'Hello, Alice,' came Stephanie's voice. 'How are you?

'I'm fine, thanks,' she lied. Hearing Stephanie on the line made her yearn for the time before she had found out about her real parents. She had been happy then.

'I was worried about you. I know you were going to visit your father today. Did you go?'

'Yes, I went,' said Alice, not really wanting to discuss it. There was silence. Alice knew Stephanie was waiting to hear more. 'I didn't actually see my dad; he wasn't in. He was at work.'

'Oh,' said Stephanie, almost with a sigh of relief, 'never mind.'

'I did see, Jane, though. His other daughter.'

'Oh.' The disappointment in her voice was audible.

'Yes, we had a nice chat. She seems really nice.' Alice still felt gloomy, and her tone of voice was flat.

'I know it's not what you want to hear, Alice, but I still don't think it's a good idea for you to meet him, darling.'

'Maybe it is, maybe it isn't,' said Alice. Then without thinking, she continued, 'I found out that Jane is my real sister, not just my half-sister. So it wasn't a complete waste of time going there today.' She wished she could take the words back as soon as she had said them.

'Oh, really, how's that then?' asked Stephanie as if she had not really been paying attention.

Alice prayed that Stephanie would not work it out. She couldn't think of what to say to change the subject.

'Alice, are you still there?'

'Yes, yes,' she said, flustered.

'What do you mean, she's your real sister?'

'Um, I... Oh, did I say that? No, I mean, yes, I found out she's my half-sister,' said Alice, hoping that she would ask no further questions.

'No, Alice, you said you found out she is your real sister, not just your half... Alice!' exclaimed Stephanie. The penny had dropped. 'That would mean that Miranda is her mother.'

Alice was silent.

'Alice?'

'Yes,' said Alice. 'Sorry, I didn't mean to tell you, it just came out. I'm really sorry.'

'Well, I don't know what to say. How did you find out? Did you meet Miranda?'

'No.'

'Does she live with your father?'

'Yes. Well, I think so.'

'Are they married?' Stephanie knew now, without having to be told, that when Roger had petitioned for divorce, all those years ago, he had done so in order to be able to marry Miranda.

'I don't know,' said Alice, remembering the parcel addressed to "Mrs. Miranda Forester." She felt terrible; she couldn't believe how many people's lives she had affected, just because she wanted to find out about her background.

'I never even considered *that* as a possibility.' Stephanie sounded distant. 'It's come as a bit of a shock, actually. I don't know why. I mean, I don't care who your father ended up with. But, I can't believe... Miranda.'

'I'm sorry.'

'Stop apologising,' said Stephanie. 'So, do they have any other children?'

'Not that I know of.'

'Are you going to go back to visit them?'

'I don't know. I was just thinking about it all now, before you phoned. I'm not sure what I think about them. I'm not too happy about the way they've never bothered to contact me. I don't know, but it seems like they never cared about me. Jane is really nice though, and I'd like to keep in contact with her, so maybe I should visit them. What do you think?'

'Oh, I don't know, dear, I'm still trying to get my head around this. I suppose your father must have been seeing Miranda, behind my back, for some time. That would explain why he left us without an explanation. I should have realised he was attracted to her when the surrogacy thing was going on. What a fool I must have been; all the signs were there. Your father wasn't keen on the surrogacy idea, but he changed his mind when we met Miranda. I was too blind to realise what was going on under my own nose.'

'But, that doesn't make sense,' said Alice, 'I mean, if they were seeing each other during the time when Miranda was pregnant, why didn't they take me with them when they ran off together? Why didn't they keep me?'

'Oh, I don't know,' said Stephanie, sounding agitated. 'Maybe they didn't want a child.'

'But they've got Jane. She doesn't seem that much younger than me. Why didn't they ever want to know me?'

'Don't upset yourself, darling; they're not worth it. They're probably both just as selfish as each other; only thinking of themselves, to hell with everyone else.'

'Probably,' said Alice, in a small voice. 'So, do you think they would want to meet me?'

Stephanie was aware that Alice probably needed to feel that she was loved by her parents, not that she meant nothing to them, so she pushed aside her own feelings about Roger and Miranda for a moment. 'Oh, Alice, they are your parents, whatever they've done. I'm sure they'd like to meet you.'

'They've never acted like parents. Why didn't they ever try to get in touch with me?' Alice fought back tears.

'Maybe they didn't want *me* to find out that they were together, maybe that's why they never made contact,' suggested Stephanie.

'But what difference would it have made if you found out about them? You were separated from my dad. You wouldn't have cared.'

'I know, but they probably thought I wouldn't agree to let them see you, if I found out about them. Then they would have had to go through the courts to be able to see you. You were legally mine and your father's, after you were born. Miranda had given up her rights over you. It would have been difficult for them.' Stephanie sighed.

'Yeah, but did they ever approach you, to ask if they could see me?'

'No, never.'

'So, they didn't know for sure that you'd deny them access. They didn't even try to find out.' Alice sounded glum.

'Don't upset yourself,' said Stephanie. 'There are always a lot of reasons why people do, and don't do, things. And time goes so fast. People's lives can get very busy. It doesn't mean they never thought about you, darling. It was all quite complicated. I mean, what with the surrogacy agreement, they were probably afraid that it would all come out in the open. Or, maybe Miranda didn't want to face me after having an affair with my husband. I don't think we'll ever know why they didn't contact you, but don't think it's because they don't love you. You are their daughter.'

'Why are you defending them?'

'You know my true feelings about your father: I think he is a selfish fool, and now I've heard about all of this, I think Miranda is a two-faced, conniving... Oh, well, it doesn't matter. All I'm trying to do is be objective. I'm trying to help you see that even though they didn't contact you, there might have been a hundred reasons—none of which would have been that they never thought of you or they didn't love you. Deep down, it must have been very difficult for them to stay away. But maybe after they had Jane, she was a replacement of sorts. Sometimes people can be fickle like that... Or maybe it was their way of dealing with losing you—replacing you and blocking it all out of their conscience. Who knows? All I'm saying is, just because I hate your father for what he did, it doesn't mean you have to hate him, and it doesn't mean they don't care about you.'

'I wish *you* were my real mum,' said Alice.

'Well, I am, in a way,' said Stephanie, feeling a lump in her throat. 'Think about it like this, Alice: there must have been a reason your parents never contacted you, just like me not telling you that I wasn't your real mother. I did it for your own good; well, so I thought—I only ever did what I thought was best. That's probably what they did.'

'So, do you think I should visit them?'

'Well, that's up to you. I can't make that decision for you,' said Stephanie. She bit her tongue, wishing she could tell Alice not to have anything more to do with them. 'Why don't you come over to mine for dinner tomorrow evening, after work, and we'll talk then. Try to forget about it all for now. Give yourself time to recover your senses before you make a decision. It can't have been easy for you finding all this out.'

'I don't know. I just feel as though I've got to meet them, before I can relax. I've got to ask them why they did it, and why they never wanted to know me. I might try going there tomorrow evening.'

'But you'll be tired after work. Why don't you leave it until Sunday. Come to dinner with me, tomorrow, darling. Give yourself more time to think about this. Don't just rush in.'

'Maybe you're right.'

'Right then, I'll see you tomorrow.'

'Yes, okay, bye,' said Alice.

'Bye.'

Stephanie sat staring at the telephone, wondering whether she had just imagined the conversation she'd had with Alice. There was nothing to prove that she had just heard what she'd heard. Nothing had changed. She was still sitting in the same chair as she had been sitting in when she had decided to phone Alice.

The significance of what she had just heard was only now

beginning to sink in. It was the ultimate betrayal. *How could Roger have done that?* She had thought he loved her, all those years ago, when they were planning to have a baby. Now, nothing seemed real. It had all been lies. Roger had only gone along with the surrogacy agreement because he had been in love with Miranda. The reality sank in with a bitter twist. *They must have been laughing at me behind my back.* Humiliation taunted her.

All those nights Roger was out late, and said he was working, he must have been with Miranda. She pushed the unwelcome thoughts from her mind and inwardly rebuked herself—*stop thinking about it! Why should I care? It's all in the past. None of it matters now.* But somewhere deep inside her, she knew why it did matter. Roger had gone behind her back and she'd had no idea about his infidelity. An old wound had opened and all the pain that had gone with it had returned. *Miranda and Roger. S*he would never have imagined...

Switching on the television, to distract herself from her thoughts, she watched as the pictures on the screen flashed before her. Her thoughts proved too persistent and she was unable to concentrate on anything else.

But, why did they leave Alice with me? The question remained unanswered: if they had been in love and had a child together, why give the child to her? She supposed they had not really wanted a child at the time. After all, Miranda had been a hippie student who wanted to travel the world and probably didn't want the burden of having to bring up a child. She had only agreed to the surrogacy for the money. But would she really have been able to give up the child of the man she had fallen in love with, to his estranged wife? None of it made any sense.

The thoughts swam around in her mind making her feel sick. She recalled the photograph she had seen of Jane in the newspaper, and how similar she was to Alice. How could Roger and Miranda have lived their lives without giving a thought to Alice? They had denied Alice and Jane the opportunity of a relationship as sisters. They seemed to have lived their lives in a vacuum, without thinking about the consequences of what they had done.

Her thoughts turned to Alice. *Poor Alice.* She had been through so much in the past couple of weeks. Finding out that the person she thought was her mother, was not, was bad enough; but finding out that her real father and mother had abandoned her and were living together... She began to wonder how Alice would be able to cope with all of this. She decided to phone Rita.

'Hello?' said a man's voice.

'Oh, hello,' she replied, wondering if she had dialled the wrong number, 'can I speak to Rita?'

'Yes, hang on a minute,' said the man. It dawned on Stephanie that she had put so much energy into worrying about Alice wanting to find her father, that she and Rita had only really discussed *her* life, not Rita's. She didn't even know if Rita was married, or if she had children. *Perhaps that was her husband who answered the phone.*

After a couple of minutes, Rita's voice sounded, 'Hello?'

'Hello, Rita, it's Stephanie. I haven't caught you at a bad time, have I?'

'No, no, not at all; it's always nice to hear from you.'

'Who was that who answered the phone?' asked Stephanie, curious.

'Er, no one. Um, my nephew.'

'I thought it might have been your husband,' said Stephanie, trying to show some interest in her friend's life.

'No, I'm not married.'

'Oh.'

'Well, I was married, but I got divorced ten years ago. My husband had an affair with my next-door neighbour. Can you believe it?' Rita laughed as if she were talking about something that didn't concern her.

'Oh, I'm sorry to hear that,' said Stephanie, thinking again of Roger and Miranda's betrayal.

'Don't be, I was waiting for someone to take him off my hands; he was such a loser. Dishonest, rude, inconsiderate... I could go on. Sorry, Steph; you phoned me and I'm ranting on about myself.'

'That's okay.'

'How are things with you?' asked Rita.

'Oh, I feel as though I'm always burdening you with my problems. Please forgive me, but I need to speak to someone and you are the only person I can speak to about all this.'

'What's happened? Is it about Alice? Has she found Roger?'

'Yes, well, she's found out where he lives. Everything is just getting so out of control,' said Stephanie.

'Has she met him yet?'

'No, but she spoke to him on the phone, and he wasn't very friendly to her. But, that's not the worst part; you won't believe this—he's living with Miranda. They're married, I think, and they have another daughter.'

'Right,' said Rita.

'You don't sound surprised. I was in shock when I heard about it,' said Stephanie.

'Sorry, Steph,' said Rita, slowly, 'I sort of knew already.'

'What do you mean you "sort of" knew? Did you, or didn't you?' Paranoid thoughts entered Stephanie's mind. Rita's friend had known Miranda, and had introduced them to Miranda when they wanted a surrogate; was it possible Rita kept in touch with her and knew all about this?

'I... I only knew what I'd heard on the grapevine—'

'Why didn't you say something before?'

'I didn't want to upset you. I knew it would all come out eventually, especially with Alice looking for Roger. I didn't want to be the one to tell you,' explained Rita. 'I wasn't even one-hundred-per-cent sure that they were living together. All I knew was something I heard a few years back. I bumped into Angela, my old friend who introduced you to Miranda. She mentioned that Miranda was living with Roger. I didn't believe her. Well, I mean, I didn't think it was possible. I thought *you* were still with Roger. Angela said she had kept in touch with Miranda, on and off, since university. I swear, that's all I knew. I didn't have anything concrete to go on. It only really clicked when I met you again, when you said you'd divorced Roger. I'm sorry I didn't say anything. I just didn't think it was my place.'

Stephanie closed her eyes and remained silent for a moment, as the information sank in.

Rita continued, 'I suppose I felt partly responsible.'

'Why?' Stephanie's eyes widened.

'Well, I was the one who told you about Miranda, wasn't I?' Rita sounded sad. 'I couldn't help thinking that if I hadn't told Angela about it, and if she hadn't introduced you and Roger to Miranda, none of this would have happened. Maybe you'd still be with Roger.'

'I still can't believe it...' Stephanie spoke softly. 'But really, Rita, you shouldn't blame yourself. One thing I know for sure is that I would not have still been with Roger. We were not right for each other. If it wasn't Miranda, it would have been someone, or something else. Believe me, our marriage wasn't working. I fooled myself into thinking that if we had a child it would make a difference, but it didn't.'

'Well, anyway, I just couldn't bring myself to tell you about what I'd heard,' said Rita. 'But, I was trying to help; that's why I was so pushy with you; telling you that you should let Alice know about Miranda, and that you should tell her everything. I knew that if they *were* living together Alice would find everything out from Roger, if you didn't tell her.'

'Oh, everything is just so confusing. I don't know what to believe anymore.'

'I know, I know,' said Rita, 'but I'm sure everything will work itself out in the end. I'm sure.'

'Alice is so upset. She can't understand why her parents abandoned her if they're still together and have another daughter. It's so hard on her. I don't know what to do,' said Stephanie. 'I think she's planning to visit them, but I don't think it's such a good idea. What good could possibly come out of it now? Am I being selfish? I keep thinking: what if she wants to be with them, and doesn't want me anymore?'

'Maybe she just needs to visit them, to get it out of her system. It's hardly likely she wants a relationship with them as parents, now, after everything they've done. She's not a child anymore. She's probably just curious,' said Rita.

'I suppose so, but I just don't want her to get hurt. She's been through so much already.'

'Stop worrying, Steph. I'm sure everything will be okay. Alice seems like an intelligent girl. I'm sure she knows what she's doing.'

'Yes, you're probably right.' Stephanie paused. 'Maybe I should go with her when she visits them.'

'Um, I don't think that would be a good idea.'

'No, neither do I,' said Stephanie, laughing. 'But I'd love to see the looks on their faces, if I did!'

'So would I. Maybe we should both go!' Rita laughed.

'Yes!' Stephanie laughed along with her. 'Thanks for cheering me up. I don't know what I'd have done without you.'

'No problem, Steph. Everything will be all right, you'll see.'

Chapter Thirteen

Saturday 23rd August 1997

Alice's alarm clock sounded at 7.30 a.m. Reaching out of her duvet, she pressed the snooze button. She had not slept very well; her mind had been so consumed with memories of the meeting she'd had with Jane, the phone call with her father, her conversation with Stephanie... Everything had been replaying in her head non-stop as she tried to think of ways around her dilemma. In the cold light of day, she felt more confused than ever. Anxiety pervaded her senses. The one thing she was sure about was that she would not rest until she had met with her parents, to talk everything through. She needed to hear their version of events.

Maybe they had wanted to look after her, but there might have been a reason why they were unable to. The thought crossed her mind that maybe they had tried to contact her, and perhaps Stephanie had refused to allow them to. Could Stephanie have been the selfish one? Had she denied them access? But Alice felt immediately guilty for even thinking that about Stephanie. *She wouldn't do something like that.* Then Alice began to question whether she really knew what Stephanie would and would not do. After all, she had kept a secret from her for so long: she didn't tell her that she was not her real mother until she said she was going to look for her father. Alice started to think that it was not so improbable that Stephanie had kept other things from her as well.

She made a decision to go to visit her parents today, aware that until she met them she would not be able to concentrate on anything else. Her alarm clock went off again at 7.45 a.m. She switched it off, forced herself to get out of bed, and made her way to the bathroom.

Looking at herself in the bathroom mirror, she saw that the last two weeks had certainly taken their toll. Her skin was pale and there were dark circles around her eyes. As she looked at her reflection in the mirror, she had a strange sense that she didn't even know the person looking back at her. Her sense of identity was muddled and confused as if everything she had once believed had been tossed up into the air and had landed on the ground haphazardly, scattered here and there; her task now was to somehow put everything back into the right order. It seemed like an impossible mission.

She made her way to the kitchen, aware that she would have to eat something. As well as losing sleep, she had been forgetting to eat, and this had left her feeling unwell. But when she opened the fridge door, she just didn't feel like eating anything. She made herself a cup of tea, and sat alone with her thoughts. Looking at the brightly coloured clock, that somehow seemed to be mocking her mood, she saw it was 8.30 a.m. She was supposed to go to work at the bookstore today; soon, Rob and Sophie Bairns would be wondering where she was.

At 8.45 a.m. she went into the living room and picked up the telephone. She spoke to Sophie, and explained that she was unwell and thought she had the flu. Sophie was very understanding, and said she would see her on Monday.

She put down the phone, and at that moment she decided to phone her dad. It wasn't planned, but it felt like the right thing to do, rather than just turning up. At least she would be able to arrange a time to meet him, so that they could talk properly. She couldn't bear to go to the house again and find that he wasn't in.

She dialled the number from memory. Since Jenny had first given the number to her, she must have read it at least a hundred times, over and over; she was just so amazed that she actually had her father's telephone number.

'Hello?' Her father answered the phone, sounding as though he had just woken up. Alice felt guilty for waking him.

'Hello,' she paused, not sure whether to call him "Dad" or "Mr. Forester" or "Ken".

'Who is this?'

'It's Alice.'

'Alice?' He sounded confused, not immediately remembering who she was. Then, he continued. 'Oh, Alice,' he sounded disappointed. 'I thought I told you the last time we spoke, you shouldn't call here. Try to forget about me. I've never been a father to you, and I can't be one now.'

'Why are you being like this?'

'It's for the best,' he said, almost in a whisper as if to avoid anyone else hearing.

'But, I have questions. I want to meet you.'

'No, that won't be possible. I'm sorry.' His voice was cold; devoid of emotion.

She felt incredulous. 'You can't just ignore me! I'm your daughter whether you like it or not. I need to talk to you. I have to have some answers.'

'Alice, sometimes things don't work out the way we want them to. It's as simple as that. People move on, people change.'

'I have to see you in person. I need to know why you left. Why you never tried to contact me. Lots of things.'

'Oh, this is stupid! You know very well that Stephanie and I divorced. We lost touch. These things happen. You're not a child anymore.'

'I don't understand how you can be so cold. It's like you're a stranger.' Alice could feel tears in the corners of her eyes.

'But, don't you see? We *are* strangers; that's what I tried to tell you the last time you phoned. Nothing good can come of us meeting.'

'Don't you care about me at all?' She held back the tears of frustration.

'It's too complicated to explain on the phone.'

'Well, we'll meet up. You can explain everything and then I'll leave you alone if that's what you want.'

'I can't meet you, I'm sorry.'

'If you're worried that Jane will find out, you don't have to. I met her when I went to your house yesterday. I went to see you, but you were out. I know everything,' said Alice, wanting to hurt him as much as he had hurt her with his careless words. 'I know about you and Miranda. I know she's my real mother, and I know you're living together.'

'Jane hasn't said anything.' He sounded as if he was thinking aloud.

'I told her not to tell you she'd seen me.'

'We've never told Jane about any of this. What did you say to her?' He sounded anxious.

'I didn't tell her much. She thinks we're half-sisters. She doesn't know the whole story. She thinks I'm your daughter from your first marriage. Aren't you going to tell her the truth?'

'Alice, listen, what we did—we never meant to hurt you. Stephanie was a good woman, you couldn't have hoped for a better mother. She really wanted you. You haven't missed out on anything really. I just think it's better if things stay the way they are.' He was almost pleading.

'Didn't you think that I would try to find you one day?'

'I don't know. We didn't think about it. It seemed like the only thing to do for the best,' said her father. 'That way, everyone was happy. Don't you see?'

'No, not really,' said Alice. 'How could it have been the best for me? Growing up not knowing my real parents, my sister... Do you have any other children?'

'No, just Jane. Listen, Alice, we never planned any of it... It just happened. Stephanie wanted a child so badly. She really did. I couldn't take you away from her. I tried to make the marriage work, for you. I know we did wrong, your mother and I, but please try to understand. We wanted you to be happy. That's all we wanted.'

'Why won't you agree to meet me? I just need to see you. To speak to you. I can't talk about this on the phone. Please.'

'If I agree to meet you, to explain everything, will you promise that you won't tell Jane about any of this? I think it's better if she doesn't know. And, I think it's probably better if things remain how they are.'

'I don't really agree that Jane should be kept in the dark. She's an adult now. You should tell her.'

'Well, exactly,' said her father, clearing his throat. 'That's what I mean... *I* should be the one to tell her, when I feel the time is right. It should come from me, not you.'

'Okay,' said Alice. 'Well, when can we meet? This afternoon?'

'Hmm... Okay. About three o'clock. Jane will be out; she's visiting a friend. Miranda will be here. We'll explain everything.' He sounded irritated.

'Great,' said Alice, 'I'll be there at three.'

Miranda Forester, wearing her peach-coloured towelling robe and fluffy, pink slippers, stood at the bedroom door, yawning. She watched her husband emerge from the spare room, with the telephone in his hands. He seemed stressed; his forehead creased into a frown.

'Who was that, Ken?' The telephone had awoken Miranda, and as she had tried to drift back to sleep, she had heard her husband's voice through the wall as he spoke on the phone. He had sounded agitated. She was sure he had shouted a couple of times. 'Who's phoning us at this time in the morning?'

'It was Alice Turnbull,' he said.

'Who?' Miranda yawned again. The name meant nothing to her.

'Miranda, let's go back into the bedroom to discuss this. Jane might hear us out here.' He placed the telephone back on the table in the landing where it usually sat, and walked past Miranda into the bedroom.

Miranda followed, confused. 'So, who's Alice Turner?'

'Turnbull,' corrected Ken. He sat on the edge of the double bed. 'Please, sit down.'

Miranda sat next to him. 'Well?' she asked, impatiently.

'Alice is Jane's sister.'

Miranda gasped. 'Oh, Ken. I don't know what to say. How did she find us? Did she just phone up out of the blue, now? Have you spoken to her before? Have you met her?'

'No, I haven't met her, but she wants to meet today.' He stood up and paced the bedroom.

'Today? Oh my God. I can't believe it. Our daughter.'

'I was trying to get rid of her, but she's insisting on meeting us,' said Ken, sitting on the bed, leaning forward, and placing his hands over his face.

'Trying to get rid of her? What do you mean? She's our daughter, Ken. She probably looks like Jane.' Miranda had a wistful look in her eyes. 'I've dreamed of this day.'

'Do you know what you're saying?' Ken's eyes widened as he looked up at his wife.

'What?' Miranda stood up and folded her arms. 'Don't you want to meet her?'

Ken stared at his wife in disbelief. 'I know this has come as a shock, Miranda, but think about what you are saying.'

Sitting down again, next to him on the bed, Miranda cast her eyes downwards.

'We have to try to forget about Alice. We agreed that, years ago, didn't we?' he said, urgently.

Miranda nodded, her lips turned downwards at the edges. She looked at her hands.

'I know it's painful, but it's for the best,' he continued. Putting an arm around her, he sighed deeply.

'I know you're right, Ken; it's just that it still hurts, whenever I remember back. It's just brought it all back to me.' She wiped her tears with the sleeve of her dressing gown. 'I gave up our child, all those years ago. Jane's sister. Now, well, hearing she's alive and wants to see me. Sorry... I'm just being sentimental.' She stood up and took a tissue from the box on the dressing table. As she blew her nose, she caught sight of her appearance in the mirror. She picked up her hairbrush and began to brush her hair.

'She knows everything,' said Ken.

Miranda turned around to face him, her mouth wide open. 'How?'

'I'm not sure, but she knows.'

Miranda, still holding the hairbrush, went over to sit next to her husband. 'How can she?' Her brow furrowed, she continued, 'We are the only two people who know everything... Even Stephanie didn't know... or... did she?'

Ken shrugged. 'Alice came here yesterday, looking for me, and she spoke to Jane. Luckily, she hasn't told Jane everything. Jane thinks Alice is my daughter from my first marriage. Can you imagine what would happen if Jane found out the whole truth?' Ken was pacing the bedroom again.

Miranda stared into the distance, as if she were in a trance. 'We should have told Jane before; years ago. We can't tell her now. She won't be able to forgive us. Oh, Ken, sit down, you're making me nervous.'

Ken reluctantly sat back on the bed.

'Jane never even knew you were married before, it must have come as a shock to her finding that out. We can't let her find out about the surrogacy, about... We just can't.' Miranda's eyes were wide.

'It won't come to that,' said Ken, his mind ticking everything over. 'I've arranged for Alice to come here today at three o'clock. Jane will be out.'

'She's coming here? Today?'

'Yes. I had to do something. She was threatening to tell Jane everything. She wants to meet me. She said that if we explain everything—why we did it—then she will leave us alone. I think she just wants to know what happened.'

'But, can we trust her not to tell Jane?'

'I don't think she'll tell Jane. Why should she? I mean, if she wanted to, she could have told her yesterday when they met, couldn't she? No, I don't think she'll tell her,' said Ken, once more, as if trying to reassure himself. 'Hopefully we'll put an end to this today.'

'I can't believe it. Alice is coming here. Our child.' Miranda smiled at Ken, but her smile faded, as soon as she saw the frown on his face.

'Miranda, face reality. We can't afford to let our emotions get involved here. We'll have to treat her as a stranger, for Jane's sake. We can't get close to her. We'll talk to her today, but then we'll have nothing more to do with her. It's the only way.'

Miranda was nodding, but her eyes were distant. 'I know you're right.'

Returning to her seat at the dressing table, she looked at her husband's reflection in the mirror. 'Oh, Ken, we did do the right thing all those years ago, didn't we? I know we don't talk about it now, but I still sometimes wonder what it would have been like if we had Jane *and* Alice. All through the years, when Jane was growing up, I often thought about Alice. On her birthday—' Miranda stopped and turned towards him, open mouthed.

'Miranda, what is it?' He frowned. 'What?'

'Stephanie. I've just realised. If Alice knows, then she must know. Does she know about—'

'I don't know,' interrupted Ken, 'that's the worst part. I hope not. I mean, I know it was a long time ago, but I'm sure it would still shock her. I'd hate her to turn up on our doorstep. Jane would definitely find out then. Stephanie had no idea about our relationship. Sometimes I think it would have been better if we'd just told her *then*, that we were in a relationship; we could have avoided all this—all the lies to cover everything up—don't you think?'

'I don't know,' said Miranda, shrugging her shoulders.

Ken appeared deep in thought. 'All these years, I've put it to the back of my mind. Now and then, I wondered why we did it. Wouldn't it have been easier if we'd explained everything to Stephanie? I just felt so guilty at the time for cheating on her, for the way it happened. She was the one who introduced the surrogacy idea, and introduced me to you. It was like, by leaving Alice with Stephanie, knowing she had wanted a child so badly, I was sort of making up for treating her so badly. Making up for all the deceit.' He bowed his head. 'I suppose it's always easier to see what you should have done when you look back on things.'

'I think if Stephanie doesn't know already, it's better if she doesn't find out,' said Miranda, reaching out to touch his hand.

'How can we avoid her finding out, if Alice knows? She's bound to tell her. I never wanted her to find out. It's all falling apart, Miranda. We thought we were doing the best thing we could, trying not to hurt anyone, but it's all backfired. The worst thing is that if Jane finds out, she'll never forgive us.'

Miranda and Ken sat staring at the ground in the half-darkness of their bedroom.

Alice walked along Oakview Road. It was only when she arrived at the gate of number twenty-seven, that she realised she was going to meet her parents for the first time in her life. As the thought entered her mind she felt nauseated, and wanted to turn around and run as fast as she could away from the house. Panic began to stir inside her, and she doubted she could actually go through with meeting them. She stood, motionless, just a few feet away from the front door, staring at the house. They were inside now, expecting her. Were they as nervous as she was? She took deep breaths, trying to calm down and reminded herself that the two people she was about to meet were the same two people who had abandoned her, years ago, without a second thought. *They* should be nervous, not her. They were the ones who would have to explain why they had done what they had done. But, somehow, Alice could not shake the feeling of dread.

She heard a noise behind her, and as she turned around she saw the next-door neighbour, whom she had met yesterday.

'Hello, Jane, dear,' said the old woman.

'Um... hello,' said Alice, not correcting her. Then, she turned and walked towards the front door to avoid any conversation with the old woman. The woman opened her own door and disappeared inside.

As Alice stood outside her parents' front door, she began questioning why she had come. She didn't feel as though she belonged there, and she knew that she was not really welcome; but somehow she couldn't leave without meeting them—they were the only ones with the answers to her questions.

Alice smoothed her black, knee-length skirt with her now sweating palms. She had dressed smartly for the meeting, almost as if she were attending a job interview. A black skirt, white cotton blouse, and her long hair tied back. Making a good first impression was important to her; so that her parents would not have anything bad to say about her upbringing. But now she regretted dressing so smartly; it felt uncomfortable, as if she was trying too hard. Perhaps if she had worn something more casual she would have felt more relaxed. She sighed as that thought entered her mind; there was nothing she could do about it now.

Almost immediately after she knocked on the front door, it opened; as if her father had been standing on the other side of the door awaiting her. She recognised his face straight away; it was the same face that she had stared at in the old, faded photograph Stephanie had given her. There were more wrinkles around the eyes, and he was slightly fatter, but the face was the same. Ken Forester smiled and held out his hand to welcome her. She noticed that although he was smiling, his eyes were sad, not lively as they had been in the photograph.

'Hello,' he was the first to speak.

'Hello,' said Alice, her mouth felt dry. She shook his outstretched hand.

'Please, come in.' He led the way along the narrow dark passage to the living room. The house smelt of freshly cut flowers.

Nerves overwhelmed Alice again as she stood at the entrance to the living room.

Someone was seated on the sofa at the far end of the room. The sofa was positioned in front of the tall, bay window. As the sun was shining through the window, the person appeared almost in silhouette. As Alice entered the room, it became clear that the person seated on the sofa was a woman. Her attention fixed on her. *That must be Miranda*, she thought.

She looked old; her hair was grey, and shoulder length. She was smoking a cigarette. Her large round glasses appeared too big for her face, and made her eyes seem twice their actual size. As Alice approached her, the woman smiled, and extinguished her cigarette into an ashtray on the coffee table in front of her. Her hand was trembling as she did so. She did not get up to greet Alice.

Ken led the way towards where Miranda was seated. He coughed to clear his throat.

Is he nervous? Alice wondered.

'Um, this is Miranda,' he said. 'Miranda, this is Alice.'

The two women nodded at each other.

Ken sat down next to Miranda. Alice continued to stand.

'Please, sit down,' said her father, pointing at an armchair directly opposite the sofa.

Alice looked around the room, but she was too nervous to take in any of the surroundings. The only thing she could focus on was the black leather sofa, and the two people sitting on it. Her parents. Eventually, she sat down. They sat in silence, the three of them. Her parents on the sofa, and Alice on an armchair facing them. Her parents were looking fixedly at the coffee table, in between the sofa and the armchair, as if they had never seen it before. Alice stared at her father and Miranda. She was scanning their faces to try to see any resemblance, any obvious family connection linking them to her. She couldn't believe she was sitting in front of her parents.

'Alice,' Miranda broke the silence, 'would you like something to drink? Tea, coffee, something cold, perhaps?'

'No,' said Alice. She looked at Miranda and realised that she didn't have any feelings at all for this woman. All she felt was indifference. After all, this was the woman who had given her up at birth, to Stephanie, for money. Alice wanted to feel some sort of emotion, but she could not really consider the woman to be her mother.

She had thought about everything long and hard over the past few days and told herself not to prejudge the woman who had given her away; she didn't know the whole story. But, as she sat here looking at her, she could not get past the fact that she seemed cold-hearted. All she had done when the daughter she hadn't seen for over twenty years walked into the room, was stub out her cigarette and give her a half-smile. She hadn't even made an effort to stand up to greet her. Her father's shaking of her hand had seemed a bit formal, but that was better than nothing at all. Alice could only conclude that Stephanie had been right about her: Miranda had never wanted her. The thought of this almost made Alice feel angry. She was the woman who had come between her parents. As far as Alice was concerned, Stephanie was her mother—the only one who had loved her as a mother should.

There was silence in the room, as if no one could think of what to say. The silence became too much for Alice to bear; it seemed to consume the atmosphere. She felt she had to start the conversation somewhere. Clearing her throat, she spoke directly to her father. 'I came to see you because I wanted a clearer picture of my background. I wanted to meet you, out of curiosity, I suppose. I know you are not keen for us to have a relationship or even get to know each other better. I was offended by that at first, but I'm fine about it now. It's probably too late for all that, anyway. But, I need some answers for my own peace of mind.' As she spoke, she began to feel calmer.

'Alice,' said Miranda.

It came as a surprise to Alice when Miranda spoke, as she had been deliberately avoiding her eyes and speaking directly to her father.

Miranda continued: 'You have to understand, we had our reasons for leaving you with Stephanie. We thought it was for the best. That way, everybody was happy, and there would be less explaining to do. We were both feeling guilty. Your father felt guilty for getting into a relationship with me, and I felt guilty about the agreement I'd made with Stephanie. It was complicated. If things could have been different—'

'But why have you never even tried to have any contact with me? Didn't you have any feelings for me at all? I mean, what about when you had Jane, didn't you think of me then?'

Miranda looked to Ken, as if for assistance.

Alice felt frustrated at her hesitation, and continued: 'I don't know *when* you had Jane, but didn't you think about me then? Didn't you ever think it would be better for Jane to have some sort of relationship with her sister? Or had you just forgotten about me by then?'

Miranda and Ken stared at Alice. There was silence again. It appeared that they were unwilling to give her any answers, or maybe they just couldn't think of any decent excuse for abandoning a child. It seemed as if she was talking but they were not listening.

It felt to Alice as though they were silently mocking her.

Eventually, her father began to speak. 'Oh, Alice, of course we didn't forget about you. How could we? I think it's best if I just explain everything to you. Hopefully then you'll understand.'

'Okay,' said Alice, 'That's all I want.' She felt as though she had made some kind of breakthrough; her father was willing to talk to her, at last. She felt as though she was on the first step to getting to know her parents better, and although there would be many steps to climb, she felt that the hardest part was over.

'The way it happened was, Stephanie and I, made a surrogacy agreement with Miranda.' Her father stopped, as if he were trying to recall everything, then he continued, 'I was still with Stephanie at the time. When you were born, I stayed with her until you were nearly two years old. I wasn't seeing Miranda at that time. When I left Stephanie, I happened to meet Miranda again by chance. We got on well, and we decided to get married. That's when I contacted Stephanie for a divorce. We decided to leave you with Stephanie because she also had rights over you... because of the surrogacy agreement. We were sure there would be a lot of fuss from Stephanie if she found out we were together, and we didn't think she'd let us have you without a battle. And, anyway, we felt guilty about getting together.' Her father stopped.

'Why? It doesn't make sense. Why would you feel guilty about getting together, if you'd already split up from my mum... I mean, Stephanie?' Alice shook her head.

'Well, it wasn't that simple. The attraction between us began at the time of the surrogacy, and we'd seen each other regularly, during that time. Stephanie was unaware of this, so I felt guilty,' said her father.

'I still don't understand,' said Alice, frowning.

'Well,' said her father, 'when Miranda and I decided to marry, Stephanie had already been looking after you by herself for a couple of years. We decided to leave you with her, because we knew we could have another child. Stephanie was a good woman. We knew she'd be a good mother for you, and we didn't want to disrupt your life.' He looked at Miranda as if he was seeking her approval for what he had said, and she smiled and nodded at him.

'You still haven't said why you didn't try to keep in contact with me,' said Alice.

'We didn't want to upset Stephanie. That was our reason at first, because we didn't know how she'd react when she found out we were together. We just didn't think she'd allow us access. It would be too complicated, and we'd have to go to court, and everything about the surrogacy would come out. We didn't want that, and we didn't think we'd stand a chance of getting access if it was discovered that Miranda had given you to Stephanie for money.'

'But, what about when I was older? You could have contacted me then,' said Alice.

'But I didn't want to confuse you. I didn't know what Stephanie had told you. I didn't know if she had told you she was your real mother, or if she had another husband and if you thought he was your father. It was difficult,' said Ken.

It was hard for Alice to see her father's facial expression as he spoke because the sun was shining through the window and making her squint. Her father's explanation of what had happened did not satisfy her. There were too many questions still remaining. He had not seemed sure of his answers, and his story seemed vague. Also, it struck her as odd that Jane was supposedly that much younger than her—maybe three or four years younger—yet she was sure that she'd heard Jane was already going to university.

Miranda seemed to be staring at the ground, trying to avoid looking at her. Alice couldn't help feeling that there was more to the story—something they hadn't told her—but she couldn't put her finger on it.

'Maybe we should have contacted you,' began Miranda. 'We often thought about you, but years pass by so quickly and we don't always do what we should. We are sorry, but surely you were happy with Stephanie?'

'Yes, I was. I still am.' Alice spoke defensively, looking Miranda in the eye. It felt to her as though the woman was trying to belittle Stephanie. 'This has got nothing to do with my relationship with Stephanie. As far as I am concerned, she is my real mum.'

Miranda looked down at her hands.

'I just wish someone had told me the truth before. I would have liked the opportunity to have known Jane when we were growing up,' Alice added.

'Sorry,' her parents said in unison, nodding their heads and looking apologetic.

'About Jane...' began her father: 'She knows nothing about all this—the surrogacy agreement, and everything. Of course, we'll probably have to tell her eventually, but we'd like to do so in our own time. We would appreciate it if you didn't say anything to her.'

Alice shook her head, not really able to believe what he had just said. 'But, now we've met,' she started, 'I've spoken to you and everything is out in the open; surely you can tell Jane? Then, we can all get to know each other. You both just said that you would have liked to have had some contact with me. It doesn't have to be on a daily basis. We could just see each other sometimes. Jane knows I exist now, so she might decide she wants to know me. If she does, I'm not going to lie to her. I'm sick of lies.'

Her parents looked at each other. They both wore frowns when they looked back at Alice. She felt as if she were at a job interview, and the two employers had suddenly decided that they didn't think she was right for the job but didn't know how to tell her.

Silence hung over them for a few moments and then her father spoke: 'So, Alice,' he said, losing his frown and actually smiling; even if the smile appeared transparently false. 'You mentioned on the phone that you are studying.'

'Yes,' she replied. Then, after a pause, she added: 'I'm doing a Law degree.'

'Oh, so is Jane!' Miranda smiled at her. Alice noticed that her smile did in fact appear to be genuine.

'Really?' Alice wasn't sure she wanted to smile back at Miranda just yet. There was something she couldn't quite trust about her.

'Yes, she'll be in her final year this year.'

Alice's raised her eyebrows. 'How can that be? I mean how old is she then? I heard she was at university, but I thought she'd be in her first year. I thought she must be about eighteen, because I was nearly two when you split up from Stephanie.' She looked towards Ken, shaking her head in confusion.

'I *said* "first" year,' said Miranda, quickly. 'Didn't I?'

'No,' said Alice, 'You said "final" year.'

'Oh, dear. I meant first year.' She sighed. Then she added, 'You'll have to excuse me, I sometimes get my words mixed up; it's my age.' She giggled.

Ken shifted in his seat, his false smile rearing its head again as he looked at Alice.

'Well, it is quite a coincidence that we both chose to study law, isn't it? I'm sure me and Jane would get on well; she seems really nice,' said Alice, still sure her parents were on the defensive as if they hadn't told her the whole truth. Perhaps they were just uncomfortable meeting the child they'd abandoned years before, she reasoned. They definitely seemed uncomfortable.

'As we discussed on the phone, I think it would be better for things to go back to how they were. I don't want you to keep in touch with us, or Jane,' said her father.

'I agree,' said Miranda.

Although not entirely unexpected, considering the cold way they had been acting towards her, Alice still felt shocked and offended by this. 'Why?' she managed to say, her mouth remaining open.

Her father stood up as if preparing to show her to the door. 'As I explained to you on the phone, it will do no one any good to rake up the past now,' he said.

Alice felt a lump forming in her throat, but she fought back the tears. She didn't want them to see her cry.

'It's for the best, Alice. Think of Stephanie,' continued her father.

'Stephanie is all right with this. She knew I was coming to see you,' said Alice. 'She understands that I would want to get to know my real parents.'

'It's been too long,' chimed in Miranda. 'You have to

understand; your father and I accepted long ago that you were going to live with Stephanie. We never saw you as our child, and I suppose, well, we can't just start thinking of you as our child now. It's too late.' Miranda stood up too.

Alice looked at Miranda's face. There appeared to be tears forming in her eyes.

'Alice, you'll have to try to understand: we don't want you in our lives. Sorry.' Her fathers words boomed out much louder to her than they were in reality *"we don't want you in our lives"*.

She felt stunned at how quickly their conversation had turned from him asking her about her studies, to him now making it more than clear that they were just not interested in her at all. It seemed incomprehensible. They were both so openly, and obviously, trying to get rid of her.

'I'll show you to the door,' said her father, formally.

Alice was still, at that moment, seated on the armchair looking up at her parents, unable to believe that they had no feelings for her whatsoever.

'I'm sure I can find my own way to the door,' she said, bitterly.

She stood up and walked away from the people who were once her parents but were now just strangers, her head bowed low. *How can this be happening?* she wondered. *Surely it should be me unable to forgive them for leaving me; they should be begging me for forgiveness. Instead, they just seem to have no remorse and no feelings at all. It's like they are made of stone.*

As she approached the front door, she heard their footsteps behind her on the wooden floor. She didn't want to turn around and give them the satisfaction of seeing they had upset her.

She reached towards the door to open it, but just as her hand touched the handle, she heard the sound of a key being placed in the lock. She pulled her hand away instinctively and the door opened.

Jane walked in and closed the front door.

Alice turned around sideways to give her room to enter, and she then caught sight of her parents' faces. Her father's eyes were wide in shock. Miranda's face had turned pale.

Ken and Miranda seemed frozen. Alice realised that they now feared she would tell Jane everything. They feared she would tell her that her parents had given away their eldest daughter for money, and had never cared about her.

Alice just wanted to get out of the house. She didn't understand why, when she had reached out to her parents—even after they had given her away—they had rejected her again. They seemed heartless. Surely, Jane was adult enough, now, to understand what had happened all those years ago? She wouldn't hold it against them. Maybe, Jane would have looked at the situation, positively—as *she* had done—and seen that she now had the opportunity to get to know her sister. As Alice stood staring at the two cold faces, she knew that she didn't care if she never saw them again.

There was no point in coming here anymore. She would leave, and hopefully be able to scrape back together the shattered pieces of her life. She realised now that her life had really been fine until she started wanting to find her father. She had always been happy with Stephanie.

'Hello,' said Jane, cheerfully, looking directly at Alice. Jane seemed pleased to see her.

'Hello,' said Alice, tears forming in her eyes.

'Darling, you're home early,' interrupted Miranda.

'Yes.' Jane nodded. 'Why didn't you tell me Alice was coming?' She smiled at Alice.

'She's leaving,' said Ken, bluntly.

Alice looked at his hard stare and closed her eyes briefly, sighing, wishing she had the guts to punch him.

'Oh?' Jane seemed disappointed. 'Why don't you stay a little longer? I'd love to hear what you've all been talking about,' she said.

'Alice is in a bit of a hurry, aren't you?' Her father walked quickly past Alice and Jane, almost pushing Alice sideways into the wall. He opened the front door.

'I could stay a little bit longer,' said Alice through gritted teeth.

Ken's arm reached out and pulled her towards the front door and then he forcibly pushed her out of the door. She looked back towards where Jane had been standing hoping she would say something else, but Miranda had pulled Jane towards the living room door and was now whispering something into her ear.

'Go now,' said Ken to Alice. 'And don't come back.'

Alice looked up at his face. His cheeks were bright red and she could not tell whether it was anger or embarrassment at Jane having turned up unexpectedly.

She turned away from him without saying a word and walked towards the gate.

The sound of the front door slamming shut behind her, reverberated in her ears.

Walking along the street, she felt as if her world had taken another drastic turn for the worse. The meeting with her parents was meant to be a new start but now it had come crashing down; an ending instead of a beginning. Their behaviour had been irrational at best, and downright evil at worst. How could they behave like that towards their eldest daughter who had come to see them after so many years apart? She searched her soul for a way to forgive them but could not find a reason. Her thoughts turned to Jane. Jane was the one saving grace of the afternoon. At least she had smiled at her; had seemed pleased to see her. Just as that thought came to mind, she heard someone call her name.

Turning around, she saw Jane running towards her. 'Alice, wait!'

Jane was a little out of breath when she caught up with her. 'I'm so glad I managed to catch you,' she said, smiling.

Alice could only stare at her, open-mouthed.

'Alice,' said Jane, 'give me your telephone number and I'll call you, and arrange a date for us to go out. I'd love to introduce you to my friends. I've already told a couple of them about you. Anyway, we've probably got some friends in common, because you were at Tony's party.'

'But... have you spoken to your parents?' asked Alice.

'Look, I think things are a bit awkward between Dad and my mum since you've returned. Dad didn't tell me about his previous marriage. My mum's finding it all a bit much. It can't be easy to find out that your husband has a child from another marriage that you knew nothing about. I can't really blame her for not wanting me to get to know you.'

'Miranda... er.... your mum did know about his previous marriage,' said Alice.

Jane frowned. 'Oh... Oh well, maybe she's just jealous. Who knows?' she said, shrugging. 'Anyway, I don't see why it should stop us getting to know each other. Er... that's if you still want to?'

'Yes,' said Alice quickly, nodding.

'Good.' Jane smiled.

Alice took her notebook out of her bag, and wrote down her telephone number. She tore out the page and handed it to Jane.

'Thanks. I'd better go back to the house; Dad will be on the warpath if he realises I've come out to see you.' She rolled her eyes. She turned to walk away and then twisted back towards Alice. 'Look, don't worry, they'll come round. I'm sure Dad will want to get to know you. He's just worried about how it will affect me if we get close, and maybe worried about upsetting my mum.'

Alice nodded.

'I'll phone you,' said Jane, holding up the sheet of paper with Alice's telephone number written on it.

'Great,' said Alice, smiling.

As she watched Jane walk away, she was left with mixed feelings. It was good to know that Jane wanted to get to know her, but the treatment she had received from her parents left a bitter taste in her mouth; and knowing that Jane still didn't know the whole truth was also a worry. Would that change everything again when she found out?

Alice turned around and began walking towards the Tube station, confusion uppermost in her mind: why did her parents hate her so much? Was it because they didn't want Jane to find out about the surrogacy agreement? But Jane seemed to have accepted her without asking for any specific details. She had just seemed to be happy to have found out that she has a sister; surely her parents could see that? Jane seemed such a nice girl, surely she would understand her parents' reasons for giving Alice away; for not talking about her? But it seemed to Alice that her parents were just not willing to welcome her to the family. They seemed to resent the fact that she had looked for them. She had shaken the foundations of their happy home—the happy home they had built on lies.

It seemed to Alice, that Ken and Miranda weren't really worried about the effect all this would have on Jane, they were just being selfish, not wanting her to find out the whole truth because they were worried that she would hate them. If Jane found out they had lied to her for so long, how would she ever be able to believe anything else they said? Alice had no sympathy for them.

Travelling home on the Tube, Alice's thoughts turned to Stephanie. She couldn't wait to see her again, especially after her experience today. She needed a familiar face, a smile from someone who cared. As she sat on the Central Line Tube train on that fateful Saturday afternoon, she had an epiphany of sorts; all her life she had defined a mother as someone who gives birth to you, but she knew now that a mother is not someone who gives birth to you, but someone who loves you, and looks after you. *Stephanie is my mum, not Miranda.*

Strangely, Alice had now managed, after meeting her real parents, to almost put herself back into the position she had been in before she had started looking for her father: she was now aware, and accepted, that Stephanie, was, in every true sense of the word, her mother; her father was now unimportant in her life, just as he had been unimportant throughout her life—it had all come around, full circle. The only thing that had really changed for her was that she had now found her sister; Jane.

As Alice stepped off the train, she found some comfort in the thought that at least she now had the opportunity to build a relationship with her sister. If her parents didn't want to know her, she would have to live with that.

Alice felt happy when she opened the door to Stephanie's flat, that evening. It felt as though she had just returned home after a long time away. The feeling was a million miles away from the sense of isolation she had felt in her own parents' house.

'Hello, darling,' said Stephanie, cheerfully, as Alice walked through the kitchen door. Stephanie had been standing at the cooker, stirring a saucepan of pasta. She was now walking towards Alice with the wooden spoon still in her hand. Stephanie kissed her on the cheek, and went back to her cooking. 'I'm making pasta with an Italian sauce. Rosie, from the salon gave me the recipe, I told her I wanted to cook something special for you.'

'Oh,' said Alice. 'That's nice.' When she heard Rosie's name, her mind went back to their recent chat at the salon. A cloud of insecurity descended. She imagined that Stephanie and Rosie must have discussed everything about her search for her father. Alice could picture the scene clearly in her mind...

'Oh, poor Alice,' said Rosie. 'It must have come as such a shock to her finding everything out in this way. I mean, she believed for all these years that you were her mum.'

'Yes,' Stephanie nodded, an upside-down smile on her face, 'I never wanted her to find out. I never wanted to hurt her. She's coming round to dinner tonight. I want to cook her something special, to cheer her up. Do you know, she wants to go and visit her real parents. I don't think it's a good idea. I'm going to try to persuade her not to.'

'Oh, poor, poor Alice. She will need cheering up. Well, if you want to cook something really good, I've got a recipe for a lovely pasta dish.'

Yes, thought Alice, *Rosie and Stephanie probably had just that sort of conversation over a cup of tea at the salon.* The feeling of humiliation would not go away. 'Mum? Does Rosie know about the surrogacy agreement?'

Stephanie's eyes widened as she turned to face Alice. 'No, of course she doesn't. Why do you ask?'

'No reason.' Alice could not meet her eyes.

'No one knows. Well, except for Rita. At the time, I told all my friends that you were adopted, but I haven't kept in touch with any of those people. I met Rosie when you were about six years old. I told her you were my child, because, well... I didn't want you to know anything at that time. Since then, I've always told people you are my real daughter.'

Alice nodded. She could breathe again. At least now she could rest in the knowledge that people she had known for years were not whispering behind her back and pitying her.

'I mean, if I'd told people that you were adopted, I thought you'd find out somehow. It was to protect you.' Stephanie had her back towards Alice as she spoke. 'So, darling, how was work?' Stephanie changed the subject, turning back towards her.

'I didn't go to work,' explained Alice. 'I went to see my dad and Miranda.' Alice could not bring herself to refer to Miranda as "Mum".

'Oh!' Stephanie dropped the wooden spoon onto the floor. 'Oh, no. Now look what I've done!'

'I'll clear it up,' said Alice, realising that Stephanie had not taken the news well.

'I didn't think you would be going to see them so soon,' said Stephanie, watching Alice clean the pasta sauce from the floor where she had dropped the spoon.

'Neither did I,' said Alice. 'I just decided this morning that I had to go and see them.'

'How did it go?' Stephanie was looking at Alice now, but her face was pale and her eyes distant.

'I don't really want to talk about it.' Alice washed her hands, and sat at the table.

Stephanie served the pasta and sauce into two large plates on the table. 'You know you can talk to me about anything that's bothering you, don't you?' she said as she sat opposite Alice at the table, a concerned frown on her face.

'This tastes nice,' said Alice, avoiding the question.

'Did your dad upset you? If he did, please don't take it to heart—he's always been selfish. I warned you, didn't I?'

'I said I don't want to talk about it.'

'I just want to know that you're not upset about anything,' said Stephanie, taking a bite of her food.

'I'm really okay,' said Alice. 'One good thing came out of the meeting, if you must know. Jane was there and she's really nice. She asked for my telephone number, and we're going to meet up again.'

'Oh, that's nice,' said Stephanie, smiling at her. 'Would you like some parmesan?' She waved the carton of grated cheese in front of Alice. 'It's recommended in the recipe.'

'Yes, okay,' said Alice, taking the cheese carton from her, and daring to believe that she would not ask any further questions about the meeting with her parents. She started to sprinkle the cheese onto the dish.

'Stop me if I'm being too nosy, but I'm curious as to what your father had to say for himself after all these years.'

Alice wanted to disappear. She had preferred it when Stephanie had been totally against her having anything to do with her real parents. Now, she seemed to have accepted that Alice wanted to get to know them. What she really wanted at this moment was for Stephanie to start saying that she should forget about them, then she could agree with her and say that she didn't want to see them again. She carried on eating, hoping that Stephanie would forget she had asked her anything.

'What does your dad think about you seeing Jane again? I would have thought he'd be against it. He's always been a miserable so and so.' Stephanie rolled her eyes. 'What excuse did he have for not contacting you for all these years?'

Tears began to well in Alice's eyes and her cheeks turned red.

Stephanie appeared to notice and lowered her eyes. 'Sorry, I'm asking too many questions. Please just let me know when you're ready to talk about it.' She sipped her glass of wine, keeping her eyes averted from Alice.

Eventually, Alice spoke: 'He said that the reason they never contacted me... Well, he said, they thought it was better if I didn't visit them. He said... *they* said... they don't want me to...' she started to explain but her words did not make sense. As she tried to explain she could not continue. She could not stop herself from crying openly. All the frustration of looking for her father, and finally finding him, and the final rejection, had been building up slowly within her, and she could no longer hold it all inside. She tried her best to stop crying, not wanting to upset

Stephanie—but the tears continued to fall.

Alice realised that she had been fooling herself that she had taken her parents' rejection well. Her true feelings had been hiding under the surface. When Stephanie had asked her to tell her about her visit, the trauma and pain had resurfaced and it was as if a time bomb had been detonated. The floods of tears seemed never-ending. She was inconsolable.

Stephanie tried her best to cheer her up, telling her that it had probably been a shock to her parents seeing her after all this time and they had probably reacted in the heat of the moment.

'Please stop crying, darling. Look, finish your dinner. You'll probably feel better after a meal. You're probably just hungry and tired after your journey.'

They ate their dinner in complete silence. The only sound was of knives and forks clanging, and Alice's intermittent sobs.

After dinner, Alice told Stephanie that she was tired and wanted to go home. 'I'll feel much better tomorrow. It's just hard facing up to the fact that they don't care about me. But I should have known that already... I mean, if they cared they would have tried to contact me before, wouldn't they?' Her brown eyes looked mournful and lost.

Bloody Roger, thought Stephanie, *I'll kill him if I ever lay eyes on him.*

'Why don't you stay here tonight?' she offered, worried about Alice's state of mind.

'No, I'll be fine. Thanks for everything.' She smiled weakly and walked towards the front door.

'Alice, forget about Roger and Miranda. Let's go back to how we were before. We were happy then.'

'Yes, I know, Mum.' Then Alice realised that she had called Stephanie "Mum", and for the first time since finding out the truth it had felt like the right thing to do. She started to believe that maybe it would be possible to go back to how things were before. Hope was calling out to her where before there had been nothing but darkness.

Stephanie watched Alice walk away. The anger she felt towards Roger and Miranda was threatening to give way to thoughts of revenge. She took deep breaths and tried to calm her mind. *How could they have turned her away like that?* She was trembling with rage as the adrenaline coursed through her. *I have to do something. Alice needs my help. But what? What can I do?* She decided to phone Rita. Maybe she could help her rationalise everything.

'Hello,' said Rita.

'Oh, Rita, sorry to keep bothering you. You must be sick of me by now,' said Stephanie.

'Don't be silly,' replied Rita, with a giggle.

'Something's happened and I'm at my wits' end. I feel like killing someone but I know that would be going too far... Well, I usually know that would be going too far, but today? I think anything is possible.'

'Steph, wait, rewind. What has happened? You sound upset.'

'Alice went to visit Roger and Miranda, and they told her they don't want anything to do with her! They don't want to know her. She was so upset. She was crying for hours. I just don't know what to do.' Her words were tumbling quickly from her mouth like dominoes falling one after the other.

'Why on earth would they do that? When—I mean, well, I wouldn't have been able to do that. If I was in that position I would have been happy to see my son... I... I... I mean my *daughter*, after all those years.'

'Do you think I should visit them?' asked Stephanie, still caught up in her own thoughts and not having really taken in what Rita was saying.

'I can't figure out how their minds work,' said Rita. 'Why would they turn Alice away?'

'Yes, but do you think I should go and give them a piece of my mind?'

'Steph, there's something I haven't told you. I didn't tell you, because of what you're going through at the moment. It would have sounded wrong if I was giving you advice about Alice, if you knew the truth,' said Rita, cryptically.

'What is it?' asked Stephanie, impatiently, not happy about the detour in the conversation, wanting to get back to the matter at hand.

'I gave my son up for adoption when he was born,' said Rita suddenly. 'The reason I left London was because I became pregnant and Peter's father didn't want anything to do with me. My parents disowned me as soon as they found out. I was an embarrassment to them because I was unmarried. I went and stayed with my aunt in Birmingham, until Peter was born. I had to give him up for adoption because I didn't have anyone to support me and I couldn't afford to raise him on my own.'

'Oh, Rita,' said Stephanie, 'that's so sad... but why didn't you tell me any of this before?'

'Because, I thought you would be upset. I knew you had tried so hard to have a child of your own, and I gave my child away.'

'But surely you didn't have to give him away. Why did you? You could have come to me at the time. We were close. I would have helped you. Why didn't you tell me?'

'I couldn't, Steph. When I found out I was pregnant, I was so shocked I didn't know what to do. Everything happened so fast. It was around the time when you were having problems in your marriage with Roger. You'd been telling me how Roger wasn't coming home, and he was working late all the time. You had enough problems. Anyway, at the beginning I was seriously thinking of having an abortion, and I didn't think you'd agree with that, not after all you'd been through trying to have a child. I didn't want to get in your way; you were so upset about everything. If I'd turned up on your doorstep, I thought I'd make everything worse between you and Roger. I never really got on with Roger, anyway—you know that.'

'But, Rita, if only I'd known. So, do you know where your son is now?'

'He still lives with his adoptive family, but he visits me. He found me a few years ago and got in touch. It was so hard living without him, knowing I had a son out there. I always thought about him. I was so pleased to see him. I just don't know how Roger and Miranda could have turned Alice away. I was so shocked to hear that.'

Stephanie remained silent and lost in thought. She hadn't even known Rita was seeing anyone at that time, let alone the fact that she had become pregnant. *How did that get past me?* she wondered. It made her question herself for a moment. Rita had always been there to listen to her problems, but it appeared she had never taken the time to find out what was going on in Rita's life.

'Steph, are you still there?'

'Yes.'

'Well, you see, I didn't tell you about this before, because I thought you would think I was being hypocritical if I said anything against Roger and Miranda. I knew you needed my support, though,' Rita explained.

'So, everything you said, you were just being a shoulder to cry on? You didn't really mean any of it, did you?' Stephanie's mind was frantically running through all the conversations they'd had recently. 'I wish I'd never told you about any of this,' she said, speaking her thoughts.

'Steph, you're letting your imagination run away with you. I meant everything I said. I only held back telling you about Peter because I knew that it would change the way you felt about talking to me. I wanted to help you, and I knew I could because I'm someone who's been through it.'

'No,' said Stephanie, 'you're someone who's been through what Roger and Miranda are going through... Wait a minute, you were the one who told me that I should tell Alice about Miranda. You were on their side all along, weren't you?'

'That's silly. No, I wasn't on their side. I wasn't on anyone's side; I just thought that it was best for Alice—'

'What would you know about what's best for Alice? You abandoned your own child!' snapped Stephanie.

'My situation was different,' said Rita in a small voice.

'Hang on a minute... You knew Roger married Miranda, didn't you?'

'No, of course I didn't,' said Rita, incredulous. 'I told you—'

'It makes sense now. That's why you were not surprised when I told you they were living together,' continued Stephanie as if she had not heard her. 'Your friend—the one who introduced you to Miranda—she must have told you, and you've been keeping it from me.'

'I haven't seen her for years—' Rita's response was in vain, Stephanie appeared not to be listening to her anymore. 'Steph?'

'Oh my God,' Stephanie shook her head, her eyes wide, 'I've been such a fool. Is that why you were so keen for us to rekindle our friendship, so you could persuade me to tell Alice about the surrogacy agreement? Come to think of it, you were very insistent that you thought Alice should know the truth. I thought you were being a bit pushy, but I had no idea then that you had an ulterior motive. How could you? We used to be friends.'

'Stop it, Stephanie!' Rita's voice boomed over the phone line and at last she caught Stephanie's attention.

Something in the tone of her voice and the way Rita had used her full name to address her, had brought her mind back to reality.

'Whatever you think of me I am not in cahoots with Roger

and Miranda. In fact, if you'd bothered to listen to me a few minutes ago, you would know that I was shocked when I heard that they'd turned Alice away. You cannot compare my situation to theirs. The circumstances are completely different. They could have looked after Alice if they wanted to, but they chose not to. I didn't choose, I didn't have a choice.' Rita was talking quickly and sounded upset. 'And, I've already told you why I thought you should tell Alice about Miranda. That was in case she found out when she got in touch with Roger. I was looking at it from Alice's point of view. I was thinking about my Peter, and comparing Alice to him. I knew it would be better for her to know her true identity. I saw how much of a difference it made to Peter's life when he met me. He felt more complete.'

Stephanie was left speechless.

'You have to believe me. The only reason I didn't tell you any of this before was because I didn't want to hurt you. I knew you needed a friend to help you through this. If I told you about Peter before, you wouldn't have taken any of my advice seriously. I think I've learnt a lot from my experience with Peter, and I wanted to help you and Alice. Anyway, you can't really compare what I did, with what Roger and Miranda did, can you?'

'Sorry, Rita. This past week has been one revelation after the other. I'm finding it hard to keep my mind from exploding.'

'It must be hard for you. It's partly my fault. I should have told you about Peter before; but I promise I was only trying to help.'

Stephanie sighed. 'I know. You've been the only person I could talk to about any of this, and I'm really grateful. I'm just shocked. I'm not thinking straight.'

'I know,' said Rita. 'It's okay.'

'So what do you think I should do, about Roger and Miranda? Alice is so upset.'

'I don't know, Steph. I just don't understand how they could have turned Alice away. I still remember the first time I saw my Peter. I grabbed hold of him and I couldn't let go. I was so happy. I was crying, and I just wanted to make up for all the lost years. I can't even begin to imagine why Roger and Miranda acted that way towards Alice.'

'I just have to do something,' said Stephanie.

When Stephanie put down the phone, she desperately searched her flat for her "A-Z Street Atlas". In the days when Alice was younger, Stephanie had owned a car and driven everywhere, never taking public transport; but one day she decided to take the Tube to work and saw that as a better option; she'd sold her car and never driven anywhere since. Sometimes, she regretted it; especially when she had to go somewhere late in the evening, or when the trains were so packed she couldn't get a seat—but mostly she liked the convenience of taking the Tube, not having to worry about car maintenance, and she'd been able to start reading again. She'd loved reading as a young girl, but life got in the way. Ever since she had started travelling to work on public transport, she'd rediscovered the written word, and could get so lost and absorbed in a book sometimes that she almost missed her stop. The downside to travelling everywhere underground, was that she was hopeless at directions now, and whilst frantically searching for her A to Z, she pondered how—since she had started using the Tube—she had never had much use for the atlas. *Hope I didn't throw it away,* she thought.

She looked through some old books that were sitting idly on the unit in the living room, gathering dust. Then she saw it. It was old and tattered, and she wondered whether the streets had changed since the late 1970s. She looked at the index. *Alice said the name of the street where Roger lives is "Oakfield"... No... "Oakleigh", no... what is it? It's "Oak"-something.* She looked down the list of road names. *"Oakview"! That's it! "Oakview Road, Finchley".*

Chapter Fourteen

Sunday 24th August 1997

Twenty-seven, Oakview Road. The address was now firmly burnt into Stephanie's mind. She emerged from Finchley Central Underground Station at 11.30 a.m. The memory of Alice, so distraught at dinner the night before, nagged at her.

As she walked towards Oakview Road, her temperature rose at the thought of how Roger and Miranda had made Alice feel so unwelcome. No doubt, they were ashamed of their past, and Alice probably brought back memories that they would prefer to forget, but she was their daughter; they owed her a little respect—all she'd wanted was to meet her parents and get a few simple answers, but they had rejected her.

By the time Stephanie reached number twenty-seven Oakview Road, she was fuming. She decided to take a few deep breaths, to calm herself down before she ventured further. For a few minutes, she sat on the low wall that surrounded the front garden, trying to convince herself that showing her anger would only make things worse. *Stay calm, stay calm,* she repeated to herself. The night before, she had hardly slept as she had been running through in her mind what she would say to Roger and Miranda. *You messed up my life, I won't let you do the same to Alice. How dare you cocoon yourselves in this lie, shutting out your own flesh and blood? Do you know how upset that child was when she got home? Do you even care? Have you even got any feelings? Of course you haven't! The woman who gave away her child for a bit of money and the man who left his wife and child to fend for themselves so that he could continue an adulterous affair!* The thoughts invaded her mind; repeating, rephrasing. In her head she had created images of what Roger and Miranda would look like now, and how they would be standing, staring at her as she gave them a piece of her mind.

She had wound herself up to almost boiling point, unable to think about them without wanting to rant and rave, and tell them what she really thought of them. Ultimately, she realised that this would not be the best way to approach the problem. Her goal was to try to make Roger see that he had been wrong to turn Alice away. She couldn't afford to alienate him further. *Surely he must have at least one remorseful bone in his body*, she mused.

She began to feel self-conscious sitting on the wall outside the house, worried that Roger or Miranda may see her through the window. She ran her hands through her hair hoping it did not look too windswept, took a deep breath and then stood up. Hesitantly, she opened the gate and approached the front door.

She prayed that she could keep up the ambience of stilted calm at least until she finished saying what she had come to say. With bated breath, she knocked on the front door. After about half a minute, the door was opened. Stephanie's eyes widened when she saw who she knew must be Jane, standing at the door. It was like looking at Alice with a different hairstyle. She noticed the plaster cast on her right arm and recalled that the girl had been in the newspaper; one of the survivors of the plane crash she had read about.

'Hello,' said Jane.

'Hello,' said Stephanie, continuing to stare at her. 'Can I speak to your father? I'm...' She hesitated. 'I'm an old friend.'

Jane looked at her, and smiled politely. 'Okay, I'll just call him. Do you want to come in?'

'Um... yes, thanks.' Stephanie felt wary and uncomfortable when she stepped inside the house, and began to wish she had stayed outside.

Jane closed the door behind her.

'You can sit in the living room. I'll just get my dad.' Jane pointed to the living room door and then disappeared upstairs.

Stephanie walked into the room. It was neat and tidy and looked freshly decorated. The sun was streaming in through the bay window. She noticed the black leather sofa, and two armchairs. There were quite a few houseplants in the room; seeing them, she remembered that Roger had always liked plants when they were living together.

After a few nerve racking minutes where Stephanie stood as still as a statue in the middle of the room, not wanting to sit down—wanting to flee but knowing she must stay—Ken walked through the door. 'Hello,' he said.

When she turned to face him, she noticed the look of surprise on his face.

'S... S... Stephanie?' he stammered. He turned bright red and cupped his face with his hands briefly.

When he slowly removed his hands, his mouth was open and his eyebrows raised. It had obviously come as a shock to him that she would visit. Looking at him, she noticed that he looked old; in fact she was quite startled by just how old he appeared. His hair was grey and thinning, and he seemed shorter than he had been. It struck her that she had, quite irrationally, been expecting to see the same man who had walked out on her all those years ago, but now she was looking at an older man. Suddenly she didn't feel so much angry as sorry for him.

'This is a surprise,' he said softly, after a few moments of intense silence.

'Hmm... I don't know why it should come as a surprise to you that I'm here after the way you behaved towards Alice.' She narrowed her eyes at him, trying hard to still the bubbling rage within her.

He appeared to be avoiding eye contact. 'Um... yes. Well, I can explain all that. You'll understand that it's for the best.'

Stephanie frowned. *He's hoping to explain it all away. Trying to convince me that he's right again.*

'Please sit down,' he said.

His voice was beginning to annoy her now.

Calm down, calm down, she told herself.

'Would you like a drink?' he asked.

Was that nervousness that she could hear in his voice?

She avoided looking at him, trying to retain her composure, and sat down on the sofa, placing her handbag next to her. 'No, I wouldn't like a drink. I don't intend to stay for long. I'll just say what I have to say, and I'll leave.'

'Fine,' he said. An audible sigh left his lips.

He sat down on an armchair to the right hand side of the sofa, his forehead was creased into a frown, and she could see the lines that time had chiselled there.

'Where's Miranda? She should really hear what I have to say,' said Stephanie.

'She's busy,' he said, and then followed his speech with a nervous cough.

'Surely, she can spare a few minutes? This is important.'

'No. You can tell me whatever you've come to say. I'll tell Miranda.' He spoke louder now, although his voice was still tinged with nervousness as if he was dreading what she was about to say.

'Hmm... okay, have it your way. Roger—'

'Call me Ken, I haven't used the name *Roger* for over ten years,' he interrupted, drumming his fingers on the arm of the armchair as he spoke.

'I don't give a damn about you, or your name. You can call yourself anything you like, it won't change who you are. You're still a selfish—' Stephanie caught her breath and paused for a moment. She breathed in deeply. Her calming technique wasn't working. Her anger was like a tap dripping into a sink until it finally overflowed. She sighed and continued, knowing that she would have to just say what she had come to say and then leave as soon as possible. The sooner she was out of this place the better. 'You haven't changed at all, have you? You're still the same. Always thinking about yourself over everyone else. How dare you treat Alice like that? Do you know she was in tears last night? She came to my flat for dinner and had to explain everything to me; how her own parents practically threw her out of their house. She's your child. She wanted to find you, to talk to you. All you could do was turn her away. You couldn't even spare five minutes of your time for her after nearly twenty years. You... You and Miranda, both of you, are so cold, so...'

'Have you just come here to abuse me?' Ken stood up. 'That's your way, isn't it, Stephanie? The world revolves around you, and if you don't get your way you stamp your feet and make a scene. Just remember that if it wasn't for you and your bloody tantrums we wouldn't be in this mess to begin with! You're the one who wanted a bloody child.'

Stephanie looked at him, open-mouthed. 'How could you say that? You don't mean that, do you?'

'Face it, Stephanie!' he said, a snarl on his face, 'I never wanted Alice; you did. Go home and take care of her.'

'You arrogant bastard!'

'This is my home,' he said leaning towards her and looking into her eyes. 'I'll have to ask you to leave if you continue to insult me.'

'Oh.' She nodded. 'You're good at that, aren't you?'

He glanced at her, venom in his eyes. 'What?'

'You're good at running away from your problems! You just can't bear to hear the truth, can you?' Stephanie picked up her handbag, and stood up. 'Don't worry, I'm leaving. I can't bear to be in your presence for a minute longer.' She turned towards the door.

'Stephanie!' He called out to her as she had her hand on the door handle. 'Wait.'

She stood motionless, with her back towards him—too enraged to face him.

'This is stupid,' he said. 'We shouldn't be shouting at each other like this.'

She turned towards him, daring to believe that he might have acknowledged his mistake.

'You have to understand why I didn't want to see Alice,' he continued. 'You're the best person to explain it to her. I have a new life now. It would do none of us any good now to open up old wounds.'

'Oh don't give me that!' Stephanie shook her head. 'Alice always has been, and always will be, a part of your life. You just have to face up to the responsibility of being a parent. You can't just close the door on her!'

'It's awkward,' he said, weakly.

She let go of the door handle and frowned. 'What's awkward? Are you afraid that I'll make problems for you and Miranda? Is that it? Is that why you didn't want me to meet her today?'

'No,' he said, avoiding her eyes.

'I don't care about you and Miranda. A lot of water has passed under the bridge since we were together. I really don't care about you anymore, Roger—sorry, Ken, or whatever your name is. I stopped caring about you when you walked out on me and Alice, twenty years ago; when you left us alone. I don't care what you do. All I'm concerned about is Alice. She wanted to meet her father. She was so excited when she found out where you live. She imagined you would welcome her with open arms, and offer to make up for all the lost years. But, no—you just treated her like a stranger, huh, worse than a stranger. She is so upset.'

'Stephanie, I can't just play happy families and do whatever Alice wants. There is more to it than that. I'm happy with my life; with Miranda and our daughter, Jane. I don't want anything to come between us, or spoil what we have.'

'Oh, how cosy! Face up to your responsibilities for once, Roger! You have another daughter, whether you like it or not! She won't just go away. She's a person. She has feelings. You can't just run away from everything, like you did all those years ago.'

'That's what all this is about, isn't it?' he sneered. 'You're still bitter, after all these years. I left you, and you just can't handle the fact that I'm with Miranda.'

'Oh, grow up! This isn't about me and you, or your male ego. It's about Alice. You abandoned her once, all those years ago. Now you've sent her away again.'

'Well, I'm truly sorry I had to do that. And, believe me, if things were different, I would have welcomed her.' He sat down again on the armchair, looking weary. 'Don't you think I would like to get to know her? Do you think I'm *that* uncaring? When I left you, all those years ago, it was for the best. All we did was argue. As much as it hurt me to leave Alice, I had to go. Don't get me wrong, I still loved you, but I couldn't live with you. I gave up that part of my life when I walked out the door. Don't you see? I can't go back. Everything is so different now. Too much is at stake.'

'But I've come here to try to make you understand that it isn't too late for you to have a relationship with Alice.' Stephanie sat down opposite Ken on the sofa.

He shook his head. 'Jane is my first priority, I have to think about *her.* All of this... she doesn't know anything about it. It would be too much for her. She's so young. She... She's been through enough trauma recently, with the plane crash. I can't just dish this out to her. Not now.' He looked weary.

'But, my understanding is that Jane knows about Alice now, Roger—sorry, Ken,' said Stephanie, calmly, realising he had become upset. 'Alice met her and they talked. Jane is okay about it. Why can't you be?'

'Jane doesn't know the whole story. She thinks she and Alice are half-sisters; that Alice is my daughter from my first marriage.'

'So, explain it to her. It won't be that difficult. If Alice has accepted it, surely Jane will.'

He looked at her as if he were about to say something else, but then he shook his head. 'I can't. Not right now—'

'When then? In another twenty years time?'

'I don't know if there'll ever be a good time to tell Jane. Sorry.'

'You're so selfish. You haven't changed. Always thinking of what's best for you.' She shook her head. 'What? You don't want Jane to realise how fickle your emotions are; how it was so easy for you to leave your wife and child for a woman you hardly knew? Is that it?'

'Our marriage had ended long before I met Miranda,' he said, looking her directly in the eye, a scowl on his face.

'Yes, because you were such a lousy husband.'

'What would you know?' he said. 'Have you found a perfect

husband now?'

'I don't see what my relationship status has to do with this conversation.'

'You're still single, aren't you?' He nodded.

'I was left to bring up a child on my own, thanks to you. I didn't have time to go out and look for another man.'

'I knew it. You know nothing about real love. What Miranda and I share is real love. But that is something you'll never know about.'

Stephanie stood up. 'I don't know why I bothered coming here,' she said. 'I came to ask you to acknowledge your daughter, and all you can do is throw stones.'

'Well, you've said everything you wanted to say.' He stood up and walked towards the door. 'I think you should leave.'

Stephanie picked up her handbag from the sofa. 'I can understand that you wouldn't want to talk to me about this. Anyway, yes, you're right: I've said what I came to say. It's your loss if Alice never wants to see you again. She's a wonderful child. You've got a chance to get to know her, but you're going to miss out. I never wanted her to look for you. I told her you'd be like this. She didn't believe me. She was determined to find you, and now you've turned her away, shattered her illusions. You say you're happy with your new family, but I don't know how you can be happy, when you've made your daughter so sad.'

'Please just go,' he said.

'Okay, I'm going. I wouldn't want to be here any longer than I have to. You're a cold, hard man, and I'm glad you left me when you did. Do you really want Alice to have this image of you? Don't you want the chance to be part of her life?' She shook her head. 'Good-bye, Roger. Have a nice life.'

She slammed the living room door as she left. From the corner of her eye she saw a figure. Turning to her right, she saw a woman wearing large spectacles, standing a few feet away. It was Miranda. Stephanie was surprised at how old she looked. Her hair was grey. Stephanie's hair had gone grey years ago, but she always dyed it a warm auburn shade; she would not dream of leaving it grey. She knew that Miranda had been listening to her conversation with Roger. Why hadn't she joined them? The conversation had been as much about her as about Roger. *She's probably too embarrassed; too much of a coward to face the truth and the consequences of what she's done,* thought Stephanie.

'Stephanie,' said Miranda, reaching out a hand and walking

towards her. As she came closer, Stephanie could see that she seemed sad, and her face had many lines and wrinkles. Stephanie turned away without acknowledging her, and left through the front door.

On Sunday, Alice spent most of the morning cleaning her flat. She had slept well, the night before. As soon as her head hit the pillow, she had fallen asleep, and she had not woken up until 10 a.m. The events of the past two weeks had left her physically and mentally exhausted; it had all finally caught up with her. The sleep had been like a tonic and had left her feeling so much better.

In the afternoon, as the weather was so good, she went to the local park. After going for a walk to clear her head, she sat on a bench for a couple of hours, reading a book. It was a pleasant atmosphere as people walked by enjoying the sun, and children ran about and played.

In the evening, Jenny phoned her. She was eager to find out about her meeting with her father.

'What's he like?' asked Jenny in her typically jovial voice.

'Um... he... To cut a long story short, I don't think I'll be visiting him again.'

'Oh, I'm sorry to hear that. What happened? That's if you don't mind talking about it.'

'He was very cold. He said he doesn't think we should keep in touch.'

'He was probably shocked to see you. Did you tell him you were visiting?'

'Yes, of course I did. It wasn't that. He just doesn't want to know me.'

'Sorry, Allie. That's shocking. But... maybe when he gets used to the fact that you are back in his life, maybe he'll change his mind.'

'I don't really care,' said Alice, and only then realised that it was true. What she had wanted was to meet him, and now she had done that. She had discovered that he was not a very nice man. She didn't really care if she never saw him again. She surprised herself with her thoughts.

'So, now you've met your dad, do you think you'll start looking for your mum? Maybe she'll be nicer?' said Jenny.

'I don't think so,' said Alice, thinking of Miranda. 'To tell you the truth, I've come to the conclusion that there's a reason I'm not with my real parents. They're just not supposed to be in my life. I don't see a reason to look for my mum. I already have a mum.'

'Good for you, Allie. I have to say, I kind of agree with that; I can't imagine ever giving away a child, and anyone who does can't be much of a maternal person. You're better off without her.'

'Hmm... I hadn't thought of it like that, but it does make sense. I mean, if she was really that concerned about me, she would have tried to find me by now, wouldn't she?'

'Yeah.'

'So, how have you been, Jen?'

'Oh, fine. Trying to make the most of the last couple of weeks before we have to go back to uni. Time has gone so fast!'

'That's true.'

'Oh, before I forget, I've got Andrew's phone number for you.'

Alice's mouth fell open. After she'd composed herself, she couldn't help the smile that played on her lips. Jenny gave her the telephone number, and Alice felt truly happy then, for the first time in weeks.

'So, when are you gonna call him?'

'Um... soon.'

'I want to be the first to know everything!' said Jenny.

'You will be.' Alice giggled.

'I've got to go, Allie, but I'll see you at uni. Oh, and try not to be too downhearted about your dad. If you need to talk, I'm here, okay?'

'Thanks, Jen. But one good thing that came out of my visit to see him was that I met up with Jane, and I gave her my phone number. So, we'll probably keep in touch.'

'That's great news,' said Jenny. 'If you do plan to go out anywhere with her, let me know—I'd love to join you.'

After getting off the phone with Jenny, Alice knew she had to phone Andrew. Somehow, whenever she thought of him she felt calm and full of hope for the future. He was like a cure for her pain.

She smiled to herself as she dialled the number.

'Hello,' said a man's voice.

'Hello,' said Alice, nervously. 'Is that Andrew?'

'No. Hang on, I'll get him.'

Alice waited, wondering whether she should put down the phone. Every second that passed made her doubt herself just a little bit more. *What am I doing? What should I say to him?*

'Hello,' said Andrew, and she recognised his voice immediately.

'Oh, hello. It's Alice.'

'Oh, Alice, hi. How are you?'

'Fine,' she said, but had no idea what to say next.

'Thanks for phoning,' he said, saving her. 'I'm glad you did.'

She hoped Andrew would continue the conversation, as she had run out of words.

'So,' he said, after a pause which seemed to last for ever. 'Would you like to go out sometime?'

'Yes, I'd love to,' she said, grateful that the silence had been broken, but hoping she had not sounded too desperate.

'How about Wednesday night? We could go for a meal. Do you like Chinese?'

'Yes, I do, that sounds great.' She could feel her heart pounding.

'Well, I could pick you up at about eight o'clock, if you give me your address.'

'Okay.' She dictated her address and they agreed to meet.

When she put down the phone, she couldn't stop smiling. All the heartache of the past few weeks faded into insignificance. She loved Andrew, and he loved her back. Nothing else mattered.

Chapter Fifteen

Monday 25th August 1997

Rob Bairns greeted Alice as she walked into the bookstore. 'Hello, Alice. So, is everything all right now?'

Her eyes widened. Rob smiled at her sympathetically.

She walked over to the counter avoiding his eyes; she could feel her face reddening. Was he talking about her meeting with her parents? How had he found out? Had Charlotte mentioned to him that she was looking for her father? Had he overheard their conversation? Had he guessed that she had gone to visit them?

Paranoia infiltrated her thoughts: 'Um... What do you mean?' she snapped back, nervously.

Rob narrowed his eyes at her, and said, 'You had the flu on Saturday. Are you feeling better?'

Alice breathed a sigh of relief, and realised how absurd her suspicion had been that Rob would know she had been to visit her parents on Saturday. She twisted around to face him and smiled brightly. 'Yes. It was terrible, I was in bed all weekend, but I'm feeling much better now.'

'Good,' said Rob, with a frown on his face, obviously now suspecting that she had lied about her illness. She kept the smile on her face, hoping that would make up for it.

The memory of the meeting with her parents was always there. If only it were possible to switch off the part of her mind that held the memory, she would do just that. The night before, she had lain awake in bed unable to sleep for a long time, thinking it over and over. For the sake of her sanity she made the decision to stop worrying about it; to accept their decision. They didn't want to know her.

It upset her when she thought of Jane, though. It was possible that her parents might use their influence to brainwash her into believing that it would be wrong to keep in touch with her sister. There was also the possibility that Jane might feel unable to contact Alice, knowing her parents were so against it—torn between her loyalty for them and her desire to get to know her sister. Alice felt it would be unfair to force the issue; she would have to wait for Jane to contact her in her own time.

The only sensible answer she could see was to get on with her life with or without any further contact with Jane or her parents. She felt almost mournful over the situation, as if some part of her had died. Although she was aware she would have to try her best to move forward, she had the feeling that she would always be looking back and wondering why. It was something she was sure she would never be able to understand.

'Alice,' said Charlotte, 'do you prefer this colour or this one?'

Alice snapped out of her deep thoughts and saw that Charlotte had placed two lipsticks on the counter. One was a dark burgundy colour and the other was cherry red. 'Um,' she replied, 'I think I prefer the darker one.'

'It's for tonight,' said Charlotte, a wide grin on her face, 'Dave is taking me to this really glamorous restaurant in the city. Apparently, all the celebrities go there. I want to look my best.' Charlotte put the lipsticks back into her pink make-up bag. 'Yeah, I think you're right; I'll wear the dark red one. It's more sophisticated, isn't it?'

'Yes,' said Alice, not really having an opinion one way or the other.

'Oh, yeah, have you called Andrew yet?'

'Um, yes,' she smiled.

The two girls were standing behind the counter in the bookstore. There was only one customer in the shop, browsing around the fiction section.

'So, what did he say?' Charlotte asked.

'Well, we're going out.' Alice blushed.

'Wow, that's great. When? Maybe we could double-date. I can't wait to meet him, and I'm dying to introduce you to Dave. He's so gorgeous.'

'Um... I don't think we could afford to dine in an expensive restaurant.'

'Hmm... Oh yeah, I forgot Andrew's a student as well. Alice, you really should aim higher, you're a pretty girl. Do you know how nice it is to be wined and dined by a rich man? Andrew will hardly be able to whisk you away for a romantic weekend on a student grant, will he?'

'Yes, but I really like Andrew.'

'I know, honey, he's your first love and you're starry eyed, but you'll learn. My Nan once said to me, it's always best to find a rich man. She said: "They all leave you in the end, but at least with a rich man you'll be left with the expensive gifts". All I'm saying is, keep your options open.'

Alice forced a smile. 'It's only our first date. I don't know anything about him really.'

'Well the first thing you need to find out is whether he has any aspirations for the future. Even if he's not rich now, he could be. Find out what kind of job he wants to do. Face it—you don't want to end up supporting him, do you? You're studying to be a lawyer, right? The last thing you want is to be married to a guy who's earning less than you.' Charlotte raised her eyebrows.

'Money isn't everything, Charlotte.' Alice frowned.

'No... you're right. But my mum always says, when you ask most people what they want out of life, nine times out of ten, people want more money. Us girls are in a position to grab ourselves a man who can make sure that we never want for anything.'

'But love is just as important,' retorted Alice.

Charlotte smiled at her. 'Believe me, Alice, I have watched all of those romantic movies too; I've even been an extra in some of them,' she giggled. 'Love is important, yes. But let me ask you this: would you want to be living on the streets with the man you love, or in a mansion with a man you don't really care that much about but who buys you lots of things?'

'Well, I wouldn't want to be living on the streets, no one would—'

'My point exactly,' said Charlotte. 'I rest my case.'

Alice rolled her eyes, and was glad when the one customer in the store approached her with a question.

Alice got home at 6.30 p.m. and switched on the television. She watched the news, and ate her takeaway meal. When she went into the kitchen to throw away the remains of her meal, she noticed the letter that she had received from the local hospital the week before. The letter was still lying on the kitchen table, where she had left it. She had generally ignored it, each day, as she sat at the table, but she knew that she would now have to make a decision as to whether she would keep the appointment or not. The appointment date was Tuesday the 26th of August.

Tomorrow. 10.30 a.m.

Alice had not felt any pain in her arm for nearly two weeks, and didn't really feel that she needed to go for any tests, but she remembered how painful her arm had been, and wondered whether she should just go to the hospital for her own peace of mind. She shrugged her shoulders and resolved to make the decision in the morning.

After watching *EastEnders*, Alice decided to phone Stephanie, and invite her over for a meal. It had been such a long time since Stephanie had been to her flat, and Alice wanted to do something to thank her for standing by her. It had been a terrible time. Alice was sure she wouldn't have survived the past couple of weeks without her. Stephanie had been on her side even when she had gone against her wishes and insisted on looking for her father. Alice dialled the number.

'Hello.'

'Hi, Mum, how are you?'

'Um... I'm fine, darling,' said Stephanie, feeling slightly concerned that Alice may have found out about her visit to see Roger.

'Good. Listen,' continued Alice, 'I wanted to invite you to my flat, for a change. I'm always coming to yours. Why don't you come for a meal tomorrow evening?'

'Oh, I'd love to, darling,' said Stephanie, catching her breath, glad that Alice had not mentioned anything about Roger, 'but I've invited Rita and her son over to dinner tomorrow. What about Wednesday?'

'I'm going out on Wednesday.' She smiled as she thought of Andrew. 'How about Thursday?'

'Yes, I think I'm free on Thursday.'

'About seven-thirty?'

'Okay,'

'Great, I'll see you then.'

'Wait, Alice; have you heard anything more from your father or Miranda?' Although she knew she was hoping against hope, she felt curious to discover whether her visit had had any affect on them.

'No, I haven't. Why do you ask?' Alice frowned, unwelcome thoughts flooding her mind. She had been trying to forget about them.

'Oh, no reason. Just wondered.'

'Well, I really don't think I would be hearing from them after Saturday, do you? They made it perfectly clear they don't want anything to do with me. Anyway, I don't care about them anymore. I don't need them.' Her mood was now dampened as she fought with her conscience once again. On the one hand, she felt guilty harbouring ill will; but on the other hand, she hated them for rejecting her so coldly.

'That's true.' Stephanie's voice pulled her out of her deep thoughts. 'You've managed quite well without them for long enough.'

'Yeah,' said Alice, glumly.

'Anyway, darling, I'll see you on Thursday. I'm looking forward to it. Bye.'

'Bye, Mum.'

Alice felt glad that nothing seemed to have really changed between her and Stephanie, despite everything.

Chapter Sixteen

Tuesday 26th August 1997

Alice arrived at the hospital early. She was there at 10 a.m. As she sat in the waiting room, she began to feel nervous, worrying about what would show up in the tests. She was tempted to leave; after all, she had not felt any pain in her arm for a while—but she remembered back to the pain she had felt and how unbearable it had been. It would be best to find out what had caused it.

The hospital was busy, and even with her appointment set for 10.30, she had to wait until 11.15 before her name was called. Her blood pressure was checked and a nurse took some blood from her arm. Then, the nurse took her to an x-ray room where Alice was told to stand behind a screen. She was left alone in the room as the strange machine took an x-ray picture. Afterwards, she was told to wait upstairs, to see the consultant. Looking at her watch, she saw it was 12.15. She couldn't help thinking back to the night of her dream. So much had happened since then.

She felt hungry as she had missed breakfast. There was a vending machine in the corridor, selling hot drinks and snacks. Walking over to the machine, she looked at the prices and found she had just enough change to buy a coffee and a packet of crisps.

She felt glad she had purchased the snack, because long after she had finished eating, she was still waiting to see the consultant. She almost finished reading the novel she'd brought with her. Finally, at almost half past two, she was called in to see the consultant. He was a friendly looking man, with a bald head, and a thick, white beard. He told her that there was nothing irregular in her blood test results, and the x-ray showed a perfectly healthy arm. He was pointing out parts of the x-ray picture, as if Alice were as experienced in these things as he was. He explained that there were no signs of any fractures or anything that could have caused her pain.

The consultant seemed confused that she had been complaining of pain. He began to ask her a list of questions about her general health, and whether she'd had any past injuries or illnesses. He generally nodded at her answers. After completing his notes, he sighed.

'Well, Miss Turnbull, I am still none the wiser as to why you were in such pain. Perhaps you strained a muscle and it has now healed. If you suffer any more pain, we'll run some further tests. I really can't think of anything else.' He looked up towards the ceiling as if for inspiration and then said, 'Do you have any sisters or brothers?'

Alice thought it an odd question, but guessed that perhaps he was trying to go down the line of finding out if there was some genetically inherited condition in the family. 'Um... well, yes, I do have a sister.'

'This is a long shot, but has she had an arm injury lately?'

Alice's mouth fell open. 'Um... ye... yes, she has... but what's that got to do with anything?'

'Well, it's rare, but it has been known that siblings can sometimes feel each other's pain. This sort of thing has never been proven scientifically, of course, but I've come across a few cases in my time. For example, husbands have claimed to feel labour pains.' He laughed.

Alice laughed nervously, too, while her brain was trying to make sense of the new information. Was it really possible that she had felt Jane's pain?

The doctor continued, 'It certainly can't be ruled out that you may have been feeling a sympathetic pain, for your sister. However, you shouldn't rely too heavily on that theory. I'd advise you to contact your GP again if you have any further problems with your arm.'

As Alice left the doctor's room she couldn't get the picture out of her head, of Jane with her arm in plaster.

In the evening, Alice was preparing her dinner when the telephone rang. She picked it up, a little annoyed at the interruption, with the intention of telling whoever it was to call back later.

'Hello, Alice. It's Jane.'

Jane? Alice sat down on the sofa, completely forgetting about her pasta that was simmering on the hob.

'Jane! Hello, it's nice to hear from you,' she said, a smile on her lips.

'We have to meet up,' said Jane. She didn't sound happy. It was more of an urgent plea. 'Are you free tomorrow? We have to talk.'

Alice felt nervous. What had happened? What did she want to talk about?

'Um... Yes. I mean, tomorrow evening, after work; about six-ish?' said Alice, remembering that she was supposed to be going out with Andrew. He would be picking her up at eight. 'Has something happened?'

'I'll explain everything, tomorrow,' said Jane, flatly. 'Do you live with your... er... with your mum?'

'No.'

'Good, because we'll need somewhere private to talk. I'll come to your house tomorrow. What's the address?'

Alice gave Jane her address, still bemused by her tone of voice.

'I'll be at your flat at about six-thirty tomorrow.'

'Okay.'

'Bye.' Jane hung up the phone before Alice could reply.

Alice concluded from the way Jane had spoken on the phone, that Ken and Miranda must have told her everything about the surrogacy. They must have told her that she and Alice were really sisters, and not just half-sisters. That would explain why she seemed to have been almost in shock. It had obviously come as a great blow to her to realise that her parents had lied to her for so long. Alice recalled the way she herself had reacted when Stephanie had told her that she wasn't her real mother, and when she'd first heard about the surrogacy agreement.

Ken and Miranda had obviously been worried that Jane would find out everything from her, and decided that it would be better coming from them. Alice remembered that she had let Jane believe she was her half-sister when they had last spoken, so, Jane obviously thought that she didn't know the whole truth.

Alice concluded that Jane was coming over tomorrow to tell her about the surrogacy agreement, and to tell her that Miranda was her real mother.

Poor Jane. Alice wondered whether she should phone her, to tell her that she already knew. At least, then, Jane wouldn't have to spend the whole night worrying about how she would break the news to her. But she couldn't bear to dial the number. What if her father, or Miranda, answered the phone? They wouldn't want her to speak to Jane, anyway. *Maybe if I disguise my voice, and pretend I'm one of Jane's friends.*

Alice looked for her handbag. Jane's address and telephone number were in there. She fished around in her bag and the first thing she saw was the old photograph of her father, smiling, as he held her in his arms. She could not help staring at the photograph again. As she looked at it now, instead of seeing her father as a happy, young man, with smiling eyes, all she could see was treachery and deceit in his eyes. Alice imagined that when this picture was taken, he had probably been having an affair with Miranda, and planning how he would leave Stephanie and Alice to be with her. She tore the photograph in half and threw it on the floor.

She continued looking in her bag, found the piece of paper she'd been searching for, and walked over to the telephone.

'Hello,' a woman answered the phone, but she could not be sure if it was Miranda or Jane. Unsure whether she should just hang up the phone, she decided she would wait until the person spoke again. Whoever had answered the phone, did not speak again. The phone line went dead. Alice redialled the number. 'Hello,' said the voice again; and again Alice could not distinguish it. She remembered though, that she had not dialled 141 before phoning, so her number could be traced. She would have to answer.

'Oh, hello,' she said in a posh voice, trying to disguise her own. 'Can I speak to Jane?'

'She's out, I'm afraid. Can I take a message?' It *was* Miranda.

'No, it's okay. I'll call back,' said Alice.

'Well, she won't be back until tomorrow. She's staying with a friend,' said Miranda.

'Okay, I'll call tomorrow.' Alice hung up the phone.

She felt disappointed that she wouldn't be able to tell Jane that she already knew about the surrogacy agreement, and the fact they were sisters. However, in a way, she felt pleased that at least this meant that Jane would be coming to her flat tomorrow. If she had told her, there would have been no need for Jane to visit her.

She was looking forward to seeing Jane again. She began to imagine how much fun it would be to have a sister around. They could get to know each other, tell each other their secrets, gossip about things. It would be great. She could hardly wait to see her.

For as long as she could remember, she had always envied people who had siblings, and often wished that she could have had a sister or a brother. Now she had found Jane, it was like having her wish granted. It was like having a dream come true.

Chapter Seventeen

Wednesday 27th August 1997

Alice sat in her living room. It was 6.15 p.m. She stared at the clock.

She had been excited all day at the prospect of Jane coming to see her. Although she had already met her a few times, this time would be different, because Jane would be visiting her flat. She was slightly nervous about whether the flat was tidy enough, or whether it would be what Jane expected.

When the shop was quiet at work, Alice had told Charlotte about Jane. At first, Charlotte had seemed really interested:

'Oh, you're so lucky, Alice! I've always wanted a sister. I've only got three brothers,' said Charlotte.

Alice noticed that the newspaper she had hidden under the counter two weeks ago, was still there; the newspaper with Jane on the front page. She took the paper out and placed it on the counter. 'That's my sister,' she said proudly. 'Can you believe it?'

'Yeah, right,' Charlotte laughed. 'So, you've just been having me on about having a sister. You definitely fooled me! But what was the point? Alice, you can be so weird sometimes.' She giggled and shook her head.

'I'm not having you on. It's true! Remember you were saying she looks so much like me?'

'Yes... but... Alice, I know it's probably lonely being an only child, but it's just weird trying to pretend you've got a sister.'

'I'm not pretending, Charlotte.'

Charlotte sighed. 'Okay, Alice, if you say so.' She rolled her eyes.

'You don't believe me, do you? Look, her name's Jane Forester, it says it here. Didn't I tell you my dad's surname was Forester?'

Charlotte frowned and picked up the newspaper. She looked

up at Alice after scanning the paper with her eyes. Shrugging her shoulders, she said, 'Well, it sounds so unbelievable, I'm not sure whether you are telling the truth or not. You'll have to bring her in, and introduce her to me one day.'

'Okay,' Alice said, grinning. For once, Charlotte seemed speechless.

As she sat waiting for Jane to arrive, Alice tried to put all the negative thoughts out of her mind. At the end of the working day, she became a little nervous; after all, she didn't really know what Jane was coming to talk to her about, and she had sounded serious on the telephone. Alice had begun to imagine that perhaps she had some bad news for her. Maybe she was going to tell her that she didn't want anything more to do with her, just like her parents had. Maybe they had spoken to Jane and somehow convinced her not to become friendly with her.

Surely Jane wouldn't come all the way here to tell me she doesn't want to see me again. She could have said that over the phone.

There was something that had disturbed her about the sound of Jane's voice the previous night, however, and so she knew she wouldn't really be able to relax fully until Jane arrived.

At 6.35 p.m., the front doorbell rang. Alice realised she had been sitting staring at the clock for the past twenty minutes or so. She decided to switch on the television before opening the door to dispel a bit of the tension from the room.

As Alice walked towards the front door, she noticed the torn pieces of the photograph of her father. They were still lying on the floor, where she had thrown them the night before. She picked them up and threw them in the wastepaper basket that sat next to the sofa.

Alice opened the door and saw that it was raining heavily outside.

'Hello,' said Jane, smiling.

'Hello.' Alice forced a smile although inside she was still nervous.

Jane seemed to be having trouble closing her umbrella, as she still had the plaster-cast on her right arm.

'I'll do that,' said Alice, taking the umbrella, shaking the rain off of it, and closing it. She placed the umbrella just inside the front door.

She helped Jane take off her raincoat, and hung it on the coat-stand.

'I can't wait until I can have this plaster-cast removed,' said Jane. 'It's such a pain. I can hardly do anything on my own.'

'Yeah, it must be a nuisance,' said Alice. 'Are you all right though? I read all about that plane crash you were in. You must have been really scared.'

'Yes, I was. I still have nightmares. It was so frightening. I go to counselling sessions at the hospital. One positive thing is that I've made some really good friends. It was such a traumatic experience that it brought all the survivors together. It almost feels like we're family.'

'I can't imagine what it's like to go through something like that,' said Alice, latching on to the word "family" which reverberated in her mind. Was Jane about to accept her or reject her from her real family?

The two girls were standing by the front door. Jane seemed nervous. Alice wondered whether she should tell Jane about her nightmares around the time of the plane crash, but it didn't feel like the right time. She was still anxious to hear what Jane had come to tell her.

'This is a nice flat,' said Jane. 'Do you own it?'

'No, I rent it.'

'I wish I was living on my own. You *do* live on your own?' Jane's eyes peered around the room, as if trying to work out if anyone else was in the flat.

'Yes, I live on my own.'

An audible sigh left Jane's lips. Then she smiled and looked at Alice. 'I still live with my parents, as you know. They mean well, but they can get in the way sometimes.' She giggled.

Another brief moment of awkward silence followed. 'Um... please sit down,' said Alice eventually, leading the way to the sofa.

Jane followed her and sat down.

'Would you like a cup of tea?'

'Er... yes, that would be nice,' said Jane, looking at the floor.

Alice could not tell from her expression whether she was happy or sad, or if she had come to relay good news or bad news. She had smiled at her a couple of times and they'd had a relatively pleasant exchange of words so far, but there was an underlying current of tension which Alice hoped she was imagining.

'Do you take milk and sugar?'

'Just milk, please,' said Jane, as if she were ordering from someone in a café.

Alice went into the kitchen and switched on the kettle. As she looked for the mugs and spoons, random thoughts ran through her mind. She pondered how she and Jane were strangers; they had lived for years without knowing each other. *Will it ever be possible to make up for the lost time, or will there always be this distance between us?* She could tell that whatever Jane had come to relate to her, she was not finding it easy; she seemed to be finding it difficult to even look at her.

Alice took the tea into the front room and handed a mug to Jane who took it and held it, staring into the mug as if she were trying to read her fortune from the tea leaves.

'So,' said Alice, trying to think of something to say to break the silence, 'did you have any difficulty finding my flat?'

'No, it was easy to find.' Jane looked at the television as she spoke. She did not appear to be watching the television programme, but seemed to be in a world of her own, as if she were in a trance.

'I was so surprised when I found out your address. We live so close to each other; only a few miles away,' said Alice, trying to start a conversation.

'Yes.' Jane's expression remained unchanged.

'Jane, yesterday, when you phoned me, you said we had to talk.'

'I know. We do have to talk,' she said, now looking at Alice pensively. 'There is something important I have to tell you, but it's difficult to know where to start. You see, I don't know how much you know about the circumstances of your birth, about...'

Alice interrupted, with a sigh of relief: 'It's okay, I already know everything.'

'But... But, when we first met you said we were half-sisters, so I thought—' started Jane.

'I know I did, but the reason I didn't let on to you before was because I knew that your parents hadn't told you the truth.'

Jane stared at her, with wide eyes. 'And you thought it was okay that they hadn't told me?'

'No, of course not. But, your dad said he wanted to tell you himself.'

'He's your dad, too,' said Jane, correcting her.

'Um.' Alice looked at the ground. 'No, actually, I don't consider him to be my dad. Your parents practically threw me out of your house on Saturday. They told me they don't want to know me. They don't want me to contact them, or you, again. Didn't you notice how keen they were for me to leave when you came home?'

'That was because I didn't know the truth on Saturday,' said Jane. 'They were worried you would tell me. When they finally told me everything, they said that they were afraid that if they didn't tell me, I'd find out from you anyway. They didn't want to tell me at first. They were worried about what my reaction would be. But, Alice, are you sure you know the *whole* story?' Jane wore a frown.

'Yes, of course; they told me everything on Saturday. Well, I'd sort of guessed everything anyway,' said Alice.

Jane raised her eyebrows and seemed surprised.

The two girls sat in silence and drank their tea, staring at the television screen. There was a quiz show on, but Alice wasn't really watching it, she was just staring straight ahead, a million thoughts buzzing through her mind. She wondered whether Jane was really watching it, or whether she was just as overawed to be sitting on a sofa drinking tea with the sister she had never known.

When the programme finished, Alice decided she would have to say something. 'So, Jane, when I spoke to your parents on Saturday they said you were going to go to university to study law, as well. Isn't it funny that we chose to do the same thing?'

'I wish you wouldn't keep calling them, *my* parents,' said Jane, agitatedly.

'We... Well, they are your parents.'

'And they're your parents too.' She placed her mug on the coffee table and leaned back on the sofa, her arms folded, legs crossed. 'You're calling them *my* parents, as if they've got nothing to do with you.'

'Well, they made it clear that they don't want anything to do with me,' said Alice, glumly.

Jane uncrossed her legs and leaned towards Alice. 'That was before they told me the truth. Now, I'm sure they'd love to get to know you.'

'I'm not so sure. And anyway, I don't know if I really want to get to know them.' She avoided Jane's eyes.

When she looked at Jane, she saw she was staring at the floor. She seemed offended.

'Look, Jane. It's different for me and you. You have had a long relationship with your—okay *our* parents—you weren't the one that they gave away or the one that they rejected again after twenty years.' Alice placed her empty mug on the coffee table.

'You sound angry,' said Jane.

'I'm not really angry.' She took a deep breath in an attempt to calm herself down, as memories of the meeting flashed through her mind. 'I just didn't feel very welcome when I went to your house, that's all.'

'I know. I'm sorry they behaved that way. I think they were just trying to protect me. All I'm saying is, they're not *that* bad. Give them another chance.'

Alice shrugged her shoulders and forced a smile at Jane.

The uncomfortable silence resumed.

'I didn't know you were studying law,' said Jane after a couple of minutes, picking up the thread of the earlier conversation.

'Yeah.'

'It is a coincidence; a bit eerie,' said Jane.

Alice giggled. 'Yeah, I suppose you could say that.'

'I'm not really looking forward to going back to university, I quite enjoy all the time off.'

'Yeah, the holidays always go too fast,' said Alice. Then, she realised what Jane had said. 'Hang on, you just said you're not looking forward to going *back* to university.'

'That's right,' said Jane, frowning. 'Don't tell me you are?'

'No, but your—our parents—said you were only going to start university this year.'

'Why would they say that?' Jane shook her head. 'I'm going to start my final year this year.'

'You can't be,' said Alice. 'I'm going to start my final year this year.'

'Yes. And?' Jane was looking at Alice as if she had just said something stupid. 'Er... why is that so hard to believe? We *are* the same age.' Jane laughed.

'The same age?' Alice frowned. 'But you are only about eighteen, aren't you? I'm twenty-one.'

Jane's expression changed then. She was looking at Alice differently now; a concerned frown on her face. 'Alice, you don't know the whole story, do you? They said you didn't. We're twins.'

Alice's face turned pale.

'Alice, are you all right?'

Alice felt strange. She could see Jane, but she seemed to be moving in slow motion. Feeling as though she would faint, she tried to focus on the television.

'Alice? Alice?'

She could feel Jane's hand on her arm, but she could no longer see her.

'Alice, I'll get you some water, lie down.'

Alice saw Jane, through a haze, as she returned with a glass of water. Slowly, she began to feel normal again. Alice finished drinking the water. They sat in silence for a few minutes.

'We're twins? I had no idea.' Alice spoke slowly as if she were trying to make sense of what Jane had just said.

'I'll have to explain it to you, how Mum and Dad explained it to me,' said Jane.

'They separated us. I don't see how there can be any justifiable reason for that.' Alice's mind was spinning.

'Mum and Dad told me that when they made the surrogacy agreement, they fell in love.'

'Oh, how romantic,' said Alice, her words edged with sarcasm. 'He was married to Stephanie. He cheated on her.' She rolled her eyes.

'I know,' said Jane, frowning. 'But there's more to the story. They really tried to avoid seeing each other. Dad did feel guilty for cheating on Stephanie. To cut a long story short, they stopped seeing each other because it was too stressful keeping their affair secret.'

'I don't really have any sympathy for them,' said Alice remembering the two stiff faces that had greeted her when she visited them. She was finding it difficult to believe that they could actually feel anything like *love* for anyone.

Jane pursed her lips and looked at her hands. 'If I tell you the whole story, maybe you'll feel differently.'

'I still don't understand how they could have been so in love with each other and yet find it so easy to give away their child.'

'Well, Mum said that when she found out she was carrying twins she threatened to keep both of us and she told Dad that if he tried to stop her she would tell Stephanie about their affair.'

'So, in other words, she wanted to blackmail him and try to get him to leave Stephanie for her,' said Alice shaking her head.

'She was in love with him, Alice; she was taking their break-up really badly.'

'Whatever way you look at it, it was an affair; adultery.' Alice folded her arms and looked straight ahead at the TV screen.

'Yes, but Dad really tried to make it work with Stephanie, despite his feelings for Mum.'

Alice shrugged.

'Anyway, listen to the whole story and then you can judge them,' continued Jane. 'Apparently, one night, Dad and Mum, got together to talk about the problem. Dad came to an agreement with Mum that she could keep one of us, and give the other to him and Stephanie. Mum needed the money, so she agreed. Mum said she was still hoping to get back together with Dad. She didn't want to give either of us away.

'Mum and Dad really thought they were doing the right thing by splitting us up, to prevent further problems because the agreement had backfired when they had an affair. They agreed not to tell Stephanie about their affair, or about the fact that Mum was having twins.'

'They did everything behind Stephanie's back,' said Alice.

'Yes, but, Dad stayed with Stephanie and you for a while after we were born. He wasn't seeing Mum at that time. The problem was that he loved Mum too much, and so in the end he had to get back with her and leave Stephanie. Dad decided to leave you with Stephanie because he thought it would cause less problems,' said Jane.

'How could they have done that? Separating twins?' said Alice, her face red.

'I know. I couldn't believe it. I was really angry with them when they first told me. I was angry because they had kept it a secret from me, and because I couldn't understand why they did it. I didn't speak to them for two days. I went and stayed at a friend's house. I couldn't bear to look at them. I really considered just leaving home, and never seeing them again. It just kept going round and round in my head. But now, I sort of understand why they did it. It was stupid, but they were only doing what they thought was right. They didn't mean to hurt anyone. Think about it, you've had a good life with Stephanie, haven't you?'

Alice nodded. 'Yes.'

'And, believe it or not, I've had a good life with Mum and Dad,' said Jane. 'Stephanie and Dad were going to break up at some stage, anyway, I suppose. I mean, Dad said they weren't getting along. But Mum and Dad really love each other. They've been together for all these years, and they're really happy together, even now.'

'But they were being selfish; only thinking of themselves,' blurted Alice, with tears in her eyes.

'No, that's just it; they weren't. If they were selfish, they would have taken both of us, and gone off to live together, leaving Stephanie alone,' said Jane.

'At least then we would have grown up together. And it wasn't fair for Dad to expect Stephanie to bring up a child on her own with no help.'

'I know, I know. I've been over it in my head again and again, and if I'm being honest I think there are things they could have done better. But I know them, remember; and I truly believe that they weren't being deliberately cruel. They were young, only a few years older than we are now. I think they thought that by giving Stephanie a child, knowing that she couldn't have any of her own, it was a kind of compensation for what they'd done.'

'I don't know how you can be so calm about it,' said Alice, tears welling in her eyes.'

Jane giggled. 'Believe me, I wasn't calm about it. I almost shouted the house down when they told me!'

Alice wiped her tears on her sleeve and looked at Jane, frowning: 'Miranda didn't even want children. She was only having a child for money. She was being selfish by keeping you, not thinking of the effect it would have on us to be split up. Why didn't they give both of us to Stephanie?' said Alice resentfully.

'Yes, I thought about that, but she explained it to me. She says that at first she saw the opportunity of the money, because she wanted to travel the world and she saw it as doing a favour to a couple who couldn't have children; but, then, she fell in love with Dad, and she just felt she wanted to be with him. They didn't plan any of this, it just happened. She ended up feeling that she would not be able to give up her child.'

'But she did give me up!'

'Yes,' said Jane, nodding, 'but can't you see how painful that must have been for her? What a sacrifice? She had promised Stephanie a child, so she gave you to her.'

'But you just said that she needed the money; that's the reason she gave me to Stephanie.'

'I didn't mean it that way. What I meant was—well she wouldn't have been able to bring both of us up, without financial support. She was only a student at the time. It was as if—I don't know—if she kept to the agreement, she would get the money, so at least she could keep one of us.'

Alice was silent, tears now falling from her eyes. She sat staring at the floor.

'I know you're angry with them. I was angry when I found out,' said Jane. 'But what's the use being angry? We can't change what's happened. At least we've found each other now, and we know the truth.'

'Yeah, but if it was up to them, we would never have known the truth.'

Jane nodded. 'That's true; but, I think they're glad it's all out in the open now. It must have been so difficult, keeping something like that secret, for so many years,' she said. 'Alice, I really think that Mum and Dad would like to get to know you better now that we both know everything that happened.'

'I don't know how you can be so forgiving. Maybe it's because you're not the one they gave away,' said Alice, bitterly.

'I've had more time to get used to it than you. I've had time to think about it. And, as for forgiving, I don't know if I have, but I think I might be able to, in time,' said Jane. 'Anyway, you shouldn't feel so bad about it. It wasn't as if they chose me over you. Look at us, we're almost identical. It could have been me that they gave to Stephanie. Anyway, I think you're the lucky one. After all this has blown over, you'll have two families. You've got Mum and Dad, *and* Stephanie.'

Alice wiped her eyes. She looked at Jane. Everything Jane had said made sense. Slowly, she began to feel a bit better.

'I'm sure Stephanie would love to meet you,' said Alice. 'She's coming here for dinner tomorrow evening, would you like to come too?'

'Well...' Jane seemed hesitant. 'Yes, okay, why not?'

Alice and Jane sat in silence for a few minutes looking at the television. Then Jane began to speak again. 'So, how did you trace us after all these years?'

'Hmm... I'm not supposed to tell you, but I don't think it really matters now: I got your address and telephone number from Susie and Tony, after I saw you at Tony's party.'

'Oh, right,' said Jane, nodding.

'It was really strange how this all started, though,' said Alice. 'I had a nightmare when you were in the plane crash.'

'Really?' Jane seemed intrigued.

'Yes, I had a nightmare, and I woke up at quarter past twelve: the time of the plane crash. I was really scared. Then I heard about the plane crash the next day. It's a long story, but basically I saw your picture in the paper, and saw that your surname was "Forester"—the same as my dad's. And, you looked so much like me. Anyway, it made me want to start looking for my dad. It's really weird, I still can't believe it myself.'

Jane stared at Alice open-mouthed. 'Wow,' she said. 'That's quite a strange story. Maybe they're right about twins having telepathic connections?'

'Maybe.' Alice remembered what the doctor had said about the pain in her arm possibly being sympathetic pain.

'Well, none of that really matters now, I suppose,' said Jane, interrupting her thoughts. 'All that really matters, is that we are together again.'

'Yes.' Alice smiled.

Just then, the doorbell rang.

'Are you expecting someone? asked Jane.

'No.' But, then, looking at her watch, she realised she had completely forgotten that she was supposed to be going out to dinner with Andrew. Jane's telephone call yesterday had wiped everything else from her mind.

'Oh, sorry, Jane, yes... I am expecting someone. It's my boyfriend. We're going out.'

'Oh, that's okay. I'll leave,' said Jane.

Alice smiled at her and went to open the front door.

'Hello,' said Andrew, kissing Alice on the cheek.

'Hello,' she smiled, blushing. 'Come in.'

Andrew seemed surprised when he saw Jane. Alice introduced them.

'I was just leaving,' said Jane, reaching for her coat.

Alice noticed that Jane was struggling and she helped her put her raincoat on over her plaster-cast. Jane bent down and took her umbrella which was sitting by the door.

'Thanks for coming over, Jane. I'll be expecting you tomorrow evening for dinner.'

'Okay,' said Jane, smiling. 'Bye.'

Alice watched as Jane walked away from the house. It had stopped raining and the late evening sun was peeping through the thick grey clouds. As Alice watched Jane, she felt happy. Finding out that Jane was her twin had been like finding the missing piece to the jigsaw puzzle of her life. She felt complete.

She turned to face Andrew.

'I didn't know you had a sister,' he said.

'Neither did I,' said Alice, laughing. 'It's a long story.'

'Yeah? Well, perhaps you can tell me all about it over dinner.'

'Okay,' smiled Alice, taking his hand as they stepped outside together into the evening sun.

Author's Note:

I very much hope you enjoyed Coincidences. If you did, it would help me so much if you could leave a review on Amazon, Barnes and Noble, or other such sites. If you're a member of Goodreads.com or other reader/writer forums, perhaps you could also leave a review there. A tweet on Twitter or a shared link about my book on your Facebook or other social networking site would be much appreciated. Another fantastic way of helping would be to tell your friends about the book. Independent authors rely on their readers to spread the word about their books.

Thank you so much for reading my novel. I hope it has entertained you. Readers are the most important people in an author's life. Thank you for picking my book to read.

Other Books by Maria Savva:

Coincidences - 1st Edition (Hardback)
A Time to Tell
Pieces of a Rainbow
Love and Loyalty (and Other Tales)
Second Chances
Cutting The Fat (co-author Jason McIntyre)
Fusion
The Dream
Short stories by Maria can also be found in the BestsellerBound Short Story Anthologies

Visit http://www.mariasavva.com for further information